KING COBRA

NAGA BRIDES #2

NAOMI LUCAS

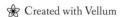 Created with Vellum

To my amazing readers.
Thank you.

BLURB

Daisy. Daisy. Daisy.

From the moment her name is spoken, it is all I can hear. Her tears of fear bring me anger. I vow to wipe them away and banish her fear. To make her my queen.

But I have to catch her first.

I have to convince her to trust me.

I have to show her she is safe.

But only with ME.

Because if any other naga male tries to take Daisy away from me, I will kill them.

And if she runs?

She'll find out there's no escape.

I've paid the price to mate her, and she needs to know a gilded nest is better than freedom in my world.

NAGA NAMES

Vruksha— Viper
Azsote— Boomslang
Zhallaix— Death Adder
Syasku— Cottonmouth
Jyarka— Diamondback
Zaku— King Cobra
Vagan— Blue Coral
Krellix— Copperhead
Lukys— Black Mamba
Xenos— Sidewinder

ONE
CAPTURED

Daisy

Gemma yanks my arm, and I stumble forward, my boots catching over a bush. Unable to regain my footing, I trip. Gemma turns back and helps me rise.

"Don't stop," she gasps, eyes darting left and right. "We can't let them gain on us!"

Panting, I chase after her through the trees but lose her.

"Gemma," I wheeze, bracing against a tree.

She comes back, grabs my arm again, and we keep running.

The forest is thick, filled with so much overgrowth it's hard to move through it. Leaves, branches, and thorns from alien plants abrade and rip at my clothes, exposing skin. Rasping, haggard breaths push my lungs to their limits, and still, I can't keep up with Gemma.

She's fierce, a fighter. She would have made a great soldier.

She's our ship's communications officer, and is being

traded to alien men for tech. As am I. Gemma's presence is the only thing giving me the slightest hope of rescue. If she's here, someone on *The Dreadnaut* will notice she's gone.

Because I won't be missed...

Someone disgraced like me unexpectedly assigned to pilot the first team to our homeworld? It was legendary. I was going to be planetside for the first time in years, and of all planets, it was going to be on Earth. My father would have been proud.

My boots catch again as the land slopes down, and we both have to pause, eyeing the sharp descent.

"It's not safe," I croak, staring at the sharp ledge, the trees between us and the top. "We'll never get away." It's almost too painful to speak.

"We have to try!" She takes off to the nearest tree and flings her body against the trunk. She does it again, bracing her feet at an angle to stop from tumbling forward. From one tree to the next, she slowly makes her way down the mountainside.

Following her lead, I take it slow at first, shunting from one tree to the next. I see her reach the bottom, way ahead of me, and she glances back. "Daisy! You can do it!" she shouts.

I fall into another tree.

Something snaps behind me. I hear a breathy hiss.

No!

Pushing myself off the tree, I rush to the next one.

I fall forward, tumbling down the slope, crashing against the side of a bush. I stare at the branches above, stunned. Pain shoots up my side as Gemma's face appears above me and she tugs me to my feet. My hair snags on a branch and rips from my scalp.

"Come on, Daisy! You can do it!"

I don't know how long we've been running or how far we've gone. The shadows are lengthening. We started running when the Earth's sun was at its zenith, when Peter and Collins dragged us out of the skiff, exchanging us for a box from the large alien male who made all of this happen. Then Peter and Collins flew away, leaving Gemma and me at the mercy of the aliens.

The big, scary one had come right up to me. He leaned down, looked into my eyes, and scowled.

He scowled like he was furious at what Peter and Collins presented him with. Me. As if he knew I was an outcast. That I was weak. And all I could do was stare. Even when Gemma grasped my hand and jerked me behind her, all I could do was stare.

Because despite how giant and frightening the alien was, he smelled really, really good.

Something crashes behind us, and Gemma sprints forward, leaving me behind. I try to keep up. I claw at my chest, grasping my jacket. I can't lose her. She's the only thing keeping me from losing my ever-living mind.

The noises grow louder. They're getting closer. A tear rips from my eye.

I can feel hands grabbing at me, catching my hair and capturing me. I'm about to scream for her when I run into her back. She stumbles forward as we nearly tumble to the ground. I drop to my knees.

She grabs my shoulder and squeezes, and I almost lose it.

"We have to climb," she gasps. "Go!"

I look up to see what she means. Right before us is a ledge and a short rocky slope of boulders. It's the only way we can go.

The sounds of pursuit continue to grow. They're

coming from multiple directions. I snap to my feet and take to the ledge. Gemma catches my foot and pushes me up. I pivot back to grab her hand, eager to finally help her, when something yanks me off the ground.

No!

I scream as Gemma gets smaller and smaller below me. My hair whips across my face as I'm jerked brutally around and into a hard, muscled chest. Pain lashes my side as a thick arm presses hard against it. The scent of musk invades my nose as trees blur past me.

The smell makes me vomit. It's bitter and sickening, like sulfur. I try to twist back to Gemma. Bands of steel stop me.

My arm snaps back as I'm flung through the air. The thing holding me hits a tree, jerks me higher in his arms, and jumps to the next one. I glimpse his face and shriek.

Yellow eyes, yellow skin, and even yellow lips. Two large fangs eclipse my vision before I'm tossed violently to the side.

Fighting with every last shred of strength I have, I kick and scream, tearing at him. He clutches me to his chest, ignoring my attempts to hurt him. My teeth snap together the next time he jumps. My neck wrenches.

He's going to kill me.

I'm going to die.

I scream for Gemma.

My nails drag across rough skin, catching on scales that rise as I touch them. Slamming my knees into the male's tail brings me more pain, and has little effect on the brute. Growing desperate when we hit the next tree, I manage to get my hands up his chest to wrap them around his neck. I don't want to die.

Tough flesh stops me from choking him with any real effect.

"Let me go!" I shout, returning to my thrashing.

He grabs a section of my hair and forces my head back. "Ssstop making noise," he hisses, snapping his fangs at me, his eyes devoid of intelligence.

I thrust back, terrified he's going to bite me when he drops us to the forest floor. Limbs locked from the sudden weightless and abrupt stop, the male releases me and forces me to the ground.

Claws rake down my body, shredding my uniform in a single sweep. Chilly evening air breezes my skin as the male tears my clothes from my body. I realize what he's doing when he gets to my boots and his nails aren't able to shred them.

I kick him hard in the face.

Rearing, the alien arcs back and grabs his face. "Rabid female!" he bellows thickly. His tail slams the ground beside my body, and the ground trembles. "You will submit! I am in pain!"

Twisting over, I hold what's left of my clothes to me as I crawl away. I don't get far. Fingers curl around my ankle and drag me back. "Gemma!" I scream for help, clawing at the ground, knowing there won't be any.

He thumps his giant, sickeningly yellow tail next to my head again, and I flinch. It's so huge it blocks out the forest, creating a wall of scales beside me. He rips my undershirt next. I try to hit the male again, but he catches my fist and forces it to the ground. The chill of the evening air hits my bare chest the same moment his hot breath does.

Shoving at his body, he's completely undisturbed by my struggles as a forked, meaty tongue lashes the air. "Female," he groans, tasting my terror.

I kick harder when he slides down my body, tearing off what remains of my pants, exposing my legs.

"Please!" I wheeze. "Please, don't," I beg.

He rips my pants off.

Something hard, hot, and thick falls upon my shin, and I cry out.

"Female," the alien groans, sliding the hot appendage up my leg. "You are mine."

I turn my head and brace for what's to come. The fight has left me. I can barely rise and can't catch my breath. All I can do now is hope I survive.

Hope it doesn't hurt, hope it doesn't last long.

The soft sensation of smoothed-out scales chafes my inner thighs as his tail forces my legs apart. His tail is so large, it forces my thighs and knees to the ground. I try to close them but can't, trapped under a wall of undulating muscle. His giant genitalia is lodged between us.

Closing my eyes with a whimper, I glimpse something shiny next to my head.

The knife.

This morning, while taking my last shower on the transport ship, Shelby, forced to guard Gemma and me so we didn't run or send a message to the Central Command, slipped a knife under my unit. I'd hidden it under my clothes...

A wet tongue slides over my breasts, fingers snaking around my neck as the alien pushes his cock to my open, dry sex. The male hisses when he's unable to easily thrust into me and bows his head down to peer between our legs, completely unaware of the knife.

Sliding my hand over to it, I grasp it, wiggling it free of its sheath and aim. Shaking terribly, I miss.

He doesn't even notice, gripping his member and trying to get it inside me. He's going to have to rip me in two to make it fit.

I bring my hand back, and a fleeting calm washes over me. I aim again.

And with everything I have, I sink it deep into the side of his neck.

I drop my hand as blood gushes from the wound.

The male jerks, his tail swipes out wildly, and he rises to meet my wide eyes as his hand releases my neck. Snatching my hand to my chest, he grabs the hilt of the knife and yanks it out of his neck.

Blood spurts from the wound and all over my face.

Run.

Twisting onto my front, I scurry out from under him as he brings the knife forward, pausing to look at it.

I don't wait to watch. Reaching down to grab at the shredded clothes next to me, I crawl away, putting as much distance between us as possible. I pray the wound is enough to stop him from chasing me.

I don't know how long I run, how many times I stop to listen, or when I find the strength to get back to my feet. I keep going until the sun sinks below the horizon and darkness blankets the forest. It's not until I'm about to faint that I collapse and curl up on my side. Bringing my ruined clothes to my chest, I sob until sleep takes me away, until my nostrils fill with the sweet scent of a different male...

TWO

ZAKU, KING OF THE FOREST

Zaku

I GIVE the human male his box of broken tech and dismiss him and his guard from my mind. He flees back to his ship and leaves. *Coward.*

Good.

Cowards are easy to control. *Yesss.*

If it weren't for their weapons, I would kill them and the rest. Only I do not know how powerful they are. I want to see them dead. I wish them all dead, or at least exiled. I am king of these lands and I do not suffer interlopers. The humans are trespassers and should not be here. They had their shot at Earth, and they will not get another. I'll make sure of that.

But the females... the females can stay.

Heading for the human ones now, I scowl as the crying one, the one with long light-colored hair held back from her face, flinches as I approach.

She cries? Why does she cry? A beauty such as her should never have a reason to cry.

Standing across from me is the most enchanting female I have ever seen. And she is not even nagakind. Except she is crying? Her glistening eyes glance at me before cutting away to the others. My scowl deepens. I want her eyes on me, and only me. Even if they are wet, even if they show fear.

They return to me like they hear my thoughts. *Good female. Keep your eyes on your king.* They widen as I move closer to get a better look at them, and it's the terror etched deep there that brings my anger to the surface.

I will not be feared by you! I growl.

Human, naga, or otherwise. Females are valuable. They bring males power, and power is all that matters. Dominion. Control. I am a king, and a king cannot rule without his queen. I have waited decades for my queen.

She holds my gaze as I stare. Pools of soft brown glitter and glint, framed by dark lashes that cling together. A teardrop forms, slipping down her soft, pinkened cheek. I curl my fingers into my palm, wanting to catch it.

I flick my tongue out for a taste.

The red-headed female comes forward and hides the blonde behind her back. My tail thumps.

"What do you want from us?" she demands, but there's a tremor in her voice. Is this one also scared? Is she trying to hide her fear?

What have their males done to them that they fear males so much? Better males at that.

Agitated that she hides the fearful one, I face her. "You will submit to one of usss."

"We'll never submit," she quips. "We're not items— we're not yours. We'll never be yours."

My brow arcs. "You will be hunted, and the best of us, the one who captures you, will covet you within his nest."

Vruksha hisses, stealing the red-headed female's attention. I stop from striking him down and starting a brawl here and now. How dare he interrupt me? This is my deal with the humans—mine! It's only out of fairness that I allow the other nagas to have a chance at one of them.

If I want both, my subjects should bow their heads and move out of my path.

"Run," Vruksha snaps. "So I may catch you," he tells the red-headed one, rising over her, urging her to flee.

"What?" she says, recoiling.

Vruksha presses into her until she's stumbling backward, trying to get away.

"Daisy," she gasps, keeping her hold on the crying one. "Run!" she shouts, and then both females are stumbling, catching their footing, fleeing into the forest.

Hoots and shouts rise up from the males, a cacophony of all the nagas hiding in the forest, waiting for this moment. This once-in-a-lifetime chance to have a mate of their own. Trees shift, branches shake, and pine cones fall. One moment I see the females, and the next? They're gone.

Vruksha surges forward, and I miss him with my tail, but I catch Vagan before he hits the tree-line. The Blue Coral spins back to me. "Zaku," he snarls.

Twisting my tail up his before he can react, I sling him over the cliff. I hear a yell, a thud, and then nothing.

Then I'm in the clearing alone.

Taking off, I sprint after the others.

Something stabs at my right, and I fling to the side, glimpsing the Cottonmouth. He rams into me and bites down on my cowl. I rip him off me before he unleashes his venom. *He is not a king*, I hiss. *He's not worthy of a female before me!* I fall atop him as he rises, raking my claws down his chest. Bellowing, he hits my back with his tail, and I use mine to wrap around his head.

He thumps me with his tail again as my grip tightens. The Cottonmouth thrashes as his skull breaks under my coiled limb.

I encounter Jyarka of the Diamondback clan next. For a moment, I pause, thinking Jyarka died long ago. Below him lies a squirming Boa that he's beating. Blood is everywhere, and my cowl flares as its metallic scent invades my nose.

I sneak up behind him and sink my teeth into his shoulder. Venom gushes as he tries to tear me off him. Wrapping my body around his, I hold him prone until paralysis takes over his limbs. He drops atop the lifeless Boa.

Four down.

I hear a noise and head in its direction, finding Xenos of the Sidewinder clan hanging limp and lifeless over a large branch. Three vicious bitemarks rent his upper back, and entire chunks of flesh are torn from his body. I smell Vruksha's venom. Slipping past Xenos, I follow the noise.

It continues ahead, leaving messy tracks for me to follow. *The females*, I lick my lips. No naga would leave such blatant marks behind.

I will kill all the other males until I catch one, eliminating my competition. I have felled hundreds, vastly diminishing our numbers over the years, I will destroy more.

"Gemma!" a feminine voice cries out. It's in the distance. My head snaps up. It's the voice of the crying one. Soft, shrill with fear, it vibrates through my chest. Her terror stabs me, constricting my heart. She does not need to be afraid.

I will make certain she knows this.

No queen of mine should ever feel fear.

I surge in the direction of her call, forgetting the tracks entirely, coming across another male I'm forced to dismember.

Soon, the sounds of the chase vanish. One by one, males are taken out by each other, and while I come upon either their corpses and broken bodies, I don't reach the females. As the minutes pass by, my frustration rises.

The slopes grow steeper. The shadows lengthen. Minutes become hours.

Where are they? My heart quickens uncomfortably.

I am like Vagan; I am not a tracker. I didn't fear this because a king is never second to anyone. There is nothing for me to worry about. I want to wring Vruksha's neck for telling the females to run before my queen had a chance to deny all others and come to me.

She was about to. I know it.

No male would take the mate his king demands. Especially when it's their king who bartered for them in the first place. They are my right. Both females are.

But I am a generous ruler and only want one.

A *king* can only have one queen. Harems breed discontent and strife. Wet eyes fill my head, and pale, ruddy skin. My tail goes rigid, forcing me to stop as the female's face consumes my thoughts. If I wasn't sure who my queen was before, I am now.

It is not the red-headed one.

Wiping my hand down my slick chest, I look down at the shaft emerging from my tail, long and thick. Spill floods into it hard and fast. The sensation rips a groan from my throat. Cupping the appendage with my hand, it grows larger until I grit with pain.

I squeeze the knot forming in the middle, overcome with intense pleasure. I knead the pressure away. I squeeze harder, wrapping my fingers as far as they'll go, and sink to the forest floor. Slicing my hand furiously, I rub violently, maddened with the onslaught of sensation.

Tears, brown eyes and soft skin is all I see, and the tension escalates. Unbelievable beauty. How was I not aware the humans brought us such a gift from the sky? I never saw this Daisy—a flower—while I scouted the facility's perimeter these past weeks. If I had...

More spill jets into my shaft. More spill than my knot as ever endured.

What—what is happening to me?

I curl on my side, brought low by something I've never experienced, needing this human female—to the point of torture. Mouth gaping, rabid hissing escapes through my clenched teeth. I rut my hand, imagining tears slipping over soft cheeks to drip from a slender jaw. Mine?

Mine. Oh yes, mine.

I take my member with both my hands and shunt into them, writhing and coiling. Imagining glistening brown eyes beneath me as I thrust savagely. I spill all over dry, dead leaves. My knot immediately fills back up. I pump it again with an annoyed rumble, using both hands to take it on, vaguely aware I need to find my mate before nightfall.

Why is this happening to me?

I release a raspy breath, my tail coiling tight around me, I beg to whatever tech is out there to make my seed stop. My pleas go unheard. The shadows deepen, and the sound of crickets takes over. Grunting, I force my hands from my swollen member and push it into my tail. Collecting my thoughts, I rise. I am wasting precious time.

I stare at my seed that's now covering the leaves beneath me. Never have I done such a thing. My member has never reacted the way it just did. *Like it sensed its mate.* I glance around, expecting to see her.

All I see are shadows, trees, and bushes. They press into my sides.

Snapping back into action, I don't know how much time I've lost. I will not let my queen spend her first night alone— or with another. Clenching my fists, I take off.

I come across a trail, and I follow it. Heart thundering, the moon rises and the light fades. Each moment, the forest darkens more and more. I must find her before it gets any darker.

Fear niggles its way into my gut, and my muscles bunch. Darker and darker the night gets, so dark that I lose the trail and roar to the sky. This is not what I planned. By now, I should have had her coiled up in my limbs. I remember my wasted spill and hiss.

I slam my tail against a tree, snapping it in two.

The tree crashes to the ground, and I spy something pale in the corner of my eye. Venom floods my fangs as I turn toward it.

A Python male lies unmoving in the brush. I recognize his pale yellow coloring and scent his blood. Poking him with my tail, he wakens and groans. His head lolls to the side. I don't recognize him. He may be new to my forest or maybe we just have not yet encountered one another. Beside him, hovering at his head, is an orb. Its blinking lights brighten his face.

"Where are they?" I demand.

Eyes glazed in the moonlight, he lifts his bloody hand and reaches for something in the grass. Turning, I find a small object wet with blood. I take it before the Python can, discovering a knife.

A human knife. It's wet. I bring it to my nose and sniff,

relieved to find that it's not human blood on it, but the Python's.

She's near. I puff out my chest.

I pluck the Python's orb out of the air and reset it so it recognizes me as its master instead.

The Python hisses low. "Are you going to kill me, Cobra?" he chokes out, blood leaking from his mouth.

"King Cobra," I correct him. "The female didn't want you," I say, turning away, happy in my knowledge that the human females should not be taken for granted. They bring weapons. They are strong and crafty.

I will not underestimate them.

I take off into the forest, leaving the wounded Python behind.

THREE
DAISY WAKES UP

Daisy

I DON'T SLEEP LONG. Moaning, I peel open my eyes, wishing I could go back to sweet oblivion, but the cold night air stops that from happening. I hug my ruined clothes, wishing for a lot more than sleep.

My bunk on the transport ship is one of those wishes, and having never left *The Dreadnaut* is another. A blanket, a cup of coffee, and the annoying chatter of the two kids who live in the rooms next to mine would be nice as well. I like those kids, more than anyone else in the universe, despite the noise they make. I promised to bring them back a souvenir...

Faces of other kids rise in my head. I shove the memory away.

In slow, jerky movements, I untangle my clothes, trying not to cry out. Placing my hand on my chest, my heart still pounds. Only now that my adrenaline's gone, the cold has crept in.

Feeling my jacket, I straighten it out and slip my arms through the sleeves. The front is torn to pieces, but after I tie the ends together, there's enough left to cover my chest. I grab my pants and breathe a thank you to whatever god is out there when I unravel them. The sides are ripped, but there's enough cloth to band it around my waist.

I slide one pant leg between my thighs and bring it up to tie it with the other one. It takes me at least a dozen tries before I manage to form some sort of loin cloth-like covering. I pause to feel between my legs and make sure I wasn't hurt... *there.*

Everything hurts. Who am I kidding? Thankfully, there's no pain when I probe my sex. I exhale. I curl up and burrow my face into my sleeve.

You were trained for situations like this, I remind myself. *Hold it together.*

Growing up in a military family, with a dad who's considered a hero—a brilliant commander before his death —it was apparent I'd be entering into the service as well, joining the fight against the Ketts. While I'd gotten into all the best academies and did okay in all my courses, I never felt any pride. I knew the entire time I was in training that I wasn't made for war. I wasn't made for death.

The first time I shot down a ship, I couldn't sleep for weeks, haunted by the beings inside it.

Still, it was *my* life, and it was expected that I give it to the demands of the greater good. There was no gilded cage for the daughter of a war hero. I was meant to sacrifice. I was not shielded. Ever.

Violence, torture, exploitation, mind control, cannibalism, and rape. I've seen it all in one way or another.

The Ketts, though unrepentant, bloodthirsty eaters,

didn't torture, exploit, cannibalize, control minds, or rape. I was conditioned to it regardless, and far more, far worse.

I press my face harder into my sleeve. A cadet never knew what colony they were going to be sent to for field training, and humans were as despicable as any other alien species. Some alien cultures are worse still.

I never want to encounter a Gestri, a horse-like species from the planet Illa that can manipulate and control a human's mind with ease. I once saw a video where they forced a man to rape himself... and then eat his genitals. It was punishment for a crime he committed, a murder of one of their elders. Still... It was a lot. It was horrible.

I pull my hand out from between my legs and wipe my fingers on the grass.

I got lucky.

But I don't have Shelby's knife anymore. I curl my knees tighter into me and wince when my scraped knees rub against my jacket.

I don't have clothes.

My boots are still on. I wiggle my toes. *And I'm hungry, dehydrated, and cold.*

I'm alive, though.

Gemma's gone.

I'm...alone.

Thoughts tumble through my head. I'm not fully aware when the Earth's sun crests, but as the shadows weaken, tweeting and chirps sound in the air. None of the noises from yesterday return. There's no hissing or shouts of pain, no hoots or calls. Just the breezy rustle of leaves and the calls of animals. I look up to see the sky through the trees. It's grey and gold.

Yesterday was a nightmare, only a nightmare... I wish I believed it.

Watching the sky change to a light, airy blue, I sit there numbly. My throbbing muscles are bearable when I hold still. Maybe if I remain as quiet as possible, the forest and everything in it will forget about me.

I peer around, and every direction looks the same. Fat bushes with berries press against me on either side. There are tiny thorns on their stems that prick my skin. Twigs and leaves are caught in my hair, and there's something wet. I reach up to touch the side of my head, and my fingers come away sticky.

Red berry juice smears the pads of my fingers as I rub them together. Sniffing it, my nose wrinkles. I wipe my fingers on the ground again and pluck a berry from the bush, spinning it. Reddish-pink, the dimpled orb has an indent.

I set it aside, not yet willing to risk being poisoned. I'm not starving... yet.

Closing my eyes, I take a deep breath. *You can do it. Just stand. You can stand.*

I shift onto my hands and knees and my body screams in protest. I bite back a groan. When I'm certain I'm not going to topple over, I bring one foot forward and shift my weight onto it. It takes me several grueling minutes.

Walking is easier—I have no idea why. I pick the direction in front of me and start heading that way. I'm on a gentle slope.

The facility is outside the gorge. There's forest on every side of it and mountains nearby. Going down is better than up, I decide. I'll know soon if I'm in the gorge or outside it. Doubts emerge anyway.

I can't be more than a couple of miles from the facility. If I can evade the aliens, I'll find my way back to it. I frown, imagining it.

Seeing the barriers, walking in, hailing the team members... And coming face to face with Peter.

Peter might give me back to the aliens.

Should I go back?

Stopping to rest, I head for a tree with large, low branches and climb under them to get out of the sun.

I need a plan.

Captain Peter will give me to the aliens again if I go back—perhaps for even more tech. The facility isn't safe for me or any human woman, and Earth isn't safe either. The only women on the planet are Shelby, Gemma, and me, and Peter wanted to give all three of us to the aliens.

The Dreadnaut will care about Gemma, since she's ranked and knows those in command, but I'm just a petty officer. A pilot. No one of real importance, and exiled. No one is coming for me; no one's going to save little ol' Daisy from the aliens. I'm insubordinate, I *care* too much, and I have too many emotions. It was my compassion that sent me from the front lines of the war against the ravenous Ketts and to serve an old support warship colony like *The Dreadnaut.*

Not even my father's legacy shielded my compassion. I tried for years to numb it, and for a time I had...

Instead of joining my teammates to battle the encroaching blobs assaulting Colony 4, coming on like a tidal wave, I spied a pair of children crying on the roof of one of the buildings below. No older than four world spins, a little boy was cradling his younger sister, a babe, behind a water barrel.

I saw the Ketts coming, the fire, the blasts. I heard screams for reinforcements in my earbuds, instead, I turned back, landed, saved the babies, and took them to base, leaving my battalion behind to fight and die alone. And they died. Every last one of them.

Within hours, I was stripped of my rank and sent to serve *The Dreadnaut*, billions of miles away. I would have been killed but my father's name saved me.

Still, those in higher castes will never help me.

I rub my face. This shouldn't be my problem. I shouldn't be here. *I'm just the fucking pilot.* I know very little about Earth. I'm not part of the team here, not really.

A branch snaps to my right, and my head shoots up. Tensing, I pull my limbs to my body and listen, hearing more snapping and the heavy fling of a tree branch. Fear hits me hard, and everything from the night before comes crashing back.

The terror, the anxiety, the assault.

Something moves through the forest ahead of me. Something giant. I force my joints to unlock and slowly slip to the ground, trying to hide, and praying the simple movement won't alert it.

It's one of them. I stop breathing.

A very long, very large tail slides by, revealing pale beige skin with thick black stripes. I recognize the coloring immediately, recalling the monstrous serpentine alien with a cowl on the plateau. He handed the tech to Peter; he stared at me and scowled like I was a disappointment. I've seen that same look so many times... My chest tightens, and I close my eyes waiting for him to pass.

I get a whiff of his scent, and my throat tightens. I nearly moan.

I dreamed of this scent. His scent.

It angers me. I want to grab my nose, tear it off, and scream.

Something like him, even his smell, shouldn't be

lingering in my head, not with how awful he is, bartering for flesh like it isn't against intergalactic law. Even those in the lowest castes, like me, are protected by that law.

His tail continues sliding by me, unending. It's big. This alien was the largest of the males on the plateau. Of all the things I recall about him and the way he looks, I recall his size. *One thump of that tail could crush me.*

I hold still, waiting until he passes and I don't hear him anymore. And then I wait a little longer before crawling out of my hiding place. Ignoring my throbbing muscles and bruises, I head in the opposite direction from where he went, hurrying my steps. Trying to be as quiet as possible, I fail horribly.

When I don't hear the sounds of pursuit, I start to breathe easier.

I lost him.

Another handful of minutes pass, scurrying as far as I can, when I see water between the trees. Excited, I dash forward until I'm at the edge of a lake.

I saw this lake when I landed the transport ship a month ago. I flew over it.

I'm still close to the facility.

Except I'm in the gorge, not outside it.

I've spent hours studying the maps of this region.

I clap my hands together at my luck and slide down the small bank to the lake's edge. I glimpse my haggard reflection as I cup a handful of water and bring it to my mouth. I'm covered in dirt and flecks of dried blood, and my long hair is a cloud of knots with sticks and leaves caught up in it. The water ripples from my hands and my reflection blurs.

I swallow greedily. When my belly is about to explode, I glance around to make sure I'm alone and scoop up water to clean my face and hands. Coyly, I clean between my legs as well.

If I follow the lake north until it ends and then go north-east from there, I'll be right back at the facility. I look behind me at the mountain slope I just came down. If I go back up toward the plateau, I can get to the facility even quicker.

I push to my feet.

"I've found you," a deep voice says.

My stomach plummets.

I slowly turn. Up on the ledge, the big one with the cowl is staring at me. The giant. The barterer. Our eyes meet and my soul shrivels. *Not him.*

I scream.

FOUR
MY QUEEN

Zaku

I'VE FINALLY FOUND HER.

I can barely hiss, barely breathe. My wicked loins leak with seed, spilling out from behind my scales. I am an idiot for taking the time to dismantle the others, for spreading my seed, when I should have been hunting for my mate.

The Python's orb mentioned only one female is near me, and I hoped it was the one who's mine. The one who hurt him... It excites me.

I feared it would be the redhead I would come upon. She seemed more likely to fight back. But it's not the redhead who has invaded my every thought; she's not the one making my body turn against me. I don't want her, even knowing the rare creature she is. She is not my queen.

My queen is scared, though not scared enough to not sink her blade into the neck of one who would have her.

All night, I searched. All night, I cursed, wanting to shout to the sky, fearing I'd lost her. Even when I used the

Python's orb and it told me there was a single human near my location, I feared.

A king does not fear.

Stumbling through the forest and toward the big lake, she does not yet know that she's been found, that she's been caught, and soon to be claimed so thoroughly that her mind will become as clouded as mine.

I saw her under the tree. I saw her staring at my tail. I've been trailing her since, learning what I can about her. Because I've begun to give off a different smell since my body turned against me, and I don't know why. She has done something to me and I needed to make sure it wasn't another attack of some kind. A sneaky attack. Something else I could admire about her.

Studying her, she looks harmless. My tongue tastes the air.

Her long, light hair is a wild mess down her back, with sticks and leaves poking out of it. Her legs are bare now, and the way the muscles move under her skin as she dodges branches captivates me.

How strange it must be to have legs instead of a tail. How limiting... How does she climb trees? Or protect her backside? Does she not have a single scale to protect her joints?

I slip through the forest behind her, keeping her in my sight, searching her skin for them.

She does not have scales that I can see... not a single one... Worry fills me. These humans have no natural armor. They have no fangs, no claws, nothing to guard themselves against those that wish to prey on them. I've seen human women in images and on the tech, and I have always wondered how such a species survived for so long without natural protection.

I shudder, imagining how easily she could be hurt.

It doesn't matter. I will keep her safe now. I have enough armor for both of us. I dig my claws into my palms, noticing the dirt and grime on her next, the smattering of blood.

It's not hers.

She dashes to the lake's edge when it comes into view. I hear her moan of pleasure, her gasp of wonder when she stops and looks across it to the mountains on the other side.

She comes from the sky... Do they not have lakes in the sky?

She drinks from the lake and washes her flesh. She dives her hands between her legs, rinsing there as well. Did she have to touch her body last night, like I? The thought thrills me. Clasping my member, I squeeze it once more before tucking it back into my tail. She is a small thing. She will bring me greater pleasure than my hand ever could.

Except I failed her.

She endured a cold night in the forest without me, unprotected. A queen should never have to endure such a thing.

She rises to her feet, pulls her yellowish hair away from her face, and smiles softly. My heart slams against my ribs as a streak of sunlight brightens her small form.

I must claim her now before another sees! Before another arrives, wishing for death!

Puffing out my chest, I slip out from behind my tree. "I have found you," I declare, claiming her outright for all to hear, making it known.

She twists toward me, and I expect her to gift me her shy smile. Perhaps her hands will go between her legs again...

Her smile falls. She screams, stumbles back into the water, and trips.

Confused, I jerk forward and reach for her.

"No!" she shouts, blue eyes wide with terror. "No!" She slips through my hands. Water splashes in my eyes.

No?

I hiss, reaching for her again. She evades and splashes to the left, moving further out into the lake.

"The hunt is over," I say, my voice straining as I try to catch her. More water hits my face, and I'm forced to pause and blink it out.

She ignores me, moving further away. I slice my tail to catch her, but her bare skin slips easily over my slick scales. I push through the shallows, hating the feel of the water sliding through them.

"Don't!" I bellow when she dives under and I lose sight of her.

I draw my tail back, flinging the blasted water off my limb. The lake is too big for her to swim across. Only a Blue Coral or Cottonmouth could manage such a feat. And there's no spare tech around for her to use. Gasps fill my ears as she emerges farther out and begins swimming into the deeper waters.

She's going to drown. My jaw pops, searching for something on the shore to catch her and bring her back. There's nothing.

Why is she running from me? I am a king.

The king. The only king.

Growling, the divide between us grows. Desperation strains my limbs as I stare helplessly after her. To keep her from drowning, I'm going to have to go in. I push into the water and dive forward, biting back my disgust. My tail sinks to the filmy lake bottom, scattering stones and silt. The water pulls at my limbs.

Closing in, I grab her ankle, and she shrieks, kicking me in the face. I rear back and slice my tail forward, but the water stops me from striking out and coiling around her.

"We will both drown," I choke, pushing my tail to the lake bottom instead to keep my body above the water's surface.

She dives under again, and I lose her. I thrash, searching the water, scanning the broken waves we've made. With the water so deep and clouded with disturbed silt, I can't see her. I can't see anything.

Water is my weakness. I hate it. There's only one pool I swim in, and it's heated, private. It's nothing like the lake early in the morning. Waving my arms wildly, I search, feeling for her. I will not lose her so easily.

I won't fail again.

She emerges again several lengths ahead of me. My lips twist, and I dive after her.

This time, when I catch her, she doesn't slip through my grip. My fingers close around her arm, banding around the delicate limb.

"No!" she screams again, kicking at me.

We drop into the dark depths as I tug her to my chest, and I feel for the lake's bottom to push off of it. When we break the surface, she's clinging to me, gasping.

"No more, female, no more," I tell her, spitting out lake water. I swim us back to shore.

Holding her tightly to my side, I fall onto the bank and pull my tail out from the lake. My mate pushes off me and rolls away coughing. I do not let her get far, coiling my tailtip around her ankle. She shivers violently and continues to cough. Turning on my side, I press into her back, seeking to warm her.

"The water freezes overnight," I rasp into her ear. "It is not a sssafe place to swim."

She shakes, pressing her limbs to her body, straining away from me.

"I will warm you," I continue, wrapping my arms around her small frame and pulling her into me tightly, draping my tail to slide up her front and closing her in. "My black scales catch the heat. Touch them. Let them take away the cold."

She's tense and doesn't say a word as we lie there in partial shade. She also doesn't touch my scales. I wish she would. I would like to make amends. If she is the one who stabbed the Python, she might be in shock from the kill. Her silence and shivers stop me from prying.

There will be plenty of time for that later. I am content just holding her, knowing the hunt is finally over.

I listen for predators as the sun rises higher, drying us. My member tries to emerge, but I keep it locked away. I won't mount my queen out in the open, on the dirty forest floor, drenched in lake water. She will mate me in my nest, one I have prepared for her, one where she belongs. She will wear my jewels and my collar when she opens her slit for me.

"Are you going to hurt me?" she wheezes after a time, her voice weak and winded and filled with so much sadness it startles me.

"I will never hurt you."

"Then will you let me go?"

I lift my head and study her. She's facing away from me, avoiding touching me any more than I make her. Brows wrinkled deep, there's a hand over her mouth as her eyes stare at the scales of my tail. Even like this, she is beautiful. So beautiful I almost believe I don't deserve her.

Ridiculous. I shake the thought away. I reach down and brush the wet hair on her cheek away.

She flinches at my touch.

"There is nowhere for you to go but to my nest," I say, hoping to soothe her with my words. "There you will rest and eat, and we will mate."

She falls silent again. I spend the next few minutes gathering her wet hair from her face and brushing it out with my claws. Strands of it dry and curl into soft waves around my fingers. I gently squeeze the water out that's gathered in the rest of it, enjoying the simple act of caring for another.

She is in my arms. She is protected. This is good.

"I waited for you for countless yearsss," I hiss. "I will never let you go. Never. You are safe."

She closes her eyes and whimpers.

She must still be cold... Rising, I cradle her in my arms, nuzzling her shoulder.

And with the sun warming my back, I carry my precious treasure home.

FIVE
CAPTURED AND CARRIED AWAY

Daisy

I LET the alien male carry me to wherever it is he plans to take me.

Fighting him, as weak as I am right now, is futile.

Wincing from the built-up water in my ruined jacket and the sun's rays burning my exposed legs, I'm hoping the elements kill me before we get to wherever we're going. They won't. I'm on Earth, after all. Humans evolved here, surviving on this planet for thousands and thousands of years. Somehow, I fear I won't die so easily. If there's anything I've learned growing up traveling through space, it's that humans are remarkably adaptable.

Even after attempted genocide.

Earth has been deemed safe now that the radiation levels have returned to normal. People stopped morphing into gross amalgamations after illegally landing here.

A shiver passes through me. Those first humans—those brave or stupid enough to return—whether for religious, scientific, or greedy reasons, had all suffered for their choice, growing extra heads, even brains, arms, toes. One human turned green before his bones dissolved.

Those humans all survived, which was the most horrifying thing of all. They suffered until death finally came.

Which means I'm probably going to survive too, and it makes me wish I had grabbed my knife when I ran. I stare at the forest canopy until it blurs.

If I hadn't let my compassion win, if I hadn't saved those babies, I wouldn't be here. I'd be dead, and they would be dead too. I take comfort in the fact that they're still alive and so am I.

Hours pass by. Not once does the alien stop to take a break or eat. He carries me like I weigh nothing, slithering away from the lake, through a forest that thickens, over one small mountainous hill, and toward a larger one—the largest mountain on the horizon. It's impossible to miss.

His hands clutch me, reminding me of the male who tried to rape me. This male could be taking me to a private place so he can do what he wants and not have to worry about being attacked.... That would be the smart thing to do, right?

I think I doze for a time, once I realize he's not going to immediately throw me to the ground and assault me. I don't want to sleep, but I'm so tired I can't help it, and the soft swaying of being in his arms. It's annoyingly soothing. I try to sniff him and get a whiff of his scent. It's gone.

The lake water must have washed it away.

I hope... My chest tightens. *I hope he won't hurt me.*

I startle awake when he sets me on the ground. Sitting up straight, I brace. Instead of attacking me, he moves away, perches on his ginormous tail, and yanks several shiny red orbs off of a tree. Once his hands are full, he returns and offers the orbs to me.

I turn away.

"Food," he says, his voice a low rumble.

I stare at the forest. Eventually he hisses, sets the red orbs down, and goes back to pick more. Soon there's a pile of them beside me.

"Eat," he says again, lowering on his tail to wind it behind my back. "Humans love these. I've seen it. They are called apples."

My brow furrows. That doesn't make sense. Humans don't live on Earth anymore. And unless he's seen them iconified from some of Earth's relics, how would he know they liked these apples?

"There's no humans here. You're lying," I say, facing him. I take in his bare chest, his groin region, where there's only smooth scales. My throat tightens. He's naked, except for his scales, and it's very obvious.

A body like his—minus the tail—would be favored by the military. He'd ascend in rank from his size alone.

Lucky bastard.

"I am not a liar," he barks, clearly annoyed at being called such a thing.

The other male had a big cock sticking out of his tail where this one is smooth. Do they not all have cocks? My pulse races as I hope for the miraculous, that he's a eunuch.

He did say we would mate...

I stare at his tail, unable to help it, too dazed to realize how long I've been doing it until the male shifts, startling me. My eyes cut to his face, and my cheeks heat with embarrassment. He's watching me intensely, his cowl pulled taut and framing his pointed face. His tail starts to move, and it's like I'm in a whirlpool of limbs.

My stomach twists and I pull my arms and legs closer.

"Why are you staring at my tail?" he asks a little too thickly for my liking.

I part my lips, closing them again after a second. I shake my head. "I don't want to mate you," I say. "I'm not going to mate you. Let's get this out of the way now. You'll have to force me, like the other one, if that's all you seek from me."

His expression shifts, morphing first to confusion and then to fury. Dark, slitted irises streaked with gold, blaze with emotion.

Fear breaks through my numbness, and I go rigid. Struggling to hold my tears in, I want to fight, to run, but I know I'll never get away. Not again, not without food and rest. I don't even know where I am or how far we've gone, and if it's not him who breaks me, it'll be the wilderness.

"Force... you?" he says slowly. "Force you to do what?" His cowl flares and the scales on his shoulders shoot outward. His face continues to darken.

I lean away, too frightened to answer. His tail shifts again, and I scramble back, pressing against it. He continues to rise over me.

I gape.

"You...were forced?" he growls.

He's so huge. One sweep of his tail would knock me across a room. One hit and I'd be on the ground. He could pin me beneath it and crush me. My fear becomes something more, something harder to fight. Dread.

Rational thought drops from my head as I shoot to my feet, sprinting head-first into the trees. Something snags my ankle. I kick hard and manage to break it off.

He roars.

I run, dashing through the forest in no direction except the one before me. The trees aren't thick anymore, and the bushes are gone. I sprint faster, realizing there are no hiding places. The terrain has changed since I fell asleep.

The ground begins to slope down, and I pick up speed, stumbling over my feet. There are noises behind me—loud, low hissing—and I know he's right there.

I'm not going to get away.

Stopping suddenly, I sag to the ground and sob, curling into a fetal position. My chest hurts so much. I can't breathe. I wait for him to strike me down, to do his worst.

So when he lifts me and cradles me gently, I lose it.

"Ssssshhhh," the male tries to comfort me, making everything worse.

"Why are you doing this?" I gasp. "Why me?"

He begins moving again, and I cry. I inadvertently press my nose to his chest seeking his scent and then whip my face away, disgusted with my actions.

"There are no females left in these lands, no females like me," he says softly, his fingers petting me where his hands clutch me. "You are precious and should belong to a male who deserves you. There is no one more deserving than I. You are beautiful. You are my chosen queen. My—" he clears his throat "—loins recognize you as such. The mere thought of you has filled them with seed. I will avenge you."

I cry harder. He has a cock and plans on using it. I'm disgusted and angry at his words, angry at myself for being too stupid to hope my luck hadn't run out yet.

Numbness claims me again when my tears dry up.

I don't know when it happens, but my mind blanks as the Earth's sun descends below the trees. As the moon climbs in the sky, I realize the trees are all but gone now and he's carrying me up a sloping mountain ledge. We're so high that by peering out over the horizon, the forest, the mountains, and even the lake comes into view. Untamed wilderness with deep greens and blues meets my eyes, cast in the golden hue of twilight.

It's so striking it should hurt. And yet, I just stare at it because it's something to distract me as he winds up the mountain.

To his home. To where he's taking me.

You can survive this, Daisy.

SIX

AN ANCIENT CASTLE AND HIGH-TECH TRAPPINGS

Zaku

THE PYTHON FORCED HER.

It's all I can think about. I want to topple the trees, tear out throats, and crush bones. I want blood in my mouth and my gore under my claws. It was dark when I came across him, and I had not taken the time to interrogate him, nor check if his member was out. If it was wet with human juices.

I'd smelled blood, only his blood. I did not think...

I had thought my female hurt him because she refused to be *his*. Perhaps that is what she means by "forced." But the way she whimpers, the way she turns from me, and what is clearly between us, tangles my mind with doubt. It brings back memories of the naga females who were forced to mate males against their will. The fear they had of *all* males afterward, the paranoia, and the sadness.

A dark, agitated, and furious rumble vibrates in my chest.

If that is what my female has suffered on her first night in my world, I have failed far more than I'd thought. Doubt niggles in the back of my skull. Perhaps Krellix was right...

Maybe we should have let the females choose.

I instantly dismiss the thought. I would not stand it if my female chose another over me; I would kill him and take her anyway.

If the Python forced her, then he committed the only crime we have.

The worst thing a naga could do.

I thought I was rid of them. The ones who destroyed us. I thought there were no nagas left who would risk doing such a wretched thing as raping a female. The dishonorable ones should've been gone from these lands. *I've killed so, so many...* The ones who cared nothing for life and only thought about themselves and their needs. It was because of these savage nagas that the naga females left. One forced mating could result in gestation, and gestation has always led to death.

Not humans, though. I cradle Daisy closer. I will make sure the Python is dead, that his meat is given back to the land. It's my duty to keep the others in line.

Scanning my surroundings with fervor, if any naga happens to be trailing us, he will die. My trust is gone.

Glancing down at my mate, I am certain if I spill my seed inside her, she will survive the litter that will result from our union. I have a human medical pod in my den to ensure her survival.

I've prepared—for years, I prepared—with hope that eventually she would come to me. I had nothing else to do but wait and prepare.

The naga females journeyed to the west, long ago. My

mother had been dead for decades by the time it happened, and I had just matured, the only one she birthed before she perished. There is not a day that has gone by that I don't carry the weight of her death.

I didn't realize then what I do now. How dearly the males left behind would miss them. If I had, I would have followed the other females west. Some tried to follow, only the females killed them or forced them to turn back. Brothers, fathers, friends...

However, if I had followed, I'm sure they would have let me join them. I am a king, after all. Nothing is higher than a king. A king is beloved by all.

My mate has been quiet for some time, and I don't know if I like it or not. She gazes off into the distance, her face emotionless.

What did the Python do to her? Did he force his member inside her? Did he spill?

Disgust fills me at the thought.

I should have made sure he died. I should have taken the time to kill him or at least cut off his tail so he would suffer, crippled, until death finally came, until the monsters of the forest found him and finished him off.

"I will gift you his head," I growl, swallowing the venom leaking from my fangs.

Her chest rises as she inhales deeply before her breathing returns to normal. It is the only response I get from my declaration. I tear my eyes away from her.

Seeing the broken path to my den ahead, I hasten only to stop, knowing that if another naga is still hunting for a mate and knows one is with me, he may have staked out my den. It is what I would do if I were not a king and had to use other, trickier means to get what I want.

Daisy looks up at me, then around, noticing I've stopped.

"Do not make a noise," I warn, lowering my voice.

I scrutinize the few trees and boulders one might hide behind as I start heading for my den again. Unlike most nagas, my home isn't tucked away, fully hidden from the world. It's out in the open, built into the side of the tallest mountain, and can be seen from certain vantage points from miles away. Though it is camouflaged to a degree, the glass walls sometimes glint while looking upon it far in the distance.

Someone important lived here once, someone who wanted to oversee all the land below.

Someone with wealth and power. Because that is what this old human home is, a place of vast power. Through a secret tunnel, one connected to the room my nest is in, is a relay. A piece of technology—a machine—that is still working from the old world. I don't know how it works but based on research I've done from the books in this place, it helps connect all the technology in this region together.

Many males have journeyed here at one point or another, seeking to take my den from me. All have failed. And they do not even know of the power source I reside over. They do not know that their precious information orbs would stop working if I wanted them to. They do not know that I keep the Earth from dying.

Me alone.

They do not know how generous I am. Only Vruksha knows, somewhat, and it is because we once hunted down dirty rapists together.

Though my home is out in the open, it is secure, and I am not an easy male to beat in a fight. Skulls litter the ground around the entrance, a warning to any who seek to take something from me I am not willing to give away.

As I near, I see nothing waiting for us in the shadows, nothing except rocky steps, tall grass, skulls, and piles of bones. I finally relax when I reach the security panel at my den's entrance. Typing in a code, the door opens.

I carry my mate into my home.

Triumph washes over me when the door shuts. Sliding to the seating area in the large living space, I lower her upon it. She pulls her arms and legs into her, curling up as if she's trying to make herself small.

She is already tiny enough. She does not need to be smaller!

My nostrils flare.

I reach out and thread my fingers into her hair. "I am not like the Python."

She turns her head so she doesn't have to look at me. "And the bones?" she asks numbly.

I hiss. "Filth I have purged."

When she shrinks further, I realize I'm going to have to prove it to her. She doesn't know me, nor my people. She doesn't know if she can trust us. She didn't even recognize the fruit I offered her. She jumped into a frigid lake at first light...

Tonight, I decide, I will go back out and collect the Python's head.

"Rest," I say, pulling back. "I'll feed you."

Staring at her for a moment longer, until I'm certain she won't meet my eyes, I head for the kitchen. Lights turn on when I move through the wide central space of my upper den. The front of the entry space is made of glass and can be seen into by anyone who braves to get close enough. The inside is minimally decorated. The humans who built this place did not like *things*. Which is why I don't mind leaving Daisy's side. There is little she can hurt herself with, and there's no escape.

White and silver, sleek with old tech appliances, the kitchen, like the rest of my home, has glass walls and a view of the mountains and forest below. Most of my den does. The walls to the outside are either glass or the rocky mountain interior.

I hear movement, and I see my mate sprinting to the exit, yanking the handle. She shrieks when the door doesn't budge, slamming her fists against it.

"It's locked," I rumble.

She runs to another door, throwing it open and ducking inside. Something crashes from within, and she shrieks again, angrier this time.

My hands clench as I hear a sob, and she comes out of the room a few minutes later. She looks at me only to avert her eyes, striding from one room to the next in the hallway off the living area. She's not going to find anything but spare rooms. This place is like a labyrinth of nothing. Quiet, perfectly preserved, nothing.

It has barely changed since I took ownership of this place. The house won't let it change. I have destroyed it before—during times of wrath. The robots that live here just rebuild it. They are as much a menace as they are generous to the house's inhabitants.

There is another frustrated scream.

Trying to calm, I force my hands to uncurl and go to open the kitchen's icebox. Inside are slabs of raw meat from my recent kills. I place the juiciest one on the counter as she heads for the last door in the back hallway.

The red one. It's thicker than the others and has a lock like the front.

She's no longer running now that it's clear I'm not going to stop her. This den is hers now as much as it's mine.

I silently slip up behind her as she tugs the handle to the immobile door.

"My nest, little human, is beyond that door. It's locked for that reason."

She startles and faces me, pressing her back to the door. Her eyes are wide with renewed fear.

With my hands slippery with meat juices, I reach beside her and type a code into the panel next to the door. The door opens, and she slinks back onto the threshold, watching me warily.

"Our nest," I declare, "lies within the spaces the robots have chosen to block off from outsiders."

Whoever once lived here... was an unusual being. The secrets of my home are why I decided to stay. That, and the robots have decided I am the home's new master.

Her eyes hood as she turns to look within. Tension radiates through me. I've waited for this moment for years. For her, and her alone, I've helped preserve the best nest in all the world. I want to see that spark of wonder finally hit her eyes when she realizes she is beloved. No one but me has gone through this door since I claimed this space.

My mate is the most beautiful. Beautiful creatures should be worshipped and surrounded by the best. It is the least a king can do for his queen.

She glances at me, and though she scents of sweat, her skin is grimy, and her hair a tousle of tangles, I still see her beauty beneath it all. She doesn't look queenly right now. She needs a bath.

I did not see, nor smell, spill on her from the Python. It may have washed off at the lake.

Was that...why her hands were between her legs?

I grit my teeth, sickened and horrified that I touched my member while she cleaned him off of her. I need to make sure she is entirely clean of him and his repulsive fluids. I want her adorned in my wealth, and as pure as the first moment I laid eyes on her. Right now, she is dirty, and it was not me who has made her that way. I don't like it.

If I want her dirty, I'd make it so. I don't, I want her beautiful, surrounded by beautiful things, and fresh to touch.

I will not only bring back his head, but I will also bring back his member, his spine, and his hands. I will rip him apart.

"Your nest," she whispers. "Not mine."

"Take a look," I encourage her, hiding my fury.

She trembles, peering down the dark, windowless hallway and the winding stairs at the end. Until she goes down those stairs, there's nothing to see except for some pictures hanging on the walls. She turns back and evades me, denying it, us.

Hissing low, I bristle.

She doesn't seem to notice as she sidesteps and heads for the kitchen. Agitated and curious, I trail her. She stops when she sees the meat.

"Food," I growl, passing her, rubbing my tail over her legs, marking her.

She jumps away. "What is this place?"

Does she not listen? "My den."

Watching me intensely, she crosses her arms, making her jacket leak with water. "How is this possible?" she says, near cowering, keeping the counter between us. "Everything is—" her eyes flick around "—brand new. This doesn't look like a... home."

Using my claws, I cut the meat into slabs. "The robots preserve it."

Her eyes dart left and right. "Robots?"

I call out, "House, initiate cleanup." Buzzing sounds fill the space and several wall panels open to the left of me. She turns as tall, thin machines with extendable arms and screens come out. They spread out as red lasers shoot from their limbs. They probe and pick at things, straightening them or dissolving them from existence. They come out on their own to keep the house the way they want it. They also come at my command.

She watches the robots, her mouth dropping open as one comes up to her and lasers the stone tiles at her boots. The water that dripped there sizzles and evaporates. I move around the counter while she's distracted.

Stepping back, she lands against my chest.

I embrace her, but she flings herself away.

Clenching my hands, I hold in my growl. "House," I call out. "Obey her." I indicate my mate. "Make her a master of this place." I turn to her, lowering my voice. "Tell them to stop if you do not like what they're doing."

"Stop!" she sputters out, and at once, all of the robots halt what they're doing. She moves further away as she takes notice. The more I watch her, the more her responses confuse me. "You'll let them respond to me?"

"Yes."

She reaches out and touches one of the robots only to pull her hand away soon after. "They will not hurt you, nor will they hurt anyone else. They will protect this place, though, keep it how it is, and that is all."

"Unlock the front doors," she says.

One of the robots heads for the door.

I grab her arm before she can bolt after it. "Stop!" I yell, making the robots pause. "Never respond to that command. Turn off," I order them next, and they retreat to their spots in the walls. Pulling Daisy into my chest, she struggles futilely. "Stop," I command again. When she continues to thrash, I spin her and grab her wrists.

"Do you understand what would happen if you run? You are far from the plateau and your human ship now. The forests are no longer clear for the hunt. The predators will have returned by now, brought in by the lure of fresh blood in the air. This mountain is home to bears, giant felines, and far worse. Even if you do not trip and fall by descending in your current state in the dark, you will inevitably face them. What will you do then?" I scan her small form. "You have no weapon, no armor, you have no scales, claws, or even fangs to defend yourself."

Her face has gone white, and I loosen my hold on her wrists. "How can you say that? Your walls are made of glass. Nothing about this place is safe," she breathes. "How do you know my name?"

I let go of her and grab the metal dining table, lifting it above my head. With all my might, I throw the table against the nearest glass wall. A loud clang pierces the quiet space of my den as the table strikes the glass and clatters to the floor.

The glass holds.

Snagging the table with my tail, I bring it back to me, right it, and settle it back into place before the robots get to it. "See? It holds. It will always hold. Many have tried to take this place from me," I rasp, "and all have failed. I leave their heads, their bones, outside as a warning to others. I am Zaku, King Cobra, king of this mountain, king of the forest, and king of all you see before you now fading in the darkness the moon brings. No one has fought me and lived. No one."

She freezes with my words.

"Now, female, you will eat, or I will force you. I will make you beautiful again."

I turn on her and take her stunned form into my arms.

SEVEN

THE SECOND NIGHT

Daisy

HE NEVER TOLD me how he knows my name...

Sitting stiffly, I stare down at my hands in the water. Warm, clear, luxurious water that fills the giant tub I'm in.

Warm water.

A tub that's within the most decadent bathroom I've ever seen. Creamy stones make up the floor, leading to a jet-black stone basin in the center. One wall is entirely curved and made of glass, but I can't see anything out of it right now. It's dark outside, and the bathroom is lit up in a golden glow.

Like the rest of Zaku's home I've seen so far—glassy, sleek, bright, and beautifully open—the bathroom is much the same. It's off one of the side rooms, and Zaku led me here after I refused to eat any more than a couple of bites from his hand. I had let him lead me, having exhausted my pride with the shame of being fed like a child.

He could hurt me here as easily as he could hurt me

anywhere in this place. It doesn't matter which room he wants me in.

The alien forced me to eat and demanded I bathe. He calls me beautiful. He calls me a queen. I grab my head as it spins.

He tried to get me inside a medical pod, which was in one of the side rooms, saying it would help me heal. He did this with a scowl on his face and his eyes staring at my legs. While I'd go in any pod on *The Dreadnaut,* I'm not about to go inside ancient technology.

Zaku hissed and took me to this bathroom instead.

He forced me to eat from his hand. I try shaking the whole episode from my head.

Instead of forgetting it, I recall the way his eyes darkened as he pressed the meat to my lips, when I relented and took a bite. I drop my hands from my head and scrub my lips clean, pumping more soap as I do.

There are gleaming silver spouts beside me, and each one is labeled in Old Human. The common tongue's origins are Old Human. *Soap, shampoo, and something called conditioner.* Testing the conditioner between my fingers, I sniff it. Vanilla fills my nose. It's nothing like the chlorinated, chemical stuff I'm used to.

It's nothing like Zaku's scent...

Pulling my limbs close, staring at the closed door and the wooden chair I leaned up against it after he left, I lather the conditioner between my hands and scrub it into my hair.

I don't know if he'll change his mind and barge in. There are no weapons in the bathroom, at least nothing that could be used against a beast like Zaku. I searched thoroughly under his gaze—as he filled the tub. He did not seem to care.

Which is concerning. I suck my lips into my mouth. How have I gone from shivering and naked in an alien forest to this? I scrub my hair feverishly.

This shouldn't be possible. This bathroom shouldn't be possible. It's one thing to encounter sentient alien life, another that they could already speak the common tongue without a translator, but this? I glance around the bathroom. This is something else.

I don't know how to handle it.

Once upon a time, did humans live this extravagantly? I almost giggle. I have no idea. I'm in one of the lowest castes in society. I haven't been near such finery since I was a babe and under the control of my father's authority.

Zaku, King of the Mountain, has everything and more. This bathroom alone has more wealth than I'll ever make in my entire life. Captain Peter and Collins would give their souls to be where I am right now. Most people would.

If I bring Peter and Collins here, perhaps they'll let me return to The Dreadnaut.

My mood sours at the thought.

I'd sooner shoot them than help them ever again. I don't like what's happening with the Ketts anymore than anyone else, but I'm not going to give a prize to the men who practically sold me into slavery.

Or matehood.

Or sexual matehood slavery. I haven't figured it out.

"What is taking you so long?" he rumbles, his voice muffled behind the door.

Tensing, I stop washing.

I might not be as afraid of him as I was earlier, but I still don't trust him. Though, if he were going to hurt me, he would have done it by now. I saw what he did with the table...

He's strong. Really, really strong.

The fact that there's a door between us means nothing—he can come in whenever he pleases.

I'm going to have to answer him or he'll come in here. Just as I think this, the lock on the door clicks.

"Wait!" I shout, covering myself. "My hair takes a long time to wash." Bracing for his entry, I stare at the door.

I hear a low, raspy hiss, and the door closes without ever opening. "I will wait," he grates.

Bending my knees, I hug them to my chest.

Maybe not all these aliens are bad.

A tremble shoots through me, and I reach between my legs to feel my sex again. The other male hadn't penetrated me, except the pressure of his cock is still there, present as a ghost. Every time he comes to mind, I feel it. I hope it vanishes soon.

I yank my hand away.

I clean my wounds in record time, and afterward, when I'm drying and watching my dirty bath water drain away, I snag the tube of moisturizer on the bathroom counter. It smells of something clean, something sweet. I could never afford something like this on *The Dreadnaut*.

Stepping up to the floor-to-ceiling mirror across from the bath, I wince. My sides are mottled purple from where the Python gripped while swinging through the trees. There are smaller bruises on my legs. My knees are scraped up, and my legs are pinkening with sun damage.

You're alive.

I quickly go to my clothes, lifting my ruined pants and jacket off the floor. They're dirty and destroyed. Grabbing the towel I dried with, I wrap it around me instead.

Reassuring myself that I'm going to be okay until I almost believe it, I head for the door and stop before it.

"Zaku—" I'm hoping I say his name right "—do you have something I can wear?" I hear shifting on the other side, and I curl my arms tighter around my body.

"Wear..." I hear him murmur. He doesn't say anything more.

Shifting anxiously, I peek out. The room on the other side is empty. Exhaling, I wait for him to return.

Soon, Zaku comes back with his arms full of various cloth products, ones vibrant with more colors and patterns than I've seen in my life. He sees me in the doorway and stops.

"Female," he purrs, his golden-glinted eyes searching my face.

"Daisy," I correct with a far steadier voice than I thought I had in me. "My name is Daisy, not female. If you know it, use it."

"Like the flower," he says.

My head tilts.

"Flower?" I ask hesitantly. "I'm not named after a flower." My father named me after my great-grandmother.

"Daisies are a common flower in my forest. They are beautiful and delicate, like you."

I'm named after an Earth flower? I furrow my brow.

Now, I long to see this flower. Flowers are rare. Swallowing, I eye the cloth Zaku is holding as the strangeness of our conversation makes me increasingly uneasy.

"Can you put those clothes on the bed?" I whisper.

He straightens and dumps the clothes without taking his eyes from me. My gaze goes to his tail. I haven't given it much attention, though I've noticed it... How could I not? Long, coiled, and scaled across a furnished room—it's so out of place. It threatens to fill the space entirely.

His tail is different from the rest of him, shifting from

beige, brown, and black stripes upon his upper chest, becoming straight black as his scales reach his tailtip. There are still stripes at his tailtip, but they're thin. Even his tailtip is thick.

I'm suddenly grateful he doesn't eat humans like the Ketts. I could fit inside his tail several times over. He'd need to eat a lot of humans to sustain a body like his.

Zaku's chest swells when he notices me staring. He lifts slightly and straightens even more.

Is he trying to impress me?

"Why do you hide behind the door?" he asks.

I grip my towel tighter. "I'm not dressed."

Heat floods his gaze.

"I wish to see you," he says.

My fear returns. "N-Not yet. Can you please step—uh, slip out so I can dress?"

His eyes narrow and his mouth twists, like my request is ridiculous.

He thinks I'm beautiful and called me a... queen? An idea forms, and I add before he can tell me *no*, "I want to look my best. For you. I... wish to hide my bruises."

He pauses.

"Please? For me?"

For a moment, I don't think he's buying it. He looks like he wants to argue. His hands open and close, and my eyes narrow in on his small claws.

"I wish to lick your bruises, so dressssss, and do it quickly," he hisses, his eyes glinting, his cowl expanding. "I will not wait much longer," he threatens as he leaves the room.

I scurry from the bathroom and fumble through the clothes on the bed, not needing to be threatened twice. They're all women's clothes, and it makes me wonder if another woman lives here. Then I remember where I am and who I'm with. If there was another woman, why barter for me and Gemma?

I hope she's okay. I frown. I hope I'll be okay.

Finding a pair of soft white slacks, a white shirt, and a loose, drapey sweater, I drop my towel and dress. I'm tugging the sweater on when the bedroom door flies open.

I jerk and face the door.

Zaku fills the entire frame and then some.

Piercing eyes trail over my body. He licks his lips, his gaze more feverish than before.

"Little human," he rasps thickly, coming straight for me. "It's time to nest."

EIGHT

THE ROOM

Daisy

"Let me down!" I snap, pushing at his chest. Zaku doesn't budge. He carries me out of the room and down the hall-way, toward the red door at the end.

"You will sleep in my nest and only in my nest," he hisses, his hold on me tightening.

I kick my legs and arch my back. It makes no difference. The doors flash by until we're passing the threshold of the red one and crossing the empty hall with walls covered in pictures. "I will not!"

"You have walked enough for today," he says, ignoring me. "I've allowed you your bath in privacy. I allowed you to dress. I have fed you and given you all you have asked, and now you will obey me. You will sleep in my nest, or you will not sleep at all," he warns, stopping and catching my wide eyes. I pause my thrashing. "What will it be?"

And then I feel it.

Pressing up, hard and probing to my backside, between

where he cradles me to his chest. Staring into his shadow-gold eyes, stunned, it takes me a moment to comprehend what's rubbing and pushing up against my ass.

His prick. His straight, hard, cock.

Hell—I writhe upward—*how is that possible?*

Zaku clutches me to his chest as I thrash even harder. Where did his cock come from?

Where did he hide *that*? It's like a dagger to my back. *No, more like a club*. And it's hot, it nearly burns.

"Calm down!" he orders, his thick voice reverberating. "Or I will spill all over your backside!"

I cower, and he tucks me back into the cradle of his arms. When he begins moving again, the pressure of his cock is gone.

"I'll sleep in your nest," I utter, still coming to terms with what I just felt. "Just keep it—that thing," I stammer, "hidden."

Without responding, he takes me down a spiral staircase. My belly jumps trying to imagine how big his cock is. It's big enough to ram into my back as he moves. I thought the other male's cock was large...

A tremble shoots through me, the ghost of pressure between my legs returning. *I stabbed him. He's gone. He can't hurt me again.*

Zaku looks down at me, and I avert my eyes.

The spiral staircase comes to an end, and I realize that there are no glass walls or windows in this new room. It would be pitch black if it weren't for the small white lights above.

Another realization hits as I turn to watch the door shut behind us.

I'm never going to be able to escape this place.

He moves deeper, and I turn to see where he's taking

me now. We're in a large seating room that's shaped exactly like the one above. Except this one has no view over a lush, alien landscape. There are no windows at all. Where the one above was bright, white, and airy—even at night—this one is the opposite in every way.

The furniture is black, the tiles and walls are a dark metal grey, and instead of a kitchen, there's a pool, lit up in a midnight purple glow. He takes me across the room and toward the only door.

"My nest," he announces, his deep voice teasing my ears as he opens it, and a dim, soft golden glow reveals the room beyond.

My chest constricts when he brings me to the center. Staring at the view before me, I can't look away. The entire back wall is a window, like above, but instead of darkness, I see Earth's moon in its glory and a sky filled with stars. I untangle from Zaku's arms, and he lets me down. I walk to the window, seeing my reflection in it as I press up against it.

A forest and a mountain range cast in silvery moonlight greet me. They span for countless miles in every direction.

But it's the abrupt drop outside the window that has my throat constricting. I try to peer downward, to see how steep it is, finding nothing except impenetrable shadows. I step back from the abyss as my stomach churns.

I turn, taking in the rest of the room, trying my best to ignore the giant male—a male who fills every room to capacity—watching me.

My eyes fall on the bed. It's huge, covered in a mess of spilled blankets and large pillows. It's near the ground, situated on a pedestal that only slightly rises from the floor. The blankets pour off it like inky black liquid, making it look overly full. Like its master.

Something glints in the corner of my eye, and I turn toward it. My brow furrows.

Gold prison bars fill my vision. They climb from the floor, stopping just before the ceiling where they begin tapering, curving to come together at a point in the center. They make a large, cylindrical shape, and inside is a swing. There's a barred door, left wide open to let someone inside it.

I notice the lock. "What is that?"

"A cage," he responds.

"Like for a pet?"

"For a human, I believe."

"Why do you have it?" I whisper, hugging my body.

"It was here when I found this place."

"What is *this place*?"

He moves to the cage and wraps his fingers around one of the gold bars as if testing it. "Do you not listen? A bedroom. My nest."

That's not what I mean but I don't say this. "And behind those other doors?"

His eyes return to me as his tail slips circles behind my back. "One is a bathroom, one is a closet, and the other, I believe the house told me, is called a playroom. I do not understand why."

I don't know what's going on anymore and it scares me. I don't want to know what constitutes *"play"* for someone who has a human cage. This isn't just a house and a bedroom...

There's something really unsettling about this place.

"I want to sleep upstairs."

"No."

"I'm not sleeping here."

"You are."

"If you think that, you—"

"My mate will sleep in my nest!" he snaps, making me fall back. He reaches for me, and I scurry away. "You will not fight me on this!" He shoots forward until he's directly in front of me, catching me. He clasps my chin and forces me to meet his eyes. "Here, female, I am king. Here, you will bow down to me and submit. I have hunted you, caught you, chosen *you* for my queen." He bares his fangs. "And now you will be one."

Gone is the male who lulled me into safety, who carried me, and gave me a false sense of exhausted comfort. His tail slides up the back of my body, trapping me in his limbs.

"I'm not your mate," I wheeze. "I'll never be your *queen*."

Fury flashes in his eyes, and I brace for him to strike me.

His mouth slams on mine.

Zaku's rough, velvety lips move against mine in a frenzy —sucking, plucking, and nipping at my parted ones. Shocked, I can't respond. I feel like I'm suffocating by what's happening. Vaguely aware I'm pushing at his chest, it's the only resistance I give.

He groans and it's thick and animalistic, making my flesh prickle. He's a predator, and I'm his prey. His growls fill my mouth and slip into my throat. They puncture my soul and vibrates it from within. It's not fair. He leans into me, pushing me against his tail. I strain my back. He's too large, too overwhelming. With his hard, muscled chest flushed to mine, he's devouring me.

I stir.

His lips move on me faster when I do, completely covering my mouth and then some, far larger than mine. Clawed fingers tangle into my air, tickling my scalp. They move downward.

His scales are hot, warming my skin where they're pressed to my skin.

He pushes my legs apart, sliding between them, and the club of his alien cock falls out. He undulates and his tail rubs over my sex. A spike of sensation rips through me, consuming my mind.

A forked tongue invades my mouth, and I gasp, finally responding.

"No!" I tear from his hold, from fingers whispering across my body, from the coiled tailtip tangled in my hair. "No," I whimper, feeling my eyes burdened with tears. I hate that they do. I reach for a pillow and grip it, using it as a shield.

I try not to cry, but my tears fall anyway.

Sobbing, everything hits me all at once, and it's like the floodgates opening. I was almost raped, I almost died. I murdered someone. Glimpsing Zaku's horrified expression as he backs away, makes it worse.

I was betrayed by my own people. Again.

I'm *lost*.

I'm alone. Again.

I'm alone when I finally fall asleep.

NINE

A BLOODY TRAIL OF VENGEANCE

Zaku

I claw my way out of my room and to the other side of my
den, putting distance between me and my... Daisy before I
do something I'll regret.

Why won't her tears leave my head? I head for the exit
of my home.

She scrambled to the other side of the room, acting like
if she didn't get away, I would hurt her, or worse. Tension
radiates from me. It wafts in the air and my nostrils flare,
scenting the new smell my body has begun creating.

She is mine! My body knows this—does hers not?

Then I remembered the Python. I remember the fear I
incite in others as I near them. I'd forgotten in the excitement of seeing Daisy dressed in clothes I provided, of
carrying her down to my nest for the first time that I am a
male to be feared.

My member is swollen past the point of pain. All I
wanted to do was grab her and shake her into her senses.

Jutting out of me now, my cock swells. I yank the wretched thing, squeezing the giant bulge expanding in the middle. All day, its pressure has tortured me. I wanted to jump my Daisy and mount her; I wanted to invade her bath and plant her onto my stem until it was she who bathed me, until she was even dirtier than before, a mess from my spill.

After, I would clean her at my leisure, satiated. I would lick her wounds and convince her to let the medical pod heal the blemishes on her skin.

Instead of heading for the exit, I turn for the bathroom Daisy had bathed in.

Waiting outside her bath, knowing she was full of the meat I hunted for her, knowing she was naked and her sex would be easy to see, easy to mount, was hellish. It had driven all rational thought from my mind. Staring at the room now, being cleaned by robots, I grip my shaft and force my seed out.

Spilling it all over the tiles, I yank my member until I'm able to tuck it back into my tail comfortably. The pressure will return, but for this moment, my mind is clearer. Shame hits, staring down at my seed.

My lack of finesse is unbecoming.

I scared her. Because another male hurt her. Because I am a male to be feared

She's crying.

Again.

My mouth fills with venom.

I tell the robots to take care of her—to *not* let her leave— as I head outside.

The sun is ascending above the mountains, and a soft pink glow is bleeding into the waning blue night when I leave. An early morning chill breezes across my scales. I hate dawn for this reason. I prefer direct sunlight.

I descend the mountain path with speed.

This is the first day Daisy is in my den. I should be with her, coiled around her. Instead, I am hunting. If I can't have her, I can at least have my bloodlust.

Only the Python's head, his spine splayed out, his fangs ripped from his skull, will sate me now.

His head will be the first of many gifts I give my female.

She will see it and worship me. She will know that I will destroy her admirers and her enemies.

Morning vanishes into noon. I know these lands like the pattern of my scales. And without a delicate, scaleless human to protect, I am unhindered. The chill of dawn fades in favor of a hot, summer day. Invigorated, I snatch a rabbit as it flees. It struggles for a moment before I snap its neck and cut my fangs through its fur, stripping it off to devour the meat.

If the Python lives, I'll need my strength to finish him off. We are hard to kill. We regenerate if we're not adequately destroyed. It's annoying.

Fury fills me for leaving him—and the rest of the nagas —alive. I won't make that mistake again. Perhaps I should have obliterated all of them. If I had, they would not be the nuisances they are now.

Passing through the gorge, I angle in the direction of the lake. I climb up a ledge and scan the treetops, locating the general area I last saw the Python. If he hasn't slithered away or been eaten by bears, pigs, or worse, he'll still be in the area.

There are worse things in my forest than animals. Creatures like *me* that I used to spend a great deal of time hunting so they would not take over my land. When I was a young serpent, there were more monsters than nagas. Now, they are rare.

But if any monsters show up...

I will kill them like I always have.

The sun is lowering when I find the very spot I captured Daisy. Stopping at the shore, my member shoots from my tail, imagining her bare legs.

Hissing, I grab it and stuff it back in, following my old trail. When snake blood fills my nostrils, I pick up speed.

Bursting through the trees, I come upon ground soaked with it, but no male. The Python's gone. Slamming my tail against the nearest tree, I crack the trunk. In the light, my eyes take in the area.

Picking up a piece of cloth the same color as Daisy's ruined pants, I grip it in my fist and bring it to my nose, inhaling her scent. I glimpse more shreds of cloth nearby.

He tore her clothes.

He left her practically naked in the cold night. She is scaleless and small!

I roar. This male forced himself upon my female, tore her clothes. I gather up everything I can, making sure nothing of Daisy's is left behind. Everything of hers, is mine. I will cherish every piece of her. I tie the cloth together, using the shirt to band everything around my arm, as I glare at the bloody spot on the ground.

It is good he did not make her bleed. My breath wheezes through my teeth. I needed to see this.

Eyeing the blood, I notice a trail leading away, in the opposite direction of the lake, and back up toward the mountain slopes. Checking the sun's position, I realize I won't make it back to Daisy tonight.

He will pay for that as well.

Once again, I must make a choice... I hiss furiously.

I go after the Python.

TEN
A HEAD FOR A HEAD

Zaku

I FOLLOW the trail until I lose it in the darkness.

The Python continues to bleed. His wound is deep. Daisy nicked a vein, and thanks to that I'm able to track his path. By staying low to the ground, his blood is enough to lead me, even in the dark.

My female is fierce and direct. I will remember this. But I am certain I'll never give her a reason to stab me. That is a mess I wouldn't like to clean. Though my member is another story entirely. It wants to stab repeatedly.

I groan as it falls out of my tail again, too big to stay within comfortably, and absently tug it as I continue. At least the darkness is good for something. It hides my shame.

The scent of the blood builds, and I lift, narrowing my eyes. I spill my seed and shove my shaft away. There's too much blood to be distracted. I slow my pace and listen. Chirps of insects sound in my ears but nothing else. I continue on until I realize it's a different scent that's now leading me.

It's not just the Python's blood in the air anymore... I taste the air. *Pig.*

Coming across a pig's corpse soon after, I pause to check it out. Mangled and broken, it's twisted into two halves. Chunks of flesh have been torn from the main part of the body—and it's still bleeding. A fresh kill. A recent one. From the way the body has been left behind, the Python caught it up in its tail and choked the life out of it. His clan wasn't blessed with venom, only strength.

If there's one pig, there's more.

Slipping into the shadows, I move on.

I come across several more in the next clearing. The branches are broken; the ground is flattened. There was a struggle here. One of the pigs wheezes, and I smash its head in with my tail. Tearing off its back leg, I don't let the fresh meat go to waste.

He's close.

I scan the shadows.

I scent him in the breeze, his sweat, his musk. There's also dirt and... rot? His scent is strange, like mine, and it churns my stomach.

Good. He's intact and alive.

I get to make him suffer. He needs to suffer. He's caused me much strife these last two days, and for that alone, deserves death. For hurting my mate, he will endure tremendous pain during his last moments in this world. Devastating, shameful pain.

Leaving my mate behind has to be worth something. She will forgive me if I bring her back the Python's head. She will look at it and smile, seeing the torment I caused in his dead eyes. And once her fear has been abated, she will embrace me and take all I have to offer. She will know.

I finish off the pig leg, flicking my tongue through my fingers to lap the blood.

Daisy won't have any choice but to accept me if I give her the head of the one who hurt her. Hissing, I slink forward. If she fears my kind, I will gift her all their heads.

Another clearing is ahead of me, and the sounds of slurping, cracking, and thumping reach my ears. Something moves, a dark shape amongst the leaves. It's bowed over another form, a twitching one.

The Python. I lick my fangs, readying for my vengeance.

Blood shoots into the air, and then it's gone.

I slither forward, careful not to make a sound as I slip my tailtip toward him through the overgrowth. He's had days to regenerate, his strength may have returned.

I hear an oink to the right of me, and a pig crashes through the trees. I still as the Python jerks back and snarls. Rabid and angry, the pig attacks him head-on. *Dumb creature.* The Python snags its back leg and yanks the hog into the air. It squeals and writhes. Its leg snaps, tearing from taut tendons.

The Python holds it there for a moment, watching the pig's misery before he slams it onto the ground and coils his tail around its body. Another crack, a squeal and a crunch, and it's dead.

The Python returns to his meal.

Feral, savage male.

My fangs drip as I approach, snaking my tail slowly through the moss.

I grab his tail and yank it hard away from him. He startles and reacts, jerking his tail back, but not before I shoot forward and throw my body atop it. My weight is enough to hold it down. He is weak from his wounds.

Our eyes meet, and his bloody scowl greets me in the moonlight. He undulates to dislodge me, but there's no strength behind it.

"We meet again," I say, clawing my fingers into the stab wound on his neck. He screams and rakes at my chest as blood gushes over my claws. His tail thrashes and thumps futilely under me.

I curl my limbs around his, sinking my fingers deeper into him.

"Cobra," the Python croaks as I obliterate his larynx. He claws at my chest, his nails biting into my scales. Eyes wide, dark slits move from my face to stare up at the night sky as I drape the rest of the way over him, keeping him beneath me.

He does not get to see the sky again. He will see me when his heart stops.

I watch him die. It's slow and agonizing, twisting my claws under his flesh, mushing his insides, prolonging it as long as I am able. He grabs my hand weakly and tries to pull it out.

"You know your crime," I say as his gaze hoods.

I wait several more minutes, ensuring his pulse doesn't start beating again and his body doesn't try regenerating. When I'm sure he's dead, I climb off him, tug my hand from his neck, and get to work.

I tear off his head first, twisting it the way he twisted the dead pigs. As I set his head aside, atop a branch in a tree nearby, I listen for more pigs or other predators that may be nearby. This much blood will attract something. The subtle breeze across my scales assures me that the scent is potent in the air, and there are creatures with much better senses than I.

Even after I take care of the Python's head, my fury is only partially sated. I dig my hand into the stump of his neck again and yank out the Python's spine. His tail twitches and coils until it's gone from his body. I lay my prize on the ground next to me. Grabbing it, I roll it around a nearby tree so any naga who comes across it will know that this male broke our one law. Now that females are back within my lands, the old icon will be a good reminder.

None have challenged me and won.

I am undefeated.

When I am done, I turn back to the Python's mangled body. It is because of him that I am not with Daisy right now, that she cries when I try leading her into a mating coil.

Knowing something will come along and eat the male brings me some comfort. As I think this, my mouth waters.

I never understood, for so many years, why I hungered for the flesh of other nagas and forest snakes over all else. My father had too, and he even shared a tail or two with me when I was young. I knew it was wrong, except my body said otherwise. It wasn't until I came across an ancient book about Earth's reptiles that I began to understand why.

There was once a reptile on this planet that resembled me. How? I don't know, but as a king, I did not like seeing a base creature in my likeness. I vowed to not be anything like these other *King Cobras,* those that do not have any human in them. It was from that book I learned of our cannibalistic nature.

That book is gone now, cracked and withered into dust after my many read-throughs. There are not enough robots in this world to preserve everything from the past.

I grab the Python under his arms and lean him up

against a tree, facing his spine. For a final trophy, I carve out some of his scales, tucking them in Daisy's ruined clothes on my arm. Afterward, I retrieve his head, just as I hear the snorts of pigs.

They can have their vengeance too.

I am benevolent.

ELEVEN
GILDED CAGE

Daisy

I SLIP my fingers across black silk, comforted by the feel of it. I've been awake for hours but haven't moved from my spot in the corner. I'm exhausted, my body hurts, I'm hungry, stressed, and sleep threatens to pull me under. I don't let it because I can't be so unguarded. Not with an alien male nearby who I don't know.

Zaku will be able to sneak up on me if I sleep.

He's not here, I remind myself.

My fingers snag on the silk—silk someone like me shouldn't be touching—and groan, knowing my exhaustion will catch up with me eventually, and then I'll truly be vulnerable. I scrub my face with my hands. I'd been trained for situations like these. All women in the military are. It's not fair, but war isn't fair. I should've been able to compartmentalize. I shiver, and I can't help it.

Zaku kissed me.

I raise my fingers to touch my lips. It was shocking... like everything else that's happened.

I reach down and clutch my new clothes—soft clothes—closing my eyes.

Zaku isn't like the other one.

Hours have gone by and despite my circumstance, I'm warm and sheltered and clean. Wrapping my mind around this has been hard. Maybe... maybe I actually am safe. He didn't have to help me. He could have hurt me instead, but he *has* helped me, and I need to remember this.

I open my eyes and I push upright, realizing it's no longer night. Endless blue skies and a bright, big sun are visible through the window, making the strange room bright and airy and open. I wince.

My gaze cuts to the door. It's still shut tight.

I glimpse the corners of the room. Stretching, I groan again. My bladder is full, and I'm going to have to get up and relieve it soon.

I eye the other closed doors. The ones I haven't been inside of yet.

He said one of them is a bathroom.

Standing, I keep my eyes on the main door. There are three doors in total. Two line the walls on either side of the window, and I assume they lead to more rooms with a view. The third door is beside Zaku's... *nest.* Though almost in the center of the room, the nest is still closest to the left wall. Between me and the nest, is the third door.

To the right side of the room is the human cage. Or an alien cage. I hope I never find out. There are people out there who like to fuck alien species, even if they're not compatible—as long as they're sentient—humans find a way. I don't know if that makes it better or worse.

Alien species have never been compatible with humans. I raise my fingers to my lips.

I haven't been kissed since I was in the officer's academy. Boys wanted to kiss me back then, hoping to steal the affection of someone who could help them rise in their careers. I stick out my tongue, remembering them. Once it was clear the military wasn't my calling—that I was too emotional, that I had no knack for violence—the boys vanished.

That was maybe... ten years ago? I took up piloting. It was a salvation I didn't know I needed at the time. I didn't have to interact one-on-one with anyone. And piloting didn't leave a lot of room for lovers. At the end of a shift in the sky, I was too tired for anything but bed, too worn down by death to want to do anything else except hide under my blanket and pretend the universe was a better place, a different place. One I could be proud of.

Petting my lips, they're dry now and nothing like Zaku's warm, full ones. It's strange being kissed again. It's been a long time.

I shake my head and walk to the door beside the bed. Testing the handle, it gives easily. Lights turn on when I stand on the threshold.

I gape.

Lucky me. It's the bathroom, but it's not like the one upstairs.

Leather brown, warm grey, and cream, one entire wall is a shower unit, with four large square spouts coming off the wall. There's no door on either side of the unit, making it easy for someone to slip in and out from either direction. Across from the shower is a long mirror with a table and sink beneath it. Upon the table are what could only be soaps, toiletries, and candles. Lots and lots of unused candles. In the back is a seating area with a sleek leather sofa, covered in silk black pillows, with a black glass table before it.

To relax and gaze upon people showering? I tilt my head. Why else would there be a sofa in a bathroom?

Like the bedroom, the bathroom's huge. I guess it has to be if a male like Zaku uses it. *His tail would fill up the whole of this space. It would run up the walls and curl over itself.*

I head for the toilet, which is in a mirrored alcove directly to my left. Seeing myself pee is something I never thought I'd do.

Whoever—whatever—once lived in this mountain palace was a strange fellow. It makes me curious about the original inhabitants and what their life was like. It's obviously nothing like mine.

I explore the bathroom for a weapon and find a nail file. Pocketing it, I wash my hands once again in wonder from the endless water. I shoot the shower a longing glance. There's no way I'm going to risk showering right now. There's also no bath. I decide I like the bathroom upstairs more. I re-enter the bedroom to find one of the robots.

It picks up the blanket from my makeshift nest in the corner, lasers it, and then positions it nicely on Zaku's bed.

Heading for the exit, I yank the handle. It doesn't give.

I yank it harder; the door holds. I search for a lock and find none. I slam my fist against the door, and it barely makes a thud. Trying the handle again, I call out for Zaku. Nothing. I pivot to the robot.

"Open the door," I say.

It doesn't respond.

I try again. "House, open the door for me."

The robot stops, scans me once over, and continues whatever it's doing.

"Hey, wait—" I follow it, waving my hand "—house, let me out!"

It ignores me.

When it enters the bathroom and begins lasering the toilet, I sigh and go back into the bedroom.

I wander to the window. There's not a cloud in the sky. I've never seen such open, clear skies in all my life. Flying toward Earth, looking down from orbit, most of the landscape was brown, beige, and dead. Though here, in this spot within the mountains, it's like the Lurkers had never touched it.

I can almost forget the dead wastes. The endless desert of dust and ruins I saw flying down from *The Dreadnaut*.

The lake is in the distance, a blue glint among the scattered mountains. It seems close, but it took an entire day of travel to get from there to here. That's a long time for me, considering I'm used to flying everywhere. I search for ships in the skies, exhaust tracks, and end with my gaze in the direction of where I'm certain the facility is in.

I wonder what's happening with the team. After a few minutes, I rub my face and turn away.

Ignoring the cage and the bed, I head for the other two doors. I aim for the one on my left first, the one on the same wall as the bathroom, saving the right door, the one beside the cage for last. I have a feeling that one is the *"play"* room.

And I'm right once again, entering a closet. I almost gape again.

The closet is twice the size of my room on *The Dreadnaut*, filled to the brink with clothes, shoes, and everything else a person could ever want. Silks and lace, velvet and leather, there are dresses and suits, underthings and casualwear. In the center is a large island covered in glass bottles, decorative candles, and jewels. Dazzled, I walk around the island, wanting more than anything to touch the beautiful things.

Why does Zaku need all of this stuff? None of these clothes would ever fit him, and there's not another woman here...

Taking a risk, I lift a sparkling sapphire necklace from where it's placed on a velvet frame. My lips part in awe. I've never seen something so exquisite...

Someone treasured this once, and then they died. I set the necklace down gently, ensuring it's perfect upon the velvet it lives upon.

There's a large locked jewelry box beside it. I test it. It doesn't open. Beside it, half covered in a swathe of silk, is a picture. I push the silk aside and take hold of it.

Several men are standing together framed by flags. Two of the men are shaking hands while facing the camera, like it's a staged moment. A photo-op. The main focus, the man in a crisp black suit, is beyond handsome with haughty features and keen eyes. I notice something is standing in the background, in the shadows.

My brow furrows as my eyes go to the creature half-hidden behind the flags. I squint, trying to make it out.

It's a Lurker.

I swallow, staring at frightening reptilian eyes that seem to stare right back at me. I've seen Lurkers in digital media before, except this one is different. There's something not quite right about it.

The word evil flits through my head. A quiet, ominous whisper.

The longer I study the Lurker, the more my uneasiness grows. Unsettled, I put the picture down and wipe my hands on my clothes, feeling icky, feeling...scared.

Glancing around the opulent closet again, I wonder why there's a picture like this in here.

This place of Zaku's has to be a human dwelling, not a Lurker one. The closet is full of human things. The knowledge doesn't comfort me. If I were in a Lurker dwelling, eventually Peter, Collins, and the rest of the team would find their way here, and I could use that to get back on *The Dreadnaut*.

For the next while, I dig through every corner, searching for a weapon. At the end, the nail file from the bathroom wins out.

The sun is setting when I finally leave the closet. The robot is gone as well, and my stomach is growling. I go to the bathroom and pour myself a cup of water from the sink. When I'm done, I'm still alone.

My stomach growls again, and I try the door to leave the room. It doesn't budge.

I call out for Zaku, and I get no response. I call for the house, and nothing. A niggling, uncomfortable sensation churns my stomach.

Where is he?

It's going to be dark soon. I chew on my lip.

Grabbing some pillows and several blankets, I set up my spot by the window this time and lie down, staring out across the landscape, hoping that someone might see me and rescue me.

No one comes.

No one.

I'm alone, and I don't know why... The Lurker in the picture steals my mind and try as I might, I can't push it out. I see it in the glass, staring back at me. Terrible, intelligent eyes that see right through me focus just enough on my soul to let me know that it's watching me.

There are scarier beings out there than the ones I'm facing. Scarier creatures that don't offer food, water, and shelter.

I fall into a fitful sleep, wishing I wasn't alone with *it*.

Wishing I wasn't alone at all.

TWELVE
ZAKU'S RETURN

Daisy

I HEAR SOMETHING BEHIND ME, and I shoot upright. Rubbing my eyes, I search for the source of the noise.

Is he back?

Moonlight bleeds through the room, and elongated shadows give the otherwise empty space an ominously quiet appearance. The bars from the cage cast dark lines on the far wall and the swing... It jostles from a breeze that doesn't exist. Seeing nothing out of the ordinary, tension leaves my shoulders.

I'm still alone.

Something moves by the door, and I pause as light pierces the gloom. A robot.

I slump, annoyed.

Facing the clear night sky and Earth's moon, I wonder why *The Dreadnaut* hasn't sent anyone else down. I shake my head and turn away. I haven't seen or heard any ships descend. And if I missed them while sleeping, they leave trails in the skies that last for days.

The robot moves toward me, and I snag my blankets and pillows close. "You can't have them. They're being used." If it tries to clean me out, it's got another thing coming.

My nose twitches, and I notice the robot holding something.

It sets a platter beside me and moves away. The wall opens up, and the robot vanishes within it before I can think of darting into the hole behind it. Dragging the platter next to the window, I scrutinize the plate.

Meat. My tummy roils with nausea even though the meat is cooked and served with one of those red orbs Zaku gave me the first day. I'm not hungry for meat or strange food, but I'm not about to let sustenance go to waste. I gorge, polishing off everything. When I'm done, I push the plate aside and go to the bathroom, wash my hands, and splash water in my face.

Sighing, I abandon the bathroom. The sun is cresting the mountains when I reenter the room.

I turn toward the last door.

The *"play"* room.

The one I haven't dared to peek inside of yet. Maybe it's because of the picture of the Lurker in the closet. Shaking out the fear that wants to drag me back down, I head for the playroom's door.

Clutching the doorknob, it gives under my hand, opening inward. I see my face staring back at me on the other side. Stepping inside the room, I'm surrounded by floor-to-ceiling mirrors on every side. There are only mirrors.

How odd.

Moving to the one before me, I study my reflection. My

brow furrows and I glance around. Seeing something above me, I walk to the side to get a better look at whatever it is.

A hook. A small one. Like something is to be hung from it...

Deep, vibrating hissing floods my ears. I spin toward the door.

My heart ramps. Leaving the playroom, I return to the main room and close the door behind me. My gaze shifts to the locked door on the other side.

He's back.

I brace for it to open, taking a step back. I don't know which Zaku I will get, the one who looks at me like he's starving or the caring one who draws me a bath and cradles me in his arms.

Maybe it'll be neither. I shift further away as the hissing grows louder. It sounds like it's coming from all around me, piercing through the walls. My nerves vibrate with it, making my toes curl.

The knob turns and the door swings open, revealing a beast. One that is dark, dirty, and covered in... blood? Dark eyes catch mine in a trap, and I gasp, releasing a shriek. The Lurker is real! Scrambling to the window, I try to get away. It rushes me, grabs me, and lifts me in his arms.

The stench of blood invades my nostrils. Flailing, I strain away. "No!" I scream, wild with terror.

"It is me! Zaku! Your male. Your king. Calm down," he barks.

I hear him, but only see the dried blood caking Zaku's large body, covering his mouth, hands, and arms. He's a different color—his pupils golden and striking and wild. I kick out frantically as I mumble his name.

"Zaku?"

I stop kicking as I take in his face.

My...male?

His gaze searches mine. "I have returned to you."

Zaku slowly lowers me, placing me on my feet. The dirt and blood on his scales have diminished his yellow coloring to the point of unrecognition. And as he leans back, removing his hands from me, my gaze trails over his giant form, making sure it's really him.

Making sure he's not another monstrous naga seeking to hurt me, or something worse.

"Zaku," I say again, almost in reassurance. It is him. I reach out and touch him with the tips of my fingers to make sure.

He's disgusting. My nose twitches from the stench wafting off of him. He reaches up to grasp my hand and I tug it away, hugging it to my body, because the gore on him is all over me now too.

He lifts his hand, outstretches his clawed fingers, and brushes a tendril of my hair behind my ear. "Your fear will end today," he says. "I promise, little mate."

I flinch.

"What happened?" I whisper, bunching my sleeve around my hand to cover my nose. "Where have you been?" Why do I even care? I back away from him, wanting to put distance between me and the blood cloaking him, not liking the way he towers over me, intimidating me. It reminds me of my father.

Still... I'm relieved. I almost press forward to see if I can get a whiff of his scent despite the coppery tang of blood invading my nose.

Zaku's chest puffs and he straightens onto his tail, commanding all of my attention. I almost smile from his obvious peacocking. How did I ever see a Lurker? Zaku looks nothing like the alien in the picture.

And then I glimpse his enormous cock.

My mouth drops. *It's outside of his tail.* A shaft of sunlight hits it directly, saying: "look here!"

It's huge! I squeak, my eyes widening, and look away.

Was that—is that—possible?

I forget about the smell, the gore, even my predicament, because what Zaku's packing is big enough to eclipse everything else. Fuck. He starts to say something that goes in one ear and out the other; I'm too stunned by his... *monstrous nether region.*

Don't look at it, Daisy. I want to look at it. Damn the light haloing it.

"—I have battled and won—"

Educational curiosity?

I try to focus on what Zaku's saying all while backing away and trying my hardest not to glance at his package. If he thinks he's getting that inside me, he'll be sorely disappointed.

We don't fit. We never will. It's not possible.

"—your king has made these lands safe again—"

I'm vaguely aware of Zaku showing off his muscles and indicating his body to me like he's a god, but his cock has literally cock-blocked him; it won't even disappear into his tail. It jerks in the periphery of my view. It's begging me to look at it.

Zaku strains, rising up, peacocking some more, and I can't help it any longer. Fuck, fuck, fuck. My eyes drop back down to his *monster*, swaying and bobbing with every one of his movements. Staring hard now, I can't help it. It's not like he's *not* displaying it for me to gaze at anyway...

"—no female of mine should ever know fear from another, only me—"

Is it... getting bigger?

I tilt my head, narrowing my eyes. There's a bulge in the middle of it that's turgid and swollen, and I swear it's growing. He keeps moving, making it hard for me to decide. Regardless, it looks uncomfortable, and I don't envy him. I'd be an angry, bloodied-up naga too if I were in his boots—uh, tail.

Liquid beads on the tip and drips to the floor.

I hold in a squeak as his seed—alien snake seed—leaks from cock's head.

Zaku stills and so does his "monster" after a final bounce. My gaze shoots to his face, and he's staring at me with an intensity that makes my soul try to shrivel and hide. I tense up when I realize what he'd just caught me doing.

Gazing at his cock...

The golden spark in his eyes gleams and brightens, making the coloring of his facial scales darken further. I inhale sharply and snap my mouth shut, discovering his gaze tracking my lips.

Suddenly, I feel his mouth back on mine.

My heart jumps into my throat.

And then I see what he must see in his head—my mouth choking down on him.

I stiffen, straighten. I'm the only daughter of a great war commander; I'll never suck a man's cock. An alien's cock. Any cock. It doesn't matter how far I fall.

"Female," Zaku rasps. And though he couldn't pose himself kinglier, he somehow does, jutting out his chin, flaring his cowl wide, and straining his muscled-packed arms.

Something in me... shifts and stutters, pauses and ponders, and then starts to warm up. I would roll my eyes if I weren't appreciating his muscles so much. My lips part and I curl my fingers into my palm to stop my hand from reaching out and feeling Zaku's arms.

This alien man wants me. He wants *me*. I don't even need the evidence of his swollen dick to know this, nor do I need his words. I see it in his eyes. I shiver, losing my train of thought as I stare into them.

I recall his muscles pressed against me. I recall his warmth.

Inhaling, and that delicious scent of his, the one I smelled the first day invades my nostrils. My skin warms, lips part. I suck it into me like I'll starve if I don't. He's bloody, disgusting, and those smells are in the air as well. They no longer bother me. All I want is to move closer to him and breathe him in.

Wrenching my eyes close, I shake my head.

Why does he have to smell so good? My skin heats even more as I breathe it in. A sensation of emptiness knots my sex, and I think it's because of his scent...

Wait? What was he just saying? Something about not having to be afraid anymore? I cover my nose.

"I have brought you a gift," he announces, his voice low, his tail coiling forward.

"A what?"

I don't get a chance to brace for what comes next because I'm suddenly face-to-face with a sagging, horrifyingly bloody, dismembered head.

THIRTEEN
THE HEAD

Zaku

Daisy recoils, bringing up her hands. The color drains from her face.

I'd just watched her skin turn rosy. She was staring at my member, exciting me. Now her face is ashen?

Gripping the Python's scalp tighter, I lift his head higher. "He is the one who hurt you and mated you against your will, and for that, I bring you his head," I announce again in case she needs reassurance. "You do not need to be afraid anymore."

Now, she will accept me. Now, she will lead me to my nest.

Daisy bows over and heaves, clutching her stomach. I furrow my brows, dropping the head and rushing to her side. "Are you hurt?" She tries to shake out of my grip; I tighten it. There's spittle on her parted lips.

I slip my tongue out to taste the air before them, my tongue a finger's width from her mouth. I long to taste her again. She is delicious and sweet, and everything I would think a daisy flower should taste like.

I glimpse her horrified expression. "Are you hurt?" I ask again, worried and frustrated by her response and lack thereof.

"Let me go—please let me go. You brought me his head," she gasps, tearing at my hands. She's making a sickened face, and I notice the dirt and blood on her, how the mess is getting all over her. Hissing, I release her.

"I brought you his head," I agree. "So you will know that he is gone and will never trouble you again."

She scurries away from me as if she doesn't hear my words, and I clench my hands to stop them from snatching her up again.

"His head..." she utters with disbelief, refusing to look at the offering again.

"Yes. The Python's head," I grunt, tossing it to the corner of the room. I've forgotten what it's like to be with another. They do not always agree or do what I want.

I thought once her fear was gone, she would sing, she would submit.

"House, prepare the bathroom," I rumble thickly. I hear the shower turn on soon after. I will clean her, clean myself, and then present her with the Python's head again. Then, she can put to rest what happened, knowing he's in the bellies of pigs, probably scattered across the forest by now, and let me finally fill her with my member.

My mouth waters. I absently palm my knot as I think this. I hear Daisy's breath hitch. She's in the corner of the room where I left her the first night, watching me warily. Color has returned to her cheeks and she's holding her hand over her nose.

There wasn't wariness on her face when she was staring

at my member moments ago. I could feel her eyes on me, petting me. I thought that she'd been pleased, earnest after my story about battling the Python. That I brought her a gift. That I planned to spoil her. Her cheeks had warmed, her eyes took me in.

I strain my muscles again, wanting her gaze back on them.

I go to her and she presses away.

My eyes narrow. "I will not touch you again while his filth is on my hands. For that, I apologize. I am—" I slip my tongue across the roof of my mouth "—eager to see you... settled."

But my frustration grows.

"Can you put that away?" she asks, catching my eyes and then glancing at my member. "Please?"

She wants me to hide *my want* for her? After I killed on her behalf?

"It no longer fitsss," I grate.

She regards me, closes her eyes hard, and opens them. Her hand tightens around her nose. I don't understand what she's doing, and at this point, I just want to get the Python's blood off of her.

I'm liking his smear on her less and less. I miss seeing her perfection, the glimpse I got of her when her tears dried after the ship left her on the plateau.

Why is the head not working? Her troubles are no more.

"I-It doesn't fit?" she asks. "Don't answer that!" She shudders, pivoting to the bathroom as if she could hide from me. "I can't believe you brought me a head!" The door begins to close, and I swipe out my tail to jar it. She hitches from within, a sound of annoyance. "I need to—"

I snap to the threshold, thumping my palm on the door,

stopping her from tugging the door closed. She startles and meets my eyes. "Need to *what*, Daisy? Relieve yourself? Wash? I have been away for over a day. I am not ready for you to be gone from my gaze."

Sliding into the doorway, I block her in. She cannot get away from me, my limbs are too big.

She steps back, continuing to hold her nose and eye me warily. Steam fills the space between us. The golden mountainous rocks that make up the walls begin glistening with humidity. I suck in the heat, letting it bloom inside me as I sneak my tailtip into the room and circle it around her.

"Zaku," she says. "I... want to thank you... for not—" she stops and shakes her head. "I can't be this way with you."

Hmm. "What way is that?"

Her soft, flimsy clothes drape her curves enticingly, showing off hints of her body beneath. Even dirty, she is enticing in them. I catch her human nipples peeking through, and I hold in a groan. I've always been fascinated by human breasts. They are large compared to the females of my kind. They also appear softer, rounder, and easier to grab, grope, or play with. I read once that human females can produce milk for their offspring.

Human females are always covering their breasts in the images I've seen, and I never understood why. Naga women wore no clothes, remaining as free as their males.

Humans do not have scales to guard their flesh...

That must be why she covers herself. For protection.

"Well, I'm a human, and you're not? I mean, half of you looks human... You speak my language..." A blush deepens her cheeks as her eyes shoot to my member and dart away. "We're not compatible. Humans have tried being with aliens in the past. It doesn't work. And that," she says, indicating my swollen shaft, "is a lot..."

"Compatible?" I ask, not quite understanding her meaning. I enter the bathroom and she stumbles back. I catch her with my tail. Why is she trying to get away from me? She pushes out of my limbs and dodges deeper into the room. I close in, pulling the door shut behind me.

I am a large male, and my den was not built for one such as me, still, I fit. I make myself fit. My tail coils up the walls. It wants to coil around her.

"Well," she says, "humans are much, much smaller than you."

"And?"

She guffaws. "That should be reason enough!" Her eyes flick back to my member, and I shoot out a jet of spill just knowing her eyes are on it. She brings her hands up to her mouth after taking a deep breath. "Zaku, I'm not ready. You've been reasonable, you've... cared for me. It took me time to realize this. But this is never going to work. I'm not staying. The first chance I get..."

"Not staying...?" My eyes narrow upon her. "Where else would you go? If you try and leave me for another," my voice lowers, "I will kill every male, human, and naga in the land until I am all who remains." Daisy's eyes go wide as I say this. "You have seen the skulls out front. I have many kills. I am unbeatable—I am king. And you... you are the most beautiful female of all, and that means you're mine. My queen."

Her mouth opens and closes several times. My tongue licks my teeth, imagining her lips moving over my scales, her hair fanned out across my tail as I bend her body for me.

"You..." she whispers.

"Me?"

"You are—" she straightens "—really thick-headed."

I consider her words and decide she's right. My skull is

rather thick. The cartilage of my cowl is heavy. "I am," I agree.

She sighs, but the hand covering her nose still remains.

Do I smell bad?

"How was I ever afraid of you?" She clutches her brow. "Because he's a headhunter, Daisy. You've been caught by a headhunter."

This word pleases me, and I pet her ankle with my tailtip. "I do collect the heads of my enemies," I say. "You have begun noticing things about me... I like this. I would decorate our den with them except the house robots..." I trail off. "You fear me because I should be feared, little female. I will be a good protector to you, the best protector. There is no other who is better."

As my tail touches her, she finally drops her hand and dances farther into the bathroom. I smirk, beginning to enjoy her now that it's not fear that keeps her from me. She just said so herself. She curses me and scampers around the bathroom as I follow her with my tail. When she climbs up on the sofa, shouting at me to stop it, I hook it around her and snag her around the middle, bringing her back to me.

"Zaku!" she pushes at my limb, legs kicking, feet straining to remain on the floor. "Let me go!"

When I have her in front of me, I arch my brow. "Never."

I carry her into the shower.

She fights, hitting me with her fists, her curses growing louder. She could never hurt me.

"I am not something that can be man-handled! I'm a military pilot, I know how to snipe, I should be feared too—" I put her under the water. She blubbers, stops fighting me and swipes her soaked hair out of her face.

I move her back toward the other shower faucet, slipping under the first, while shifting my tail behind her to keep her from escaping out the other side.

"How dare you!"

She starts struggling harder while I find the soap spout hidden in the crevices of the mountain rock, pumping the liquid in my palm. I lather it between my hands until it's bubbly. She's pushing at my tail some more but not nearly as hard as she could be; she's watching me instead. I think she likes the warm water. When I bring my hands toward her hair, she jerks back.

I pause. "I will wash you."

She shudders, then glances at my member again. "I can't give you what you want, Zaku," she whispers. "Even if you spoil me, take care of me, even if what you say is true... it can't be."

"It can. You are mine now. That's all that matters."

Her tongue peeks out to swipe at her wet lips. She's so stiff that I'm afraid she'll break if I move my tail too quickly.

"Submit?" she asks with hesitance. Water droplets gather in her lashes. She wipes her brow as water continuously showers her from above. I span out my cowl and rise higher, trying to shield her eyes, touching the ceiling.

"Yesss, female. I will take care of you, and your worries. You only need to let me. I can be your king too."

Her eyes flick to my soapy hands, then back to my face. "What happens if I submit? Will you... will you listen to me?"

"Listen to you?"

She glances behind me. "I don't want to be hurt again."

"I will never hurt you."

"I don't want to be locked up anymore either... I want freedom. I don't want to be left in the room alone with that..." she trails off.

"With what?"

She shakes her head.

"With what?" I demand.

"The head!"

I nod. If that is all she needs to give me what I want, then that is easy to grant. "You will have access to my den, and I will not bar you from any room, though the entrance will remain locked. I will not budge on that. You will not go outside without me."

"You said the land is safe, didn't you?"

I hiss. "Until it is not."

My logic is sound.

She searches my eyes, and my nostrils flare, waiting for her to finally accept me. My spine stiffens as the seconds lengthen, and my tailtip presses into the floor. Water continues to drench us, and the humidity thickens with the steam. The heat on my skin doesn't diminish the throbbing of my member as I hoped.

I know she is small. I know I am large.

That won't stop me from lodging inside her, from spilling my seed within her. From filling her womb with many litters.

"I want one more thing," she says slowly.

"Anything."

Anything. I will give her anything; I will give her every-thing except her release.

"I want to decide when we first mate."

"Fine," I snap, bringing my hands to her hair.

She startles. "Fine? Wait, what?" She tries to tug my hands off her. "You're not going to argue that? Wait—"

"No," I rasp. "No more waiting." I know she fears mating me. The Python made her fear it. I do not want to wait, even though I must for her sake. There are other ways to find relief until then. My mood sours despite my excitement. "She's mine, finally mine," I whisper to myself, awed.

Daisy winces. "I thought..."

Gathering the rest of her long yellow hair, I bring it closer to me, liberating it from the water, and soap it up. *The feel...* I groan as it catches on my claws. Daisy grows even tenser, holding her limbs close to her body, but she's no longer trying to get away. She looks deep in thought.

I will take it. It doesn't matter that she's holding herself prone and away from me. I don't care.

"I will let you decide when you wish to mate, but I will decide the rest. Right now, I will wash you, and you will wash me. Afterward, you will lead me to our nest and lie with me while I sleep. I have earned this. I will have you naked when I want, I will touch you when I want, you will touch me when I want. You will allow me to prove to you that I will protect you, that I will destroy your enemies. And you will stay and be my beautiful queen.

"You will help me rule these lands, and I will remain the envy of every male in our world."

"Zaku... You really are thick-headed."

"Yes. It is thick." I squeeze her gently with my tail. "If you try to leave me, I will know."

I *will* know.

Because from this moment on, she'll never be away from my side again. I tremble at the thought.

FOURTEEN
LIFE ISN'T FAIR

Daisy

HE'S SO NAÏVE it's almost painful.

Only there's a fire in his gaze that I can't ignore. His claws gently scrape my scalp, making my skin prickle. It's a lot. He's a lot. It feels good and I wish it didn't. Biting my tongue, I didn't expect him to so easily accept my terms, hoping his swollen cock would give me more time to figure something out.

Who can think straight when they're horny?

I'm not the craftiest person. I'm not creative. I'm reactive, living in the moment, with seemingly every instance ruled by my annoying emotions, so being trapped by a massive, turned-on male covered in gore has not been an easy moment for me to wade through. Not without appreciating the specimen who's trapped me.

If circumstances had been different, I'd be more open to Zaku's advances... *Maybe*. I like men who know what they want and aren't willing to manipulate others to achieve their goals. I like *kind* men. But I've given up thinking those types of men existed. I've been manipulated my whole life. I'm sick of it. Only, Zaku's not like any male I've ever known, stiff, cold, keeping his thoughts and feelings closed off. Seeing me as a means to an end, and then not seeing me at all after they got what they wanted. Which is usually something I never planned to give in the first place.

No, Zaku's an open book. Too open for my comfort.

It makes me nervous. I've never dealt with anyone like him. He's so blatant and forward about what he's thinking that I almost think it must be a trick. It has to be, right?

He doesn't seem like the type to be tricky, though.

He believes that by catching me during some cultural mate hunt, we're destined to be together. I get that now. Sleep has helped. Also, his insistence that he won't hurt me —over and over again—has helped a lot as well.

I believe him. I'm beginning to, at least.

He should keep his thoughts to himself... Zaku would never survive on a ship like *The Dreadnaut.*

But it means I can get free of him if I'm patient enough.

I inhale, remembering the rotting head in the bedroom, how he thrust it in my face, and the stench of decay coming off of it. I don't want to become what I hate. I don't want to manipulate Zaku, even if it means my freedom. I also don't know him very well. *He's the reason I'm in this situation to begin with.*

He's the one who came to the facility and brokered an agreement with Peter.

Thankfully, the water has taken Zaku's scent away. It was muddling my thoughts. houghT I find I'm missing it, hoping for another whiff. I'll have to be patient. He's reactive too. He's willing to kill for me.

What else is he willing to do?

My belly flutters.

He's waiting for me to respond... His hands tug and grip my hair, lathering it, making my body warm. The water feels good.

"I won't run," I lie. I will, but not now. I can hold him off for a while, though I'm certain I won't be able to forever.

His tail coils tighter around me. *He's watching me.* Bubbly soap trickles from my over-lathered hair, soaking my shirt.

"I know you won't," he rumbles, his voice heating. His eyes go to my breasts again, as if he could stare so hard that he'll see under my arms and through my shirt.

"I will have you naked when I want, I will touch you when I want, you will touch me when I want... And you will stay and be my beautiful queen."

An idea forms. His claws softly graze my scalp again, and I stop the moan that wants to leave me.

I can ingratiate myself to him, give him what he craves—within reason—and maybe by doing so, he'll want me so badly that he'll give me whatever *I* want.

He says I will touch him when *he* wants, though he can't make me do that against my will. As far as I'm aware, neither the Lurkers nor ancient humans had developed tech that could control another's mind.

God, I hope.

If these nagas are anything like the Gestri...

Feeling empowered suddenly, I desperately want to hold onto the feeling.

Slowly, I uncoil my arms from my chest and place my hands on his tail.

His eyes glaze, and his kneading, tugging hands halt in my hair, tightening into fists. My chest constricts as a hungry fervor etches across his face. The water from above trickles down his cheeks, and I catch a glimpse of his forked tongue sliding over his fangs. His scales glisten, wet.

"I will touch you when I want," he says, as if reminding me of our agreement, his voice a mumble.

I shudder, and it's not because I'm scared.

It's because I want him to touch me. His hands in my hair feel good. I recoil at the thought and strain back. Only his hands untangle from me and cup my breasts instead. I go still, shocked. His hands are huge, his fingers having to curl inward to cup me better, covering the entirety of my torso. Every fiber in me is on edge. I don't know if I'll bolt or give in—my thoughts war. What I should want and what I really want are refusing to align.

He gently squeezes my breasts, and I'm still waiting to react. To run. To burst into tears.

I don't.

A low, guttural, and deep hissing fills my ears, blending with the patter of the shower. I press the pads of my fingers into Zaku's tail, testing, feeling the velvety grooves of his scales. His eyes flick to mine as I do so, and my fingers lift from his hide.

Without saying anything, eyes locked on mine, his tail around me loosens, and I bare down on my feet, able to stand on my own once again. The pressure between my legs diminishes from the loss, and my sex clenches, hoping to bring it back. I reach up and grab his wrists.

I can't even curl my fingers around them.

His hissing lowers even more. Suds trickle from my hair and down my body, gathering over his hands on my chest. They slip down his wrists, slickening them. I slowly, damnably slide my palms up over his hands and press them into me.

Giving in, just a little.

"Daisssy."

His fingers find the top of my thin sweater and the shirt beneath it, gripping the material of both. His claw grazes down, drifting down from my neck, ripping the fabric. I gasp. He grins and, with new vigor, tears both open, baring my breasts completely to his view.

He pushes me backward into his tail and puts his mouth on one of them, lapping wildly. I cry out, straining from the abrupt assault of his tongue. I grab hold of his cowl and arch my back, trying to find purchase—anything to help me when everything is slippery—but then the thick part of Zaku's tail pushes my legs apart, sliding between them.

This is more than a little!

Straddling him, half-lying backward upon his tail, Zaku's upper half rises over me, his mouth suckling my left breast, then my right, and then back to my left. He laps at me like a man starved, and I'm too stunned to do anything but let him do what he wants.

He hisses my name again, licking up and down, the fork of his tongue flicking my nipples. I hitch. His tail writhes under me like a wave, each undulation putting pressure on all the right spots.

I whimper.

It's not fair.

It's really not.

I turn my thoughts off and close my eyes with a moan. For a final moment, I glimpse the Python's head in my mind, then Peter's awful smirk, and finally Zaku's hungry eyes. His tail comes next, his enormous cock—that will never, ever fit. The images can bring me back to reality—

He pushes my breasts together and thrusts his tongue up and down my cleavage, forcing my eyes to snap back open. The spray of the shower dews my lashes, and I blink rapidly to clear them.

He looks at me as his tongue whispers over my breasts again.

"Oh, hell," I moan, digging my nails into his cowl. It's thick and hard, like the rest of him.

I can give him this. I can—

Zaku flicks my nipples faster. I squeeze his tail with my thighs, pushing up into his face. *This is wrong, Daisy.*

But his tongue...

He releases my breasts, sliding them down my body, moving so gently they don't even disturb the bruising on my sides. He tears apart my pants, pulling them off me.

Zaku moves my body between his, laying me fully on the length of his tail. His eyes are almost human, and for an instant he's just a man of my species, but then his forked tongue appears again.

"Beautiful female," he says, licking the air. "You have made me happy. I am honored. You rest naked and wet and open on my tail. I am *pleased.*"

I grow warm from his words.

I've pleased him.

Zaku's eyes drop back down to my chest, and further still, wandering to the rest of my body. I curl my toes realizing the position I'm in and how vulnerable I've become.

How did this happen so fast? How? His tail undulates again, and I feel him everywhere. His scales, his heat, his muscles...

Something hot splashes my belly, something much hotter than the water.

I strain my head to look between us and see his cock poised above my splayed sex, the head angled toward it. Seed is leaking from the tip and onto my body.

Fear returns hot and fast.

"No!" I jolt upright, pushing at Zaku's chest and climbing off his tail. I turn to face him, plastering my body against the glass wall that separates the shower from the sink, blocked in by both sides of the shower, by his tail. I curl my arms over my breasts again, a hand protecting my sex.

"No," I say again, almost whimpering. "We have a deal."

He reaches for me, and I turn away.

"I was not going to..."

His hands never meet my skin.

I hear him hiss—and perhaps inwardly curse me. "I can't," I whisper.

I need to know he'll be true to his word. I need to know he won't betray me like Peter, like my own kind.

I'm desperate... to be able to trust someone again.

I feel him move away, feel it in the way the shower sprays me as he slips out. The air cools without his presence.

Without opening my eyes, I sense that he's gone, that he's left me alone. I slide down the glass with a soft sigh... and suddenly I'm splaying my fingers through his seed on my stomach and rubbing it into my skin.

I've lost my mind.

But...

I can trust him.

FIFTEEN

Daisy

It takes me some time to wash the soap out of my hair and clean my body. I make doubly sure any grime that has gotten on me is scrubbed off. I don't have any open wounds, only scrapes. I clean them thoroughly anyway, not wanting to risk infection. An alien bacterial infection. I gulp. I don't want to get sick here on Earth.

I'm also hoping that if I scrub hard enough, long enough, I'll scrub the way Zaku's making me feel, scouring it right out of me.

It's his damned scent. I know it is.

Though I don't smell him right now, I still can't get him out of my head.

I can trust him. Hope constricts my chest.

Wrapping a towel around my body, I leave the shower and peek out the bathroom door. Zaku's on the other side, wet and dripping and splayed out in sunlight that's beaming into the room through the window. With his cowl wide around his face and arms crossed over his chest, he's leaning back on his tail. He looks like a god. A strange, alien snake god.

He straightens when he sees me.

And puffs out his chest.

"I need new clothes," I tell him, checking him out, sliding my eyes to his pelvic region. Relief fills me—and perhaps a little regret—when I don't see his *monster*. "I'm going to just... go to the closet over there." I point toward it. He won't deny me clothes, will he?

"I have something for you."

I suck on my lip. "It's not a head, is it?"

His eyes glint. "No, not a head. Another gift. One you might like better."

I see something in his hand as his fingers uncurl away from his palm. Whatever it is catches the sunlight and flashes with brilliance, shooting rainbows across the room. I flinch, shielding my face, thinking he's shooting me with something. When nothing hits me, I lower my hands.

Rainbows streak across Zaku's tail, his rippling muscles, all coming from the thing he's holding. My lips part. He jangles it, and the room glitters with another burst of brilliant color. Dazzled and curious, I blink rapidly, clearing my eyes.

Whatever he's holding doesn't look like clothes.

It looks like—I squint as my eyes adjust to the sparkling light—strings of jewels? *Maybe crystals...*

Or diamonds?

My whole body goes on alert. If what Zaku is holding are diamonds... adding that to the wealth of jewels I'd seen in the closet... he might be the richest being in this galaxy. Maybe all the galaxies.

Diamonds are exceedingly rare, especially those from Earth.

There's a whole other reason *The Dreadnaut* has been sent to Earth, and it's not entirely for lost technology. Every human in the universe knows of the wealth that's been trapped on our home planet, wealth that's unguarded, unprotected, and ripe for the taking. A lot of people want that wealth, and no one more than the government and the royals. I'd heard enough chatter in the academy to know that the government isn't just going to let people return to Earth and steal that from them.

Greedy bastards, all of them.

I hate working for them. I only kept piloting because there were innocents out there—children—who needed saving, and also because if I quit, I'd sink to the lowest caste. I'd be a dregger.

I'd do anything to not be a dregger. Dreggers have no rights.

Zaku curls his fingers, and the sparkles—the rainbows on the walls—vanish. My chest feels lighter once they're gone. He shifts from his cocky posturing and slithers to me and out of the sunlight. I sniff the air, and when I smell nothing, I open the bathroom door a little further, clutching my towel and stepping out.

His eyes drop to my body. I hold my towel tighter.

"You'll wear this," he hands me the glittering thing he's holding, "and I will enjoy the sight of you while I rest. I will enjoy your beauty."

Taking the sparkling thing from his hand, making sure I don't accidentally touch him, woven chains fall from my fingers, each attached to a black leather band. "This... isn't clothes." Stretching the thin chains out, my eyes go to the crystals. "This won't cover any part of me," I mumble, trying to see how something like this would even be worn, mesmerized all over again.

"I don't want you covered."

I gulp, bringing the jeweled chains to my chest. "I don't think this is safe. I can't accept this, Zaku." Not at all. Not. At. All. What he's giving me is little more than jewelry and nothing else. I'd be exposed, completely. The chains cover nothing.

I also don't think I deserve to wear such wealth, if my pounding heart has anything to do with it... I hope it's only crystals that I'm holding.

Zaku lifts his hand and twirls a strand of my damp hair with his finger. "If you're afraid they will chafe your scrapes, I will pet and soothe your skin. I will enjoy it. It will give me time to learn you."

"I can't."

"You can. You will. It is what your king wants."

"What about what I want?"

Zaku tilts his head. "Your freedom?" He indicates the door to the room with his chin and my gaze snaps to it. It's open. "The house is yours. The robots are yours. They will listen to anything you ask of them, except opening the front door. They will not release you."

I shiver. "And you promise it's my choice—" I lick my lips "—when, uh—" and I feel my cheeks heat "—when we—"

"Mate?"

My eyes flick back to his. I nod.

"It is your choice," he says.

"Can I go outside, ever?"

"With me by your side, you can."

I glance at the chains in my hand, the black leather band. "How long do I have to wear this?"

Zaku gently pulls the chains from my grip, letting them fall between us. "Until I have had my fill of your beauty. Until I have memorized you."

That's not a good answer. He may want to gawk at my human body for weeks—months. I startle, realizing I might be here for that long, or more. But my skin warms at his compliment, and I am intrigued.

If Zaku were a human, I would think he was playing a huge joke on me, except he isn't a man, and he's not. "Okay."

His gaze smolders at my acceptance. He lifts the chains above my head, unclasping the collar. "I will give you more gifts than this," he rumbles. "Gather your hair."

Digging my nails into my towel, I swallow thickly. "You don't need to win me with gifts. Kindness is enough."

"I have already won you."

My lips purse.

I eye the exit behind Zaku and swallow again. The room is warm, my cheeks warmer, and my belly is twisting up with starflies.

"I can be kind," he says. "I am out of practice, but I can be kind. I think."

My gaze goes back to him as he sends the starflies dancing.

I let my towel drop to the floor and gather up my hair, meeting Zaku's waiting eyes.

He keeps them despite my nudity and works the delicate chains over my head, over my arms. I shimmy, threading one arm through, and then the other, helping him out, knowing all the while, every inch of my body and all its flaws are exposed. Zaku positions the open band around my neck and latches it at the back. Once it's on, I let my hair fall.

Tense, neither of us move as silence fills the space between us.

I drop my gaze from his to look down at my new adornments.

There's one thick central chain that falls from the band, down to my navel where it forks, draping around my hips before returning up my back. Thinner chains drape from the collar, landing like necklaces, falling across my collarbone and breasts. They stop an inch above my nipples. From those thinner chains, two branch off, wrapping my upper arms, accentuating my neck and chest, my curves.

Throughout the piece, there are jewels. *Crystals*, I reassure my mind. More than I can count.

"Beautiful," he says.

I bring my arms up to hide my breasts. He's looking at me like I'm the sun, the stars, and the magical nebulas of space. His hands open and close. His tail coils around my ankle.

I wish my body was as beautiful as he says it is. I wish my bruises were healed. I'm glad he knows nothing about my past...

I lower my face.

His fingers clasp my chin and lift it, forcing me to meet his eyes. "It is time to rest now, Daisy. I am tired. I want to enjoy you. I want you to enjoy me."

"Okay."

What else can I say?

He smiles, revealing his fangs. "Good." His tail strokes the sensitive skin behind my ankle. "Lead me to my nest, female." His fingers drop from my chin. "It is time for my queen to give her king a gift in return."

I step out from his tail and start walking toward the bed. He grabs my arm.

"Take my hand," he says when I look back at him. His eyes trail across my backside.

It's only several steps. I grab the hand he offers me.

When I'm at the edge of the bed, I stop, waiting for another cue. Why am I so nervous? I realize I'm waiting for the ball to drop, for Zaku to do to me like Peter has, like others before him have. He slides into the bed and lies back upon the silken pillow. With his hands behind his head, he looks at me.

Once again, he looks like he could be a god. All gold, all big, all potently male.

His tailtip slices through the air and tugs my hair, making my whole body jerk. The sun catches the jewels on my chains, filling the bedroom with sparkling wonder. I gasp, and he lets it go.

Awed, I turn away from him and walk into the sunlight.

Zaku doesn't stop me, though his tailtip follows, stroking my ankles. Mesmerized, warmed, and feeling oddly freed, the rainbows streak over the floors and walls with every move I make.

After a while, I forget my nudity. I forget the aches in my body, the bruises on my skin, and even the circumstances I'm in, unable to look away from the splendor. I've never created anything before except tears.

The sun begins to set as my hair dries in silken waves down my back, as I hold onto this moment as long as I can.

When the sun lowers and my sparkles vanish, I press up against the window and watch Earth fall into a purple twilight. It looks empty and serene—peaceful—like no matter what happens, everything will be okay.

The room is in shadow when I face Zaku again.

He hasn't moved, though his gaze is hooded, dark, like molten fire.

He looks wicked.

I feel beautiful.

For an instant, I consider crawling up onto his tail and straddling him.

"Come here, Daisssy," he hisses my name when I just stand there.

I walk to the edge of the bed, and his tail coils up my leg. He reaches out for me to join him.

Staring at his outstretched hand, I slowly take it, climbing into the bed with him. *A bed he calls a nest...* Zaku shifts and herds me to his side, his giant tail moving to drape around all sides of me, closing me in. He presses me up against him, and I wait for him to do more as his hand cups my shoulder.

But his breaths even out and his hand loosens, slipping down my arm a short time later.

My heart calms, and I relax.

Sleep takes me away.

SIXTEEN
MORNING LIGHT

Zaku

I WAKE, warm and content. The past weeks have seeped from my limbs. Twirling a silken strand, I have the most beautiful female in all the universe at my side, her leg hooked over my tail and her hand on my chest.

She is asleep. Against *me*. I have never slept next to another. My mother did not birth a full litter, and so I never had to share my mother's nest with siblings.

I'm sharing my nest now, and it is everything I have dreamed about.

Rumbling a low hiss, I release Daisy's hair and play with the chains at her back. Her skin is flushed this morning, the red of her scrapes now a soft pink, and her bruises are yellowing. She will become more beautiful as she heals. I long to see her in all her glory.

I envy *me* for claiming her. No male deserves the most beautiful female in the land more than I.

I only want to be surrounded by beautiful things. I deserve the best.

My rumbles deepen. I have earned them.

Soon we will mate, soon my member will be lodged deep inside her, and she will remain on it, the flower to my stem, forever. She will give me young, gestate many litters—live well and long by my side—and raise our offspring.

It's been so long since I saw a young naga. Decades. The female young who were birthed were adopted by unmated adult naga females and taken west. Males, like me, were left behind with their fathers.

I do not have to worry that Daisy will die like the females of my kind. Humans have safely brought children into this world far longer than I've been around. They will continue doing so long after I'm gone. Her being here is proof of that. I have a human medical pod just in case...

Though... I have never seen a pod that could fit a naga. I wonder why.

Catching a new strand of Daisy's hair, I rub it between my fingers.

Seeing the humans' ship descend from the sky has changed my plans. I'd thought about journeying west again to search for the lost ones, to try and help them. I expel the old plans from my mind.

I am glad I waited.

Everything is perfect—everything except my swollen member. I glance down at where it's sticking out like a slightly curved pillar from my tail. I clutch the base with my free hand and slide my palm up my length, squeezing the bulge that has only grown. Seed bursts from my tip.

I grit my teeth.

Some of the seed drips over the side of my tail and onto the bedding between Daisy and me. Groaning, I do not want any more of it to go to waste. I gather what I can and rub it over her skin.

She mumbles and shifts. She doesn't wake up.

Excited, remembering our deal, I drop my hand, coiling my tailtip around my member.

I yank my shaft while I lift, shifting so I'm on top of her, gently positioning her below me. Arching my tail so my member won't bump her, I squeeze my length hard, imagining so much more.

I hiss low and deep. My nostrils flare as my knot grows from the attention. I gather as much seed as I can endure, staring at Daisy's slumbering, soft face. Slipping my tongue out from my mouth, I lash the empty air between our faces, wishing I was lashing her body. But if she wakes, she may stop me, and though I have every right to do as I will up to the point of mating, she might balk and try to flee.

I can't let that happen. This moment is perfect.

She's under me, soft and sweet, so small she could be nothing more than another pillow on my nest. Yet she's in it, and she remained in it the whole night, letting me enjoy her warmth. My gaze streaks to the chains bunched up around her breasts and the glittering diamonds that tease her nipples.

I grip the bedding on either side of Daisy's head, tearing it with my nails, rocking my hips, rutting my coiled tailtip.

She moans, brings one of her hands up, and swats her nose. Tensing, I go still, waiting to see if she wakes up. She moans again, and I lean on my right arm, deciding to shift to her side. I never get a chance to.

Her eyes flutter open.

Widening, they land on my face. The glare of sleep vanishes from her irises instantaneously, and her body loses all its sweet looseness.

We stare at each other. She's stopped breathing. Her lips part and I can tell she's trying not to scream—trying not to move. Because she knows if she does, even a little, she'd still be trapped under the cage of my arms, and right now, I'm barely touching her.

If she tries to flee, I'll grab her and pull her against me. Daisy fears our differences, I sense it.

Her eyes flick down between our bodies, stopping where my tailtip is curled around my shaft. She stares and takes a deep, shuddering breath.

I wait for her reaction yet all she does is stare. I puff out my cowl, delighted that she wishes to watch me. She takes in another deep breath. Pulling my shaft harder, I wonder how far I can go before she tells me to stop.

"What are you doing?" she whispers. Her hand slides up to cup her nose but not before her cheeks pinken.

"Relieving the pressure in my knot," I growl, releasing the tip of my shaft and spilling all over her thighs and legs.

She jerks, shimmying her legs, trying to get out from where my seed is leaking onto her. I reach down and clutch her hip. "You wear my diamonds—you will also wear my seed. See? It is nice when you wear it." I tilt my head at the glistening cum on her skin. "It is yours."

Daisy stops moving, her gaze snapping to mine. Her other hand comes up to grasp the chains tangled at her neck. I pet her cheek, pull her hand off her nose, and while she winces, she remains where she is, sucking in another deep breath. She even relaxes.

"Zaku... this is..." She inhales deeply again. "So wrong. We don't even know each other."

"Wrong?" I check to make sure I am not limiting her airflow, but finding I am still fully above her, I move my gaze back to her face. Her eyes hood and dart between us, down to where I hold my member.

"I..." She brings the hand I pulled off her nose to join the other one clutching her chains. "I'm scared," she whispers. Her chest rises and falls quickly.

My ardor cools, and I release her hip, bringing my hand up to cup her face. The other pets her tousled hair. "I know, but you don't have to be. Our deal still stands."

"Promise?"

"Yesss," I hiss.

Her eyes search mine. They're a light brown that complements her yellow hair and pale skin. I don't know why I haven't studied their depths until now, but they're as alluring as the rest of her.

I smile, caressing a line from her cheek to her lower lip with my thumb's claw. She relaxes a little more, and I lower my throbbing member to rest against her thighs, pressing my body to hers.

She tenses again, though it doesn't last. Her body is heated. She takes in another heavy breath, and her flesh warms even more. A delicious scent rises to my nose. It's one I have never encountered before. I like it. Immensely. I push my tail into her legs until she has no choice but to open them and let me lie between them. When she does, the scent blooms in the air.

I groan, my tail swaying gently.

It's her arousal.

She wants me. I have aroused her!

I am king.

Uncoiling my tailtip from my member, I thrust once excitedly against her thigh. The sensation of her flesh along my bulge forces a winded groan from my throat. I empty my spill all over her.

She gasps as I spill and spill and spill. There is little pleasure from the action itself except for the release of tension deep inside me.

I rise and, grabbing my shaft with my hands, staring down at Daisy beneath me, I spill even more. Daisy's gone tense again, but she lets me have this. Her fingers loosen on the chains and her hands drop to rest on her chest.

She's panting wildly. I notice dabbles of sweat forming upon her brow.

Thrusting into my hand, I cover her with my essence. Fluid falls over her legs, her belly, her arms, her chest. It pools and trickles over her curves and dampens the bedding. I spill until the aching bulge is gone from my shaft. And still, I clutch myself, wanting to soak her, working all the built-up tension from my loins. Releasing my member long enough to remove her arms from her chest, needing to see all of her, I groan, wanting more than anything to sink my fangs into her shoulder and mark her and engorge.

She squirms, rubs her nose, and gasps again, stopping this primal need of mine. I spread my seed over her breasts instead, her neck, and even smear it on her lips.

The shock on her face excites me.

When her tongue sneaks out for a taste of me, I lose it.

Grabbing her thighs, I press her knees to her chest, drawing back to plant my face between her legs, needing her taste on my tongue.

She cries out, and her hands grab a hold of my cowl. Heels dig into my back as she tries to close her legs, undulating her hips all the same. "What's happening?" she whimpers. "To me?"

I think I hear a twinge of fear in her voice and I glimpse her face to make sure. It's not fear I find. Her face is flushed with fervor and...excitement?

Have I excited her as well? Pride wells inside me.

"Pleasssure," I answer, helping her come to terms with this thing between us.

When she doesn't try and flee, I spread her open wide, and take in her delicate human sex. Yellow curls glisten with dew, framing a soft pink slit. There's a nub at the top that beacons my tongue, but it's her little hole that brings my saliva forth. It's wet and quivering. It's small and delicate. And it's open... For me.

For her king. Satisfaction joins my pride. I have chosen well.

"Zaku!" she whimpers my name, body straining against mine.

"Daisssy," I hiss back, petting her opening with my fingertip. I lean forward and slip my tongue into her, pushing through tight, tender flesh.

She cries out again and her hips shoot upward at my invasion. I grasp them and hold her there in the air. The angle gives me even better access to her sheath. Sliding my tongue everywhere, tasting her, drinking her, I learn her from the inside out. Pressing my fork as far back as I can into her tightness, I reach her body's end. I swirl my tongue.

A deep, satisfied groan bursts from my throat.

"Zaku!" Clawing and clutching my head, my cowl, her nails bite into my scales as she shrieks my name. Her little body writhes and she jerks her hips up and down like she's trying to dislodge me or seek more of my attention.

But my mouth is planted firmly on her opening, my lips kissing it, refusing to move. My tongue is lodged deep.

My little flower needs watering. She needs to bloom to fit my stem.

She is small. And so is her sex. She will need lots of watering.

Pressing her back down to the bed, I glimpse her overly flushed and stunned face, her wild hair. Her eyes are wide and heated. I lick harder, and she hitches.

She's not trying to remove me anymore—she's doing the opposite. I smile against her dewy folds. Daisy bears her sex down onto my face, gripping me tightly. Careful not to hurt her, I open her legs wider and push her back until she's sprawled out like a meal.

I could accidentally hurt her, so easily, a niggle of worry enters me. Perhaps her fear of mating is sound...

Her eyes close and her body hitches again, banishing my worry. She shunts into me, and when she does, I roll my tongue in deep circles. Her moans build, her gasps heighten. Her little noises excite me. Her body wants what I can give it. I know because her arousal thickens over my tongue. It gushes, and I quickly remove my tongue to swallow it, only to thrust my tongue back in for more.

Groaning, I feast.

Her hand comes down between her legs to pet her nub. Wondering what she is doing, I exhale a hot breath through my nose, staring as she works it. She moans, and I massage her thighs where I grip them.

The Python might have gotten here first, but I'll be here last.

I'd kill him all over again if I could.

I lick her harder, faster.

"Zaku," she breathes my name again, and my spine straightens, waiting for direction. There's a rigid spot inside her that makes her moan when I flick my tongue to it. I use it so she stays put. "D-Don't stop!" Her fingers quicken on her nub.

Good.

Her sex clamps down on my tongue, and Daisy arches

her whole body, going abruptly silent. She flings her head back; and I look up, mesmerized. Her mouth purses as her chest arches. I'm tempted to pull away but I don't want to stop licking her. Her body convulses, and she takes my tongue with it.

She writhes on my face, and I give her the leverage to do so.

Sweet essence floods me.

My knot expands hard and fast from the assault, and I spill again, lapping it up.

Slowly, her convulsions subside, her breathy panting the only sound in the room. I hungrily swallow everything she gives me. If I could sustain my body with hers, I would. From this morning on, I will see if it's possible. I will drink her down and see if we're even more compatible than she wants to believe.

"Zaku..." she says, sagging into the bedding of my nest. She pushes my head out from between her legs. Sliding my hands up to grip hers, I swirl and lick her sex one last delicious time.

I will seed you soon, sweet flower. I kiss it goodbye and pull my tongue out, swiping at her outer folds as I do.

"No more." Clamping her thighs together, she turns on her side, bringing her hands to her face and rubbing it. "It's too much, too sensitive," she whines. "I need... I need to think."

I crawl over her until she's within the cage of my body, my large tail coiled around us. She's such a small thing compared to me. My worry returns. I have to be careful. So easily, I could ruin her. My hands, from claw to palm, span from her chin to curl over the top of her head. I carried her body for hours the first day, never tiring.

She's all soft curves and lush breasts, softness personified, and a perfect contrast to the hard scales and ridges of my body.

She also has no natural armor; I don't even know how she is alive right now without armor. I take in her scrapes and bruises. I take in the tangled chains gathered around her throat. I span my fingers out to grip them, pushing my fingers under the collar around her throat.

I will need to feed her well and often so she becomes more substantial. Daisy will need the extra sustenance if I plan to keep her nested for many years to come. If I plan to feed from her slit.

Her panting subsides as she slips her hands from where she has them pressed over her eyes to look up at me. The pink glow of her cheeks has yet to disappear.

"We're only just beginning," I say, leaning down and licking her jaw, gripping her collar.

But first, she needs food.

SEVENTEEN

A VISITOR

Daisy

THE NEXT COUPLE of days bleed into each other.

Pressing my palms to the glass in the foyer, I debate if I've been here for five or six days already. Maybe more? It's hard to keep track, even with the windows. Time is different on Earth than it is in space. Things are faster here yet somehow slower too.

Gazing at the bones in the yard, I make up stories about them in my head. Fierce battles, bloody deaths, and booming last words. Only for those words to vanish on the wind as Zaku ultimately wins. The more he wins in my head, the more I want him to win. The more I like thinking about it and imagining it.

Everyone has their heroes. Mine was supposed to be my father except putting him in that role in my head only infuriates me. I sigh.

Zaku's out hunting and foraging to refill his stores and I

wonder if he'll battle today as well, perhaps bring home another trophy. I shudder, uncertain if I like the idea of it.

He says I'm too small and wants me to eat until I'm bursting. He needs more food for that.

I sigh, annoyed that I haven't even tried to escape now that I'm alone.

Being alone is easy, safe. I became a pilot for that very reason. I can spend entire shifts alone in my cockpit, never encountering another soul. Though right now? It's making me uncomfortable. Imagining a whole day alone churns my stomach.

I suck in a clear, unscented breath of air. With Zaku's absence, his scent has vanished. I curl my toes, not certain I like that it's gone. His scent makes me happy—happy, of all things. It does something to me. At first, it was frightening, but now, not so much. It's not always in the air. It's not always spinning my thoughts. I've come to realize the scent only comes around when Zaku's overly aroused. *I don't think he realizes...*

Most of the time, though, he's producing the smell. And, I, desperate to trust him—to trust in *something*—keep testing his limits, keep searching for a reason to distrust him like those I've worked for.

I'm waiting to be betrayed all over again.

Closing my eyes, I bring my hands to my face, rubbing it hard.

I should be trying to escape. I should be looking for Gemma.

Except all I want to do is pretend the world outside these walls doesn't exist. My hands fall from my face to clutch the collar around my throat. I haven't taken it off since Zaku placed it upon me. The diamonds and chains have been unhooked, but the collar remains.

I blush, remembering this morning how I gripped at his cowl and dug my nails into it, writhing on his face as he held me up on his shoulders. As his scent flooded my nose, warmed my body, made me ache feverishly, and almost had me screaming for sex. As his tongue slammed into me, dizzying my world.

Each day, I get to sleep for as long as I want, bathe in hot, scented water for hours, eat the freshest food, and *relax*. Throughout it all, Zaku's touching me, massaging the aches out of my muscles, and trying to part my legs for his pleasure and mine. I stopped caring because it's a distraction—*he's* a distraction.

I'm growing complacent.

My hands fall from my collar.

Sex is commonplace amongst agreeable, contractual humans. It's even encouraged to grow our numbers. Women, despite being soldiers, are still pressured to have at least two children in their lifetime. The father's identity doesn't matter. It's the numbers that count. There's always a need for more soldiers, for workers.

If I were to stay here on Earth, Zaku would be a great companion. He's strong. He'd keep me safe until I learned how to keep *myself* safe. He's not cold. If he were human, he'd give me strong children—he'd provide for those children, I'm sure of it—except he's not, and interspecies relations have never resulted in gestation.

I can't be with him. I want to be a mother someday. I want to raise my children the way I was never raised. With love, affection, and perhaps... dreams. I want to prove there is more to life than war and death. My fingers twitch.

Who'd want someone like me? I can't offer anything anymore. The best I can hope for is a contractual relationship with a man who will impregnate me and leave, to impregnate another. I could do the same for a man who wants children, but then I wouldn't be able to keep my baby, which is out of the question.

I don't have the looks to entice a higher caste man. One who would willingly *life partner* with me. And then there's the problem of barely having enough rations to take care of one, let alone a child.

It's not in the cards, Daisy. It never was.

I inherited nothing from my father except his genes, his appearance. Everything he earned, he donated to the military. It was the first time I felt betrayed. When he died, I had no idea what was happening, begging for him, confused as to why I was being handed off from one official to the next. They didn't even let me keep one of his medals to remember him by. My father was there, and then he wasn't. He and the military taught me not to rely on anyone in the most brutal way possible, through innocent, childish confusion.

Zaku could teach me things. Different things. How to survive here. He could make *me* stronger.

Feeling my eyes grow heavy, I force my tears away. I've gone years without crying. Earth, Peter, and the Python unraveled all of my hard work and I hate them for it.

Zaku could show me how to use the tech. He could teach me about this land. I suck my lower lip into my mouth and chew on it, knowing I'm trying to convince myself of life here on Earth. That living here is a possibility. Glimpsing the scars on my hands that I've sustained over the years, guilt floods me. I brush them with my fingers. Zaku cares a lot about the way I look. I don't understand why. I'm not particularly beautiful for a human woman, but he doesn't seem to know that.

I can't help wondering if his affections can be easily

shifted, and if they are—if there were more "options" —
would he still think I'm beautiful? I scrunch my face.

You're not staying here, Daisy.

I groan, turning to the stake right outside where the
rotting stump of the Python's head is decaying. It's been
covered in maggots for days, surrounded by bloated flies.
One of the flies crawls into its mouth. Looking away, my
eyes go to Earth's sun.

Where is Zaku?

Does Central Command know I'm gone yet?

Is Gemma okay? Shelby?

I hear a sizzling sound behind me. Turning toward the
kitchen, there's a robot preparing food.

Something thuds on the glass, and I twist back. A blue
shimmer catches my attention as a rock tumbles away from
the window.

Zaku?

Suddenly the blue blur comes charging toward me from
out of the trees. My heart jumps into my throat and I fall
into the room and duck behind the sofa. *A naga male.* The
blue one from the plateau. I close my eyes and press my
hands to my mouth.

Please go away.

There's more thudding on the window, louder than
before, and I flinch. I press my hands harder to my mouth. I
wait, even pray. After a few minutes, the thudding stops. I
wait some more and it doesn't come back.

Slowly lifting my head, I peek over the sofa cushion...

I stiffen, and my chest constricts with fear.

The male sways on his tail when he sees me. He presses
one of his hands flush to the glass. His palm is a brilliant
orange, like his face, like his hair. Stunned, we stare at each
other for a time, taking each other in. This one's not like

Zaku at all. The only thing this naga and Zaku share are their forms.

Where Zaku is a giant with a cowl and dull colors, this naga has a short tuft of wild orange hair on his head that matches the brilliance of his face and his hands, his body bearing a longer, thinner tail. The orange upon him is striking with the sapphire and indigo blues of his body and scales.

His eyes are black.

I can't decide if the male is either stunning or uncannily terrifying. Or both. He reminds me of the lake. Of deep blue water and all the creatures hidden within it.

Swallowing, my fear ebbs. *The glass will hold.* It will...

The allure of his coloring, though, screams for me to keep my distance. If I've learned anything from visiting numerous planets, it's that the prettiest, brightest creatures are the most dangerous.

Wanting to get closer, I move into the open space of the room.

What will he do if I show courage? If I stand up to him?

Will he *fear* me?

I've met two of these nagas so far, and both were different. Maybe he will be too?

He stares at me intensely, and I curl my arms over my chest. When I'm standing mere yards from him, he says something to me that I can't hear through the glass. One of those little white orbs floats around his head.

He bares his fangs and says something more, the intensity going into his expression.

I shake my head.

He slides his hand down the glass, bringing the other forward. He's holding a knife.

Shelby's knife.

I forget the naga and search the yard for Shelby. A fist pounds on the glass, startling me. I look back at the male. His flaring nostrils, the frustration etched on his face, sends my pulse racing. I take a step back. He looks around, finds a large rock, and flings it at the glass.

Thump!

I recoil as the rock tumbles to the ground.

The male glances at something behind me, and I turn to see the robot holding out a plate of food. An idea forms.

Zaku programmed the robots to listen to me in all things except for letting me leave.

"Robot..." I say, pursing my lips, trying to find the right words to ask for what I want, trying to keep my anxiety from showing. "I want to speak to him." I indicate the male outside.

The robot scans me, scans him. Then it scans the white orb hovering beside him.

"Connecting," it says.

I glance at the trees around the yard, searching for Zaku. He could return at any moment. I don't know what he'll do if he sees this other naga speaking to me, but I assume he'll kill him and put his head on a spike with the other. Or maybe he'd just let it rot on the ground with the others scattered about. If his talk about domination is to be believed, he won't let this naga live. Facing him, I straighten my shoulders.

If he wants to risk his life, then so be it. He might have news of the outside world. He has *something* because he's holding Shelby's knife. I'll take something over nothing.

A crackling noise fills my ears, and then a voice.

"Female... where... Zaku?"

My flesh prickles with excitement. It worked! But I

shake my head again at him. I sure as hell am not giving Zaku's location away.

I like Zaku.

More than most people or beings I've met.

"He's around," I say softly. "Stop making noise or he'll hear," I lie.

The male snarls at me. "Open the door," he demands. "Let me speak to him." His voice is clearer now coming through the house's robot. "I am owed."

Owed?

"I'm not an idiot. I'm not letting you in, and even if I wanted to, I can't," I say a little louder.

The male pounds his fist on the glass, clearly annoyed.

"Where did you get that knife?" I ask, pointing to the weapon in his hand.

He pauses, looking at it. "The forest."

"It's mine," I say, growing more confident.

His eyes come back to mine. "It's *mine* now. Open the door. I am owed!" he shouts, thumping his tail.

I flinch. Absolutely not. If he's near Zaku's home, where there are remains scattered everywhere, then he's not afraid of Zaku.

Maybe this male is that terrifying. Or maybe he's stupid.

But then if he's stupid... if I try the door with his help, perhaps I'd get *free*. I could trick him.

I could run.

I could make it back to the facility, take the transport ship, and return to *The Dreadnaut*. There I could find reinforcements, save Gemma, and get my vengeance on Peter and the others.

Zaku will never let me get that far.

I'm mad at myself for even considering such a terrible

plan. These males aren't stupid...and if they were, they're strong enough to counteract it.

"No," I tell him.

The male's lips twist. His eyes go wild with desperation, making my heart race. The scales rise on his neck and shoulders. "He promisssed me a female!" The male strikes at the window again, and I take a step back. "He lied. I will have what I'm owed!"

A cold sweat breaks out on my skin. I shake my head again. The male hisses, flings his long tail like a whip upon the glass.

The window shudders, the sound louder than the thump of the rock. "I will have what I've been promised! I will have her!" his roar thunders through the robot, making my soul quiver. I back up until my butt is against the kitchen counter. "He promisssed me! A so-called king," the naga spits, "never breaks a promise!"

The further I back up, the angrier he gets. He slams his tail against the glass over and over. Harder, heavier, the pounding rumbles through my whole body, filling me with terror. He thrashed, beating at the window.

I hear the glass crack.

"I will have what I am owed!"

EIGHTEEN
BROKEN PROMISES

Daisy

Glass shatters, and I dart to the side, sprinting to the red door. I slam it closed behind me, frantically searching for a lock, a weapon, anything. There are only the paintings on the walls and the spiral staircase on the far end that leads to Zaku's nest. Nothing else.

Then I see the panel next to the door. Pressing buttons at random, I pray it locks.

I hear more glass shatter, growing louder by the second. *The glass isn't working,* my thoughts reel. *The door isn't going to keep me safe. I can't stay here.* I pivot to flee below when Zaku's voice stops me.

"Vagan!" he bellows, the sound eclipsing all else.

There's another crash, and I stop.

"I gave you what you needed, and you deny me my prize!" Vagan roars. "I bought her, not you!"

Bought...her? Anger streaks through me. *Who?*

Sliding my damp palms on my pants, I crouch as I hear more things break and shatter.

After a time a thunderous hiss pierces through the door and straight into me. *Zaku's hiss.* It slithers through me and over my flesh, entering me and invading every nerve ending. I lick my lips and open the door to peer outside.

Shaking, I find Zaku in the middle of the room, towering over the other male's form, and the naga, Vagan, coiled, glaring up at him.

Shelby's knife is sticking out of Zaku's chest. Fear rips through me.

They're poised, the both of them, waiting for the other to make the next move. Zaku's tailtip sways tensely from side to side above his shoulder.

I clutch the door as the blue naga hisses, "We had a deal."

Slowly, Zaku lifts his hand and grips the knife. "You dare enter my den? Attack my queen?" he grits. "Any deal we had is gone for your foolishness."

"Gone? It was my tech. Mine! I will have what I'm owed!"

Zaku's lips curl and he pulls the knife from his chest. "You are owed nothing. You did not capture a female. The hunt was fair."

"Fair? There was nothing fair about it. You threw me off the mountain. You denied me the chance," the blue one sneers. "I will take yours in compensation," he hisses.

Zaku lifts the knife and stares at it. Just like the Python had that first night. Blood spurts from Zaku's chest.

Transfixed, fear cramps my stomach.

Zaku's cowl flares, his eyes darkening when they return to the blue male. "You will never have my queen, Vagan. And for this intrusion, I will make you pay."

Vagan rises to face him. "Dishonorable sssnake," he says. "You're the one who will die today, and I will claim your female upon your corpse! I will take her as your punishment for your deceit!" He attacks, and I shove open the door, screaming when his tail snaps behind Zaku and comes down.

Zaku braces against the hit, tenses at my voice, and strikes out, thumping Vagan in the face. Vagan roars, and then there's nothing but a flurry of tails and limbs. I hear grunts, snarls, and groans. Vagan flings away and twists in my direction. He rushes for me.

He abruptly stops and is dragged back by his tail. I dodge behind the door and close it again, sliding down the frame with a whimper. I need to do something. I need a weapon.

There's no fucking weapon in this house!

"I will have what I'm owed!"

"She is not the one you want," Zaku bellows.

"You allowed the human males to leave without delivering her, without giving her to us! She is mine!"

"She is gestating. How was I supposed to know this? Do you want a human litter to fend for?"

"The human males lie. She is not gestating!"

They're talking about Shelby.

"I can't give you what I don't have. The hunt was fair, Vagan. Leave now and I will let you live," Zaku growls. "For the history we share, I can be merciful."

"Merciful? You don't know the meaning of the word. You owe me, King Cobra. You owe me. Help me! Help me steal her. Now that would be mercy."

"I'd rather see you maimed."

Abruptly fighting returns, louder, wilder this time, and closer to the door. I fall back when something crashes through it. It cracks, shattering, wood splintering everywhere. Fleeing, I race for the safety of Zaku's nest.

A tail wraps around my ankle, jerks me, and I drop hard to the ground, hitting my head. Crying out, I'm dragged across the floor and into a cage of arms.

"Release her," Zaku snaps, poised in the doorway, a hand clutching his chest where his blood spurts. Sharp claws press into my neck.

"I want my mate," Vagan wheezes against my ear, lifting me against him. Corded muscles press into me. His claws push into my skin and I wince.

Zaku strains but remains where he is, meeting my eyes. "Don't hurt her."

"I will do more than hurt her," Vagan threatens, "if I don't get what I want."

"Shelby," I rasp. "You want Shelby."

Vagan goes taut, his chest pushes into my back. "Ssshelby," he repeats her name. "The one with bright eyes."

Zaku's tail inches closer.

"Yes!" I burst out, focusing on it. "Shelby, you want her, don't you? Her eyes are special," I say, distracting Vagan.

"Ssspecial?"

I lick my lips. "Very special. They're... they're enhanced, her eyes." Vagan's claws lift from my skin slightly. "She's very special. Only one in a million have eyes like hers."

"She is," he agrees. "She excites me. She... she has turned my body against me. Why?" he roars, sending my hair flying from the ferocity. "Why is my body quaking!?"

Zaku's tail gets even closer. I feel Vagan's tail coil up my leg and something hard digs into my lower back, something more than his chest.

Knowing what it is, I try not to be sick. "How does she excite you?"

Vagan grunts and his cock grows harder, bigger, wetter. "She makes me want to mate. Tell me more about her eyes. Tell me anything. I want to know everything. I need—"

Vagan's hold on me drops, and I fall forward. Zaku catches me as Vagan is ripped back, pulled away by Zaku's tail. Zaku thrusts me behind him, and I tumble to my knees as he jumps atop Vagan's form, his fangs sinking brutally into the blue naga's arm.

Vagan screams, clawing at Zaku, refusing to give up. Zaku's entire body twitches, straining against the place where his fangs are deep in Vagan's skin. I scurry away and into the foyer, not wanting Vagan to grab me again. Zaku's fangs hold.

Vagan rolls onto his back, his eyes glazing over. They meet mine and he hisses weakly, "Shelby." Like he is satisfied dying on her behalf. For a woman he has never even met.

I frown.

Zaku slides his tail over Vagan's form, pulling his fangs out as Vagan falls unconscious. Zaku presses his hand back to his wound. Minutes go by—minutes that feel like an eternity—and Vagan doesn't rise.

Zaku slumps to the floor, keeping the heaviest part of his tail draped across Vagan's chest. His eyes hood, finding mine. They dull further as I rush to him. There's blood everywhere, pooling from his wound. It's all over his scales.

"Zaku," I whisper, spanning my fingers, uncertain if I should touch him.

"Vagan... will not be out long." He sags, his hand sliding down his chest. "You... must hide."

"We need to stop your bleeding," I say. I sprint into the

front room, grabbing some towels from the kitchen, and when I do, I spot dozens of robots everywhere. They're picking up the rubble, the broken furniture, and the glass strewn about. Some are beginning to repair the walls. I don't wait to watch, returning to Zaku's side.

His eyes follow me as I press the towels to his wound, staunching the blood as best I can.

"We need to stop the bleeding. Do you have anything that can help?" I call for the robots when he shakes his head. Soon, several come to my aid. "Help me," I beg them.

One of the robots scans Zaku. "Emergency medical aid has been called. They are on the way."

Zaku reaches for me. "I will regenerate."

"Hush. The robots said aid is coming—we need to put pressure on your wound. We need to stop the bleeding. Try not to move."

"Aid isn't coming. I need... sleep. Rest. You need to hide. Vagan will not be down long. My venom—"

"Not without you. I'm not going anywhere without you."

He just saved my life. There's no way I'm leaving him, but if what he says is true and Vagan will soon wake, he'll kill Zaku and finish the job. He'll come after me. He'll go after Shelby.

I need a weapon. Straightening, I run back to the front rooms and find my knife. Covered in blood, I wipe it on my pants and return to Zaku.

He eyes me and the weapon. I go to Vagan's side.

I poise the knife over Vagan's chest and sink it in, putting my weight down on it to push it through the naga's muscles and organs. I hit bone. He groans but doesn't wake. I yank it out and stab him several more times in the gut.

"Shelby will never be yours," I whisper, "You'll never

hurt her baby." Pushing my knife into Vagan once more, I leave it in. "You'll never hurt her or her baby."

I turn back to Zaku. He's slumped over, and I crawl to him. "What about the medical pod?"

"I... will not... fit."

Glancing at the robots gathered around us, Zaku grabs my wrist, forcing my eyes back to his.

Slowly, he lifts, pinning me with his eyes, towering over me, blood spurting between his fingers when the towels plop to the floor. Some of it gets on me. He tugs me to my feet, and my mouth slackens as he drags me toward the stairs.

"What are you doing?" I choke. "You're going to hurt yourself further. You'll die!" He leads me toward his nest, his grip tightening when I try to pull away. "Stop, Zaku! You're making yourself bleed more!"

"If you will not hide—" he wheezes. "I will make you hide."

Zaku falls against the wall, taking only a moment to steady his body with his arm. I gag, glancing back at the trail of blood he leaves in his wake, his tail slipping through it, half tumbling down the stairs.

"Please stop," I beg him. "Please. I'll hide, I promise, just stop!"

He uses the wall the rest of the way down.

A robot is waiting for us at the bottom. Zaku groans and stares at it. I try yanking my wrist from his grip again. "Why are you doing this?" I gasp.

"From this... point on," he hisses at the robot, "you will follow no one's... commands but my own."

My brows furrow. Zaku drags me into his room and toward the golden cage. He thrusts me inside. I catch my footing and turn as the cage's door closes.

"Sssafe," he says. He tumbles to the floor.

I rush to the bars. "No," I cry, reaching my arm through them. My fingers brush his scales. "Zaku!"

He doesn't respond.

"Wake up!" I scream.

NINETEEN
TRAPPED

Daisy

I LOSE MY MIND.

I scream, I rattle the cage bars, I curse. All the while, Zaku's blood slowly covers the floor, making the cage feel even smaller.

The stench of it fills my nostrils. I can't stop breathing it in, no matter how hard I try. I can't get away from it. My clothes are soaked with it. I shout for Zaku to wake up. I scream for the robots that no longer respond to me. I vomit up bile, nauseated with fear.

I climb onto the swing in the cage when the house robots enter the room, fearing it's Vagan back from the dead to finish the job.

The robots clean the blood. They wash the walls. They laser the ground. They even wipe the blood off Zaku. I beg them to let me out of the cage but they leave me be, cleaning what they can through the bars.

The smell of blood remains.

When the robots are done, I move to the lock and try it. Only I can't get a good look at the mechanism on the outside. I can't reach it with my fingers. Straining, pushing I still try, giving up before I hurt my hand. Holding it to my chest, I curse some more. My attention returns to the giant, unmoving male and my heart constricts.

He hasn't stirred, his coloring continues to diminish. The yellow, browns, beiges, and even his black scales have gone grey. I calm, staring at him, or go numb, I don't know anymore. His bleeding has stopped, but he's also still not moving. I gaze at his motionless form, begging for him to wake up and then cursing him for putting me in this situation. Eventually, the robots leave.

And I'm alone.

One returns and brings me food. It's the same plate from earlier. One look at it, and I hack up empty air.

Wiping my mouth with the back of my hand, I notice Zaku's chest quake. He expels a heavy breath, shudders, and goes still again. But soon after, he breathes once more, easier this time.

"Zaku," I whisper, expelling my fear. Deep-seated fear that's been drowning me from the inside, thinking he had died...

I clutch the bars, frighteningly relieved and excited. I grip the bars harder.

Safe? This isn't safe.

I can't do anything inside a cage. I can't even help myself!

And then it occurs to me that perhaps putting me in the cage is to keep Zaku safe. From *me*. It makes sense. Unconscious, I could easily stab him to death like I did Vagan, and he'd not be able to stop me.

I could also run. And right now, with the way I feel, I want to stab Zaku all over again for throwing me in here. My numbness gives way to fury, and for a long time, I glare at him. I glare and tell him if he dies to spite me, I am going to find him in the next plane and kill him myself.

The night comes and goes. I don't sleep. I can't. Sticky, cold, and miserable; there's not enough space for me to lie down without touching blood. Most of it is dry now, but that's not any better. It's crusted on my clothes, and I contemplate stripping, eventually deciding against it.

Resting my head on the bars, I begin telling Zaku stories I heard as a kid just to fill the deafening silence. Legends of space pirates, marauder kings, and princesses who fell asleep only to be woken up by a lover's kiss. He stirs, and I grasp onto the hope that he's listening, that he hears my voice.

"Live," I whisper. "I'm not worth dying over." I tell him if he comes closer to the bars, I'll kiss him. It's stupid, but maybe fairy tales have some truth to them. I'm willing to try.

He doesn't wake, he doesn't move closer. And before long, I run out of stories. I was never told very many of them when I was a kid. I try making a couple up, stumbling over words, saying silly, ridiculous things. I give up when it doesn't work.

My fear ramps up again in the silence. I've been around silence for far too long. I've been alone for longer, and I can't do it anymore. I don't want to be alone anymore. Tears fall, and I angrily wipe them off my cheeks.

When the picture of the Lurker pokes at my brain, when it finally makes its return, I sit in terror thinking that he's real... he's real and he's watching *me*.

So I fill the silence and tell Zaku about my horrid life, to keep my tears, the fear, and the silence at bay.

"My dad was a commander," I begin but then stop, sniffling. "I hate crying. I grew up in the military," I say, starting over. "I don't have any brothers or sisters, at least that I know of... My mom was... well, she had a contract with my father to give him a child. She wasn't in my life after I was born. I might have siblings," I ramble.

I lie down on the floor despite the blood, pressing up to the bars nearest Zaku where it's cleaner. "I was forbidden from seeking her out. Even after my dad's death, I was forbidden. I was my father's daughter and no one else's. There are rules. Strict rules where I'm from."

Why do I keep coming back to my dad?

I start over a third time. "I grew up on a ship called *The Prime*. A sister ship to the one hiding behind the moon right now, but newer, faster, closer to the front lines of wherever the war is taking place. It was an honor to be born on such a ship. I had access to the best training. I was born privileged, and I was told such every day. Not every child is lucky enough to be born into a high caste..." Pulling my limbs close to me, I curl them into my body, finding I'm able to keep from focusing on the Lurker in my head if I focus on talking. "But I hated it. I hated every single minute of my life on the Prime," I whisper.

"It was worse when my dad passed. I cried a lot. I missed him. I thought I hated him, but once he was gone, it was different. I was six. I had no idea about the world. No one cared. I had no friends, no family. And crying is a sign of weakness, and someone like me shouldn't have been weak. Not with who my dad was. Daisy Downer is what the other military kids called me. They tried to beat it out of me. I took up piloting to get away. I could be alone if I was flying a ship. No one would see me cry there, no one could hurt me. I didn't like being alone, but I learned to live with it."

I pause, swallowing, hoping Zaku will rouse so I don't have to go on. When he doesn't, I rub my eyes, hard.

"When I was thirteen, it was pretty evident that I wasn't going to live up to my dad's name. Everything got worse. I had to start paying my keep, so they put me in the field. I was sent on my first mission." I hate remembering those days and how terrified I was. I was just a kid. "I shot down my first ship on that very mission, killing over a dozen aliens."

I lift up and look at him, begging him to wake up. *Please, wake up.*

"And do you know what I did, Zaku? I cried. Fuck, it was the worst thing to ever have happen to me, my dad, and then *that*. I didn't want to live. I wasn't cut out to be a soldier. I had no idea who was on that ship, nor what they had done. I was confused and the ship's doctors told me that someday it would all be clear to me. It didn't matter. I had killed them. The guilt was horrible. I vowed to bury that Daisy forever. I didn't deserve to be sad, not after that. I didn't cry again for years.

"I buried my emotions, and life became... tolerable. I began to understand why everyone was so cold, so walled. They learned that lesson much sooner than I. I rose in the ranks and became a petty officer, and life was... okay. But the war caught up to me eventually, and I was shipped to the *real* front lines. My life is pretty boring, isn't it? Pretty sad. No wonder you won't wake up," I say, lying back down.

I stare at Zaku's tail. "Please wake up." He stirs briefly at my voice. I wait another minute hoping he'll stir again. He doesn't.

"I was sent to join a fleet of ships that were being

deployed to help stop the wave of Ketts taking over Colony 4. I was supposed to die there, give my life to the war, just to hold them off another day. Only, I saw children on a rooftop as I was flying by." I press my hand to my mouth, guilt flooding me. "I'd be dead right now, if I wasn't so emotional... I should be dead. I'm not worth dying for. I saved them. I couldn't *not* save them. They were crying, like me, like when I was a kid. Everyone in the fleet died that day but me and those kids." Tears bud on my lashes, and I let them fall this time. "So many innocents died. So many lost souls."

Thinking of those babies, silence surrounds me again like a heavy blanket. "They had clung to me, wanted me to protect them, and I wanted to keep them," I murmur. So badly, it hurt. I wanted to be their mother from the moment I saw them. I wanted to give them the protection they sought but I never even made an argument for them because I knew it was futile.

No one was going to give me two healthy, land-born children.

I was a disappointment after all. A failed prodigy. I couldn't provide for them.

"Now I'm here. With you," I say. "Begging you to survive."

When the sun lowers and my eyes start to hood, when I'm bracing for another night in misery, for more silence, I hear a moan.

"Zaku?" I say his name almost hesitantly.

His tail twitches and moves, pulling into his body. I sit up.

He moans again, and his eyelids peel open. For a moment, he stares at the ceiling.

"Zaku?" I gasp, excited.

His tongue leaves his mouth to swipe his lips. His eyes slide from the ceiling to mine.

"Daisy?" he groans, tilting his head in my direction.

"You're awake," I breathe, unable to believe it myself. "You're seriously hurt, Zaku." I grasp the bars.

Zaku slowly lifts his hand from where it rests on the floor and presses it to his wound. He winces and then raises his hand to his eyes. It glistens with fresh blood. "Nothing I won't recover from," he rasps.

I guffaw. "You should've died. You bled—a lot."

He places his hand back on his chest. His gaze narrows as it slips from it to me, and over my form, checking me over. "Are you hurt?" He tries to coil his tail under him. More blood leaks from his chest.

"Don't move!"

He doesn't listen, pushing up, opening his wound even more, and coming to me.

"Zaku, you're going to make it worse."

"Are you hurt?" he asks again, his voice gaining strength.

"I'm..." I trail off, having no idea. "I'm hurt, all right! I'm furious!" Everything in the last day and a half expels from me. "How dare you," I growl, sitting up on my knees. "How dare you put me in this cage where I have no choice but to watch you bleed out! How fucking dare you."

He stares at me like I've lost my mind.

I've lost it, all right.

"You bled out all over the floor! You left me here to rot, all the while soaked in your blood, and for what? Safety? I'm not safe in here, nor are you out there! You stupid, stupid male!"

He doesn't say anything as I do, and only when tears

burst from my eyes and I sink to the floor, does he reach through the bars. He catches a tear with his claw.

I hate him so much for it; I hate that the simple gesture comforts me.

"I could not lose you. I am sorry I've been asleep for so long... Do not cry."

"Fuck you! I'll cry if I want. A day and a half, almost two," I whimper. "Two days where I've been drenched in your blood, no idea if I was going to die alongside you." More damning tears fall.

"Vagan must have pierced my heart. I did not think it would be so long."

"Well, you should have thought about that before you passed out." I wipe my cheeks. "Please let me out. I promise I won't run."

He draws his hand out from the cage and presses it back to his wound. "I can't, not until I've gained my strength."

"What? I can't stay in here!"

Zaku rests his shoulder on the bars. "You are safe in there. My den has been compromised, and if something catches the blood in the air before the robots finish repairing it, that something will follow the blood trail here. Nothing can get to you behind these bars. They will have to go through me."

I'm still not sure I'm hearing him correctly. "You can't possibly leave me in here like this," I whisper.

His head rolls, his chin lowers to his chest. I sit up straighter.

"If I lose you..." his words slur, softening. "I will never let that happen—" He slumps.

"Zaku?" I say his name, getting no response. "Zaku?" I say louder.

I reach through the bars and shake his shoulder. His

cowl shifts and his eyes are closed, and I notice the blood steadily trickling between his fingers.

"Zaku!" I shout. "Don't leave me in here!"

But I already know he's gone, and I'm once again alone, left to wait. Something snaps, and I scream and scream. I scream until sleep finally takes me away.

TWENTY
NO LONGER HUMAN

Daisy

Hearing a strange sound, I peel my eyes open. They're crusted, raw, and my face is dry. I rub my eyes hard and groan, pulling my aching body up from the ground to look around. I've gotten weak, being unable to eat and getting no rest. No good rest, at least.

My nose twitches. The air smells fresher.

Rubbing my face even harder, I wonder how long I've been asleep.

The first thing I see is a hot plate of food outside the bars, and a little further away, a large lump of fresh meat on the ground beside it. My brow furrows.

The kitchen is fixed? Why that comes to my mind first, I have no idea. But it no longer smells like blood. It smells like food. My stomach knots, and I'm suddenly starving. Hearing the robot leaving the room, I fixate on the food.

There's a large shape moving out of the corner of my eyes. I know what's happening—the sounds I'm hearing indicated as such—but haven't mustered the courage to look at Zaku head-on.

Wet groaning, rasping, growling, and hissing fill my ears. The sounds of a wild animal feasting on a kill.

Slowly, my gaze moves from the plate.

Zaku's hunched over, his hands clutching a red, dripping husk, and he's tearing into it. Chewing and ripping, ravenous hunger shudders his giant form, and I go still, awed by the sight of an apex predator. He sinks his teeth—his fangs—into the husk and yanks a huge piece from it. He doesn't even swallow it before he's ripping off another chunk.

And there's more blood. It's back upon his hands and all over his face. Forcing my eyes from his mouth, I notice hunks of meat surrounding him. As I stare, the wall opens up, and another robot enters carrying more. I press my hands to my mouth as the bloody leg of some animal is dragged across the floor.

I think about saying something but don't, lowering my hands. My stomach growls.

Zaku drops the husk he's holding and snatches the leg.

I flinch when the bones snap, as he devours the entire limb, including those bones. His throat bobs and expands, his belly growing bigger, pushing out his abs, and as it swells, the color returns to his scales.

His wound is closed.

His cock's out.

I swallow thickly, heat blooming my cheeks. My stomach growls again despite the gorefest. Staring at his turgid member, I appreciate it and the primitive nature of him. For a moment, I wish Zaku had been with me that day on Colony 4. If he had, those children would be mine because no one would deign to stand up to a male like him.

He'd protect them like I would have... Glancing at the bars around me, I see them differently. Maybe his methods are mad, but he still managed to protect me.

When the leg is gone, there are two more body parts already waiting for him. Where the robots are getting these limbs, I have no idea, and I'm not sure I want to know. I'm just happy they look like animal parts.

Zaku reaches for one, and I absently reach for my food. I eat my cooked meat as he works his way through the new offerings.

His eyes shift to me when the meat runs out. His eyes twinkle gold and then darken. I stiffen. His tongue swipes out to taste the air in my direction. He rises onto his tail, and his cowl flares outward, laying his large shadow over me. I straighten as he nears, as he does something with the lock, and opens the door.

He yanks me into his arms. I let him, even knowing he just ate my body weight in meat, possibly twice over. Even knowing he might still be hungry for more... I press my nose to his chest, and breathe him in.

And there it is. His musky, soothing smell. It's weak, but it's enough.

I moan, nuzzling him.

"Daisssy," he hisses.

"You're alive," I whisper, my voice dry. "Did you get enough to eat?"

He doesn't answer me, carrying me to the bathroom instead, and turning on the water. He slips us both under it and lowers me to stand. Keeping my hand on his chest so I don't fall, he tears my dirty clothes off with his claws.

Weak, I brace my other hand on the rocky wall, dropping my head to my chest, and simply enjoying the sensation of water and warmth, the heat building inside me, and his scent.

Zaku washes me thoroughly, reverently. His hands scrub my hair clean, tugging and pulling and gripping it. They move to my breasts, my arms, my belly, giving every inch of my flesh attention. I spread my feet when he moves to my sex, lathering it with slick soap. When that's done, he lowers and lifts one of my feet to wash it, massaging it as he does. Holding onto his shoulders, I moan when his thumb pushes into my arch. Then he moves to the other foot.

As warmth returns to my body, I lift my face to the shower and open my mouth, letting the spray fill it. I drink, lick my lips, and drink some more.

"My little queen is a killer," he says thickly, running his hands up and down my legs like it excites him. "I will have to watch you more carefully."

I hum, too tired to respond. I am a killer. In his world and others. I'm glad one of us likes it. I'm glad he's a killer too. If I'm going to be a killer like him, I hope it's only ever in self-defense.

His fingers sneak between my thighs. Turning my face away from the water, I peer down to see what he's doing. His giant tail is partially coiled around me, up against the walls, and the rest of it outside of the shower, filling the bathroom. Water sprays over Zaku's cowl and face, rinsing the blood off of him. His fingers swipe back and forth over my slit, teasing me, coercing me to open for him.

"Zaku," I breathe, leaning into the wall.

And then he finally answers me.

"I hunger," he groans.

"I know."

He pushes a finger into me, and I sigh happily.

TWENTY-ONE
COAXING DAISY

Zaku

SLIPPING my finger into Daisy's sheath, I shudder with need.

Every second I grow stronger, and it's because of her.

She chose me. She chose to save my life, and remain by my side. She will forgive me for the cage. I had not planned to kill Vagan, only maim him—he has many secrets I long to know, and we have history—but Daisy chose to protect us. How can her mistake anger me? When it was done to protect her mate?

Over and over I see her stabbing him on our behalf. I see his body slump.

No one has ever killed for me before. It is an exciting thing.

What a delicious gift she has given her king.

My member engorges with fresh, hot spill.

I heard her words, her story. I heard everything. Daisy is a killer, and I now know why she stole my attention on the plateau. She's a survivor. She's kept herself alive. She saved children.

She will make a great mother to our many litters.

And she made it across the vast skies to *me*.

My eyes fall to her collar, thick and banded, still around her neck. It's dirty. Even in the shower, she leaves it on. It's the only thing she wears. I did not have a tiara to give her—or a crown—but that collar and its diamonds are part of the treasures stored in my home, and I want them to be hers. I have kept them safe all these years. For her.

The robots can't replace everything...

Grunting, I swallow the saliva flooding my mouth. I am hungry. The meat my house robots brought to me was barely enough to sate me. Daisy will sate me instead. Her swollen sex will. Only... I have no more jewels that I haven't already given her, and she already has reign over the entirety of my den. Now that my strength is returning, I will give her access again, but only once I've made sure the robots are done repairing the walls and windows...

I have nothing left to give my queen—only my member and my devotion. Finding the rigid spot inside her that makes her thrash, I begin rubbing it.

She moans softly for me.

I growl, wrapping my tailtip tight around my aching shaft, yanking hard.

In the days she has let me explore her sweet sex—bringing me closer to my madness without realizing it—I have memorized it. I have pushed and pressed and licked and loved it with my fingers and tongue, wanting to know my female and what works for her best. If she is pleased, she will let me do more, and then we both get what we want.

I like getting what I want. I always get what I want. I want to spill inside her.

She insists it will never happen, insists that we'll never fit. Does she not see that I have been preparing her?

And now that I know she will kill for me, I need to claim her. I need it, or I might crumble into dust. If I can't claim her, no one can.

I almost lost her.

I can't wait any longer.

My mind is clouded, and I am making too many mistakes because of it, mistakes that will get us killed. I also made her a promise...

And she is a small, little thing. A breakable flower, unwatered, and in need of mastery.

I push another finger inside, forcing her to open for it, and join it with the first in petting the sweet spot within. Her sheath is tight, having lost all the work I've put into it, devouring her arousal for sustenance.

"Zaku!" she squeaks my name. But she pushes into my hand and I smile, knowing I will soon get what I need from her.

Her arousal on my tongue... I am also in need of watering...

I lick the air, tasting her despite the steam and water. She may have cursed me to death, but she will soon understand why I caged her. It's not even my cage, though I'm glad I have it. It is useful now that I have a mate to protect.

Rubbing her gently, I add a little pressure, letting her know I will take it slow. My wound still aches. It will take another meal to finish regenerating. That and another night of solid rest.

Rest can wait. Food can wait.

I haven't moved in days, and my muscles need exercise. *So do Daisy's...*

"Zaku," she whimpers my name again when I stuff another finger inside her, forcing her to take it.

The worst of her bruises have yellowed and her scrapes are all but gone. I run my free hand up her leg, feeling the smoothness of her skin. She is bare of hair everywhere below her neck, and I... like it. She is like me in that aspect. Our differences are not as much as she fears.

I *will* master her.

Daisy rests her brow on the wall, languid with the pleasure I'm giving her. Her eyes are closed, her lips parted. When I press my fingers—hard—into her spot, she gasps, jerks, and tries pushing my fingers out.

My smile widens. "They are just fingers," I purr.

I release the pressure of my fingers and go back to rubbing her gently, stretching them slightly as I do.

Oh, how wet you are, little queen.

"Too much," she breathes. She brings her hands to the wall, placing her brow on them instead of the wall, and rubs her face against them. "I'm so mad at you," she mumbles weakly.

I hiss. I stretch my fingers a little more.

She will fit me eventually. Human females can expand, and expand a lot. I read it once in a book about human reproduction. She can take me. She will take me. Sliding my hand up and down her leg, I soothe her.

Daisy rubs her face some more against her hands, but her feet part to give me better access. Pleased, I speed up my fingers and contemplate adding a fourth.

"It was for your safety and mine," I groan.

"So you did... put me in there because you thought... I'd hurt you," she murmurs through soft moans.

"You would not have hurt me, but you could have run,

and that would upset me. I will not have you run from me."
I quicken my fingers.

"I—" she swallows, "I..."

"You?" I rub her harder, seeing her hands fist and her spine straighten. I yank my member hard before sneaking my tailtip up her front to slap her nub, sensing her imminent undoing. Spill dribbles from my shaft.

"I won't be your captive forever!" she cries out, pushing away from the wall.

Her sex clamps down on my fingers, squeezing them; her hips buck on my hand. She drops her hand to grab my tailtip, tearing it away from her nub as her body shudders deliciously. I grip her hip and steady her, keeping her upright as she bucks and quivers.

Her sheath dances beautifully around my fingers. "I need—I can't—" she gasps.

I pull her into me, stretching my fingers as wide as I can get them inside her. "Let me take care of you," I say, clutching her body, rubbing my swollen member over her backside. "You can take it."

I will not lose her. I will lie and beg for it. I don't think I can go another day without her.

If Vagan had stolen her from me... If I hadn't returned in time...

She moans loudly as I force a second orgasm from her body, but this next one is weaker. She is exhausted. If what she says is true, I've been unconscious for days.

The cage is not a comfortable place.

I resolve to remedy that after she's forgiven me.

"Freedom," I rumble in her ear. "Freedom for your surrender."

Daisy shudders at my voice, her legs splayed, and I'm half-holding her up by my hand, pressing into her back. I run my free hand up her chest, her breast, and cup her neck and the collar there, continuously working her sheath, waiting for my answer.

I will coax another orgasm if I must. I will coax a dozen.

"I will never cage you again," I add, licking her ear. It's a lie, though in truth, I hope it's not. I never want a reason to cage her again. I will if I must. "Forgiveness is next to godliness," I say, remembering reading that line somewhere long ago.

She grasps onto me, trying to support her weight. "You're using my exhaustion against me." Her head falls back onto my chest. Climbing over her to look upon her from above, I slip my hand from between her legs and cup her breasts, rolling her nipples between my fingers.

"You've gone through a lot, little mate. Give in and let me rule you. Let me take it all away."

A king should never have to beg...

"I will never give you another reason to cry," I purr.

She doesn't say anything for a time, resting against me while I roll her nipples and move my palms along the curves of her body. I wonder if she's asleep, letting me work the tension from her muscles, because her head rolls to the side. But when I lift her, moving my tail between her legs so she straddles me, she leans forward upon it. She rests her cheek on my scales.

Leaning back, I take her in.

She's facing away from me, and her ass, her sex is open and on display, dewy wet and being sprayed on by the water from above. Her feet barely touch the ground on either side, hanging off me where she sits. I slide my hands down her back to cup her behind, pulling her cheeks apart to open her up.

She wiggles, and I grip her hips, sliding her backward so

her sex is flush against the length of my shaft. I undulate slowly, rubbing it back and forth over her slick folds.

She still hasn't answered, but she lets me play.

My hunger festers.

I won't let this gift go away. If this is what happens when I get hurt, I will seek pain to have her so amenable toward me. Just enough for her affection; not enough to bring her tears forth.

I rub my knot over her slick sex, piercing it with my fingers when she sighs, and it quivers for me. I thumb her sensitive nub and her backside, even after she swipes my hand away. I like her responses.

I am the luckiest male.

All the while, the warm water of the shower sprays upon her, while she cuddles my tail. Cuddles it!

It's almost too much for me to bear. She is teasing me, torturing me. She has no idea what she's doing to me, pushing me to the brink. I milk another orgasm from her body and yet, she still does not give me an answer.

I grit my teeth, sinking my fangs deep into my lip. I position my tip to her entrance. I nudge it.

She tenses immediately. "Zaku," she whispers my name, fisting her hands.

I grab my member and glide my tip up and down her slit, and when I'm done, I press it to her little hole again, sinking the tip in. "Answer me," I growl.

She looks back, blinking water from her lashes. I press into her a little more. Her sex clenches deliciously and I moan.

Her lips part.

We stare at each other. I don't move my eyes from hers as I reach out with one hand and pet her spine.

I dare to push a little further. Tight, swollen flesh fights against my invasion. I hiss, deep and hurried, as the pressure of her sheath tries pushing me out. I refuse to let it win, keeping my tip seated.

"Daisssy," I beg.

Hooded eyes staring at me is all she gives me. Wildly, my heart thunders, knowing how close I am to my own ruin.

"Freedom," I whisper, pushing a hand between us to tease her nub.

Her brow furrows.

Daisy

I HAVEN'T FELT this relaxed in longer than I can remember.

Zaku's finger rubs me, and I whimper. Overcome with exhaustion, I've been open to his gentle caressing, the orgasms he's worked from my aching body. I'll take the pleasure he offers greedily, having been denied any pleasure or comfort for days.

His tip is inside me. I tense around it, feeling it press back, keeping me stretched. It scares me, but I feel so warm... so relaxed.

And his smell... It's heady. The water washes it away, but it doesn't stay gone. I breathe it in, wanting it to fill me up. Except every time I try to inhale it deeply, there's never enough.

Zaku's hand pets my spine. We stare at each other. He's waiting for me to give in, he's taking advantage of me, and I should hate him for it, but I don't. I want the pleasure he's giving me to continue. He's alive. Yet...if I let him try to put his cock in me, my last defense against my captivity and my capturer will vanish. I'd be powerless.

Keeping my gaze, he dares to press further into me. I constrict, not ready to allow him access. I ache for so many things. I don't know what I want anymore.

He rubs my clit faster in response.

Gasping, I accidentally shunt back onto his cock. It sinks further in, and I strain backward. Zaku groans and I fist my hands harder. I jerk forward into his rubbing fingers, and his tip loses its purchase, slipping out of me.

He growls and stops flicking my clit, hooking an arm around under me and stopping me from moving. He pushes his tip back into me, lodging it in place, stroking my clit so I won't fight it.

"Zaku," I moan.

He answers by thrumming my nub hard and fast. Hitching with pleasure, I jerk upon him, feeling another orgasm build.

Terrible male. He's a terrible, terrible male. He's not being fair.

But neither am I. I have tested him, pushed him, using his want for me against him to see if he'll keep his word. It's worked against me just as much as him. Because I want him. I want him so badly it stings.

He's given pleasure, and more, he's saved my life. I've given him nothing in return.

He hoists me, taking my feet off the floor. I hold my body over him precariously, crying out as he works another orgasm forth, trying not to slip over his slick scales. I rock my hips, desperate to be... *full*. He stops his thrumming, and I cry out again, rocking on his tip. I press back, searching for the pleasure I've lost. He grabs my hips to help me, and his claws bite my skin.

"Yesss," he hisses as I shudder upon him. "Yesss. Use me."

Use him?

"Yes," I whisper.

My legs slip on his tail and he sinks into me. I hitch from the abrupt, brutal stretch as I fall onto him to his massive bulge. He goes rigid, his hands tightening on my hips, and I tense, alarmed by the sensation. His bulge presses against my opening—so big that I'm practically perched on it, seated on it.

I scrape my nails across his tail. "Zaku!"

He holds me upon him as I adjust to his size. I try to widen my legs but can't, my feet sliding, my heels slipping. His tailtip coils around my right foot and holds it away from my body.

"Don't move," he rumbles thickly, keeping me precariously over him. "You will make it worse. Trust me."

"Trust you?!"

I reach back and grasp his cowl. I try not to move, knowing if I do, I might slip further onto his cock. I might break.

"Trussst me," he hisses.

Hot, blistering heat shoots up inside me. Zaku growls, filling me with his seed. His scent returns thick and heady. I heave, taking as much of it as I can into me.

Squeezing around him, I brace. I want my orgasm.

"I need—" I gasp, "I need... more!"

TWENTY-TWO
A KING NO MORE

Zaku

"Zaku! I can't stand it any longer," she begs.

Daisy milks my member, twitching upon it, rolling her hips. I push her forward to lie down on my tail so she can relax.

"Relax," I order her. She's so tense. Her body is fighting me, making it harder for her to take me inside her. Even as she cries out for *more*, her sheath is refusing to accept *more*. I bare my fangs, staring down between us, where she's stretched upon me. Where the seed I've released is trapped.

Watered. I growl inwardly.

Her hole is tight around my girth, gripping it hard. There's no way I'm going to be able to push further in. My knot is thicker than the tip of my shaft. A lot thicker.

She can't take it. Already my bulge is pushed hard to her opening. It's so full it'll never breach her as is.

I groan as a niggling thread of doubt enters me.

"Please," she mumbles, and while I hold her still, she shakes.

I shake with her, salivating, tasting the humid air, the aroma of sex, her arousal, and my spill. A delicious miasma to drive me insane. Nudging further, her sheath gives me no access.

I dig my claws into Daisy's hips, trying to retain a modicum of control. She cries for more than I can give her, and my lips twist. I slip out and flip her over, trying again. It doesn't work. I bare her to the floor and try mounting her from above, finding I'm able to get even less of my member in her in this position. I swipe my tongue across my fangs.

No matter how much I spill, it's only ever gotten bigger. Glaring at it, I snarl where it's blocking my complete mastery of her.

She is right.

We do not fit.

Disappointment ravages me hot and fast. Hauling Daisy into my arms, I put her back on my tail to straddle me again. She shimmies her hips, undulating in tiny sways, reaching down and grasping my member, seeking what I can't accomplish. She pushes onto my bulge, and I grit out an annoyed moan.

She lowers but can only take half my shaft. She rides my tip, and it's almost too much for me to take... I need my knot inside her.

My tip is not enough.

Clenching my hands, I hold them away from her body so I do not accidentally hurt her.

Turning her head, she blinks the water from her eyes, finding mine. Her hair is plastered beautifully over her shoulders and onto my tail, and I love it. I just can't love it enough...

"Zaku?"

The way she says my name is enough to nearly turn me into a rabid beast.

I yank her off my shaft and place her on the ground.

"Zaku?" She calls out for me when I slip out of the bathroom. I need to put distance between us. I need to get away from her. I don't know what I'll do if I don't. She cannot fit me, and the pain of that knowledge is too much to bear. The pain in my loins will make me do something terrible. She's all I want, the only being I crave, and we are not meant to be.

We aren't compatible.

She doesn't follow me, and I'm glad. If she did, I might jump her, mount her, and destroy her. I do not want to hurt her. I never want to hurt her. Seeing my empty nest twists my stomach.

I am not a king.

I am not *her* king.

I am a naïve, monstrous male, one who seeks to force a union where there isn't one. I have wronged her. She kills for me, and I lock her in a cage because I cannot bear letting another have her, even if I perish. Fleeing, I head for the rooms above because if I turn back, I will force my knot inside her body, and she will suffer great pain. I hiss long and furiously, scraping my fangs across my lip.

Let her leave if she wills it. I snap. She has earned her freedom. It is the least I can do. It's not her fault that I am what I've been made to be. A brute, even to my own kind.

A murderer.

I strike out, slamming my tail against the nearest wall, reopening my wound. Gritting my teeth, I press my palm to my chest to staunch the new blood. The pain feeds my sense of failure. Not only must I suffer this loss, but I have to live with the scar of it until my last breath? I finish ascending the staircase and enter the hallway where Daisy stabbed Vagan.

It's as good as new. The pictures on the walls are perfect. There's not a crack, a scuff, a scrape from the fight. Even Vagan's body is gone.

It's what I expected.

The robots that maintain this place have always repaired it. They go into their walls and come back out with magic and lasers and materials from the storage hidden high in the mountain. Seeing them angers me. They can keep this place perfect, they can abide by my wishes, but I have never been able to fully master them either.

Like I can't master Daisy... *my* female.

The robots never stop. I have wrecked them, and they don't stop. New ones arrive and repair the ruined ones. I gave up long ago. I shove open the brand new red door.

The foyer, the kitchen, everything is back to normal. There are a half-dozen robots still working and I fall upon them, tearing them to pieces, scattering their parts across the room. Roaring, I turn my attention to the real source of my misery. My throbbing, swollen shaft.

My knot is enormous.

How had I not noticed? It's bigger than it's ever been, bigger now that I'm full of sustenance. Curling my fingers into my palm, I stop from tearing the whole appendage off and being done with it.

Wiping the sweat from my brow with the back of my hand, I calm, trembling, and cup my knot instead. I squeeze it until I grit my teeth from pain, and then I squeeze it harder, forcing the spill out. I take no pleasure; I feel no pleasure. My hand is not Daisy, and now that I've felt what it's like being inside her, I'll never find pleasure from my hand again.

I work my bulge, hissing like the base savage I am, spilling seed upon the clean floor of my home, wanting to ruin the robots' work.

I reclaim the space, taking back control, jetting out spill all over the broken robots, the furniture, and even the glass windows, trying to empty my bulge of all it has stored. It makes no difference. I curse my misery, thrashing my tail. And when my shaft is red and aching from violent fingers, when everything is marked and claimed by me, I take to the wilds outside. I leave Daisy and my den behind.

Tonight, I will be what I've always known I am.

Not a king.

Not an honorable naga.

But a primitive animal. A reptile. The one I've buried deep within. The one that needs to be far, far away from its mate. Because if it's not?

I shudder, not letting the thought of what would happen come to my mind.

TWENTY-THREE
ALONE

Daisy

DROPPING to sit on the shower floor, I stare after Zaku, waiting for him to return. I press my hand between my legs and thrum my clit, clenching around nothing. The loss of his cock has me reeling. Zaku's scent vanishes. I was so close to the edge that now I'm consumed by the fall from it, but as the seconds turn into minutes, and Zaku doesn't reappear, I pull my hand away with frustration.

I stand and figure out how to turn off the showers, my nerves twitchy and pent-up. I'm tired, annoyed, and desperately pushing the last few days out of my mind. The blood and the cage—the Lurker—are invading my thoughts again.

I dry off and step into Zaku's room, wrapped in a towel. I expect to see him, but the room is empty. I avoid looking at the cage and the robot within, who's lasering the inside, and head for the closet.

And I pause, staring at the island of baubles, my gaze

going to the picture. Feeling my blood pumping, I slowly go to it and pick it up. Hands shaking, I crush it between my fingers and rip it in half. *Stupid ghost. You're not even mine.* I tear it into tiny little pieces and cup them in my palms. Heading back to the bathroom, I flush them down the toilet.

A fitting end.

Returning to the closest, emboldened but still angry and confused, I put on some loose black slacks and a long-sleeved shirt. When I leave, I'm still alone.

My gaze falls on the open door across the way.

I still. Is it a trap? Is Zaku testing me? It has to be a trap, right?

Or is there really a ghost haunting me?

I walk to the door. Zaku isn't devious enough to try and trick me. He's practically an open book. Peering into the room beyond, my eyes go to the stairs. I hear the buzzing of a robot out of my sight.

"Zaku?" I call out. I get nothing except the robot's whirr in response.

Heading up the stairs, I frown, coming across the robot repairing the wall.

The blood trail is gone.

I slip past the robot and enter the hallway of the upper level of the house. Everything is gone from the fight. It's like Vagan was never here, that I never stabbed him, that none of that happened at all. There's no corpse to greet me, no rubble and plaster. There are only the sleek edges of a sparsely decorated home.

The red door opens when I turn the handle.

On the other side, everything is exactly the same as it was the first day Zaku brought me to this place. Almost.

Instead of seeing broken furniture, a shattered window, and the markings of a fight. There are broken robot pieces scattered across the floor. Some twitch and spark. Amongst them are several robots gathering the pieces and taking them into the walls of the house.

I recall Zaku mentioning the robots repairing it, but I never imagined they'd be able to do so to this degree…

When I step out, Zaku's smell floods my nose.

My skin heats furiously and my eyes contract. A whistle of air escapes through my lips as his smell falls upon me thickly. I bring my hands to my chest and drop to my knees, sucking in, needing more of it, all of it, right now. The world tilts, and my swollen sex quivers erratically.

My knees slide apart, slipping on the stone, and I press my hands to my sex. I moan loudly, practically salivating.

Zaku's scent has always warmed me, though it's never been like this, never been this overwhelming. I can't get my hands under the waistband of my slacks fast enough. My fingers slip through wetness, seeking my opening and my clit at the same time. Thrumming hard, shoving my fingers into my body, it's not enough. I paw at my sex, thrusting my hips helplessly. My arousal gushes.

"Zaku," I moan weakly, scared. My sex constricts around my fingers, and I lean forward until my cheek is pressed to the floor. It's wet and sticky, but down here, his scent is even more potent. "Zaku," I say again, calling out for him.

I push my palm to my clit, rubbing hard.

It's not enough. I lick the floor, knowing it's his seed beneath my lips.

He tastes as good as he smells.

Writhing like an animal, I inhale him. His smell is changing me. I don't know what's happening to me, and my fear builds. I need him badly. So badly it hurts.

Where is he? I whimper.

I clean the floor with my tongue. I tug my hand from between my legs with a cry and wipe my fingers through his seed, returning them to my sex and pushing it inside me. I don't know why I do it—it's just right.

And after I do, my body cramps. Pain tightens my stomach. I curl into a fetal position until it goes away.

My lust returns furiously, my sex crying out for more of his seed. For hours, I crawl from one puddle to the next, fighting the robots who come near me for it. A wild thing, inhuman, desperate for more. I beg for Zaku, but he never comes to me, never relieves my torment, and as the day falls to evening, the robots finally win out.

His scent slowly vanishes from the air.

I don't know how long I lie there, staring at the ceiling, touching myself. No matter how many times I come, it's not enough. It's not what I need. The robots clean me up like I'm part of the room, like they cleaned Zaku when he was unconscious. I'm too tired to stop them.

When it gets dark, I crawl up onto the sofa and pass out.

I wake with a start, forgetting where I am.

Snapping upright, my eyes darting around wildly. I yank my hand out from my pants where it must have wandered in my sleep and suck in fresh air, realizing where I am and how I got there. Heat and shame colors my cheeks.

Zaku would never let me sleep here. He always made me sleep in his nest.

He's gone.

The thought jolts me, and I push my legs over the side. It's day again, and the robots are gone. I look around the room absently. There's a plate of meat and fruit, and I grab the apple as I stand.

"Zaku?" I call for him again.

My eyes slice to the window—the completely fixed window—but he's not there. Instead, there's a pile of rotting corpses that weren't there before.

Squinting, I see pig corpses. Lots and lots of pig corpses.

What I don't see is Vagan's corpse.

"House," I call out. "Why are there pig corpses outside?"

A speaker answers from one of the walls. "The pigs entered the house, and as a source of meat that needed replenishment in the icebox, the house accepted the resource."

My fingers go to my mouth as nausea threatens. "What about Vagan?"

"I don't understand. What is a Vagan?" the house responds.

I walk down the length of the window, trying to see around the pile for a shimmer of blue. "The other creature that attacked the house," I say a little nervously. "I killed him."

"Except you, all beings who entered the house have either left or have been used to replenish the house's resources."

"And Zaku?"

"What is a Zaku?"

I sigh. "The house's master," I correct. "Where is he?"

"The current master left yesterday at 11:18 a.m. He has not returned."

11:18? I tilt my head. I don't know the ancient time system. But that was yesterday, and he still hasn't returned. It confirms that he did leave and isn't just hiding in one of the numerous rooms in the house.

Why would he leave? And in the middle of a shower?

In the middle of... My confusion builds. Had I done something wrong? Had I said something?

Did he... did he not want me, once he had me? I couldn't take him, but...

I lift my hand to my nose. His smell did something to me, made me delirious, mindless, and lusty. As the memories resurface, I drop my hand. I would have done anything to take the heat between my legs away. I would've begged.

I licked the fucking floor. I scrub my face with my hands and run back to the kitchen. Grabbing a cup from the cabinet, I fill it with water, gulping it down and pouring another until my mouth feels clean again.

"Where did he go?" I ask the house, not expecting an answer.

"Relay Two's current master went west."

"West? Relay Two?"

A robot comes out of one of the walls and takes my empty cup away. It also lifts one of its long arms, and points in the direction of the gorge. "West is that way. Relay Two is one of three relays in this area," it answers.

Turning, I can just see over the cliffside outside the house's grounds. Searching the lawn, I realize the same rocky pathway Zaku climbed to bring me here the first day is in that direction. The same path I would need to take to go back to the facility.

"Thank you," I say.

"You are welcome." The robot drops his arm and leaves.

I check for Vagan's corpse again. I still don't see it.

Could he be alive?

My fingers twist, remembering the feel of stabbing him in the stomach, the way his muscle fought me. The pressure it took to sink the blade in. Zaku regenerated from a stab wound to the chest, a deep wound that bled for hours. He hadn't died. Instead, he went unconscious until the wound closed, only rousing when it had.

The Python's head... My eyes dart to the skulls on the lawn. There are some other bones among them, but they're mostly skulls.

Vagan could've regenerated like Zaku.

Impossible.

The blade nicked Zaku's heart...

My fingers twitch.

I swear I stabbed the Python in the neck and through his jugular. Both Vagan's and the Python's wounds should've killed them. Zaku's wounds too. Yet none of them had died.

Realization sinks in.

I only know for certain the Python is dead because his rotting head is on a stake. Swallowing thickly, I bring my hands to my mouth.

Shelby's in trouble.

A shudder zips through my body. Vagan's after her. He wants her badly enough to break into Zaku's home, nearly killing me, nearly killing him for *her*. Zaku owes him a debt for the tech. And Zaku's gone. They both are. My chest constricts.

Shelby's pregnant. She can't fight without risking her child. She shouldn't take the risks I've been able to. She can't risk the child.

Vagan doesn't care if she's with child... I saw it in his madness. The faces of the children I saved on Colony 4, their frightened eyes, their tears, their hopelessness hits me like a punch to the face. I see the Ketts approaching in the distance, the fleet unable to stop them.

I run to the door, praying it'll open, and when it does, I don't question it. I race to the ledge and look out.

I have to warn Shelby before it's too late.

I have no idea what happened or why Zaku left. *If he is with Vagan...* I shake my head.

I will protect Shelby's baby, even if it's from him.

TWENTY-FOUR
GONE

Zaku

I GO to the human's facility in my torment. Intending to tear it down, to locate all the males across the land, human and naga, and rip their heads off. They deserve pain and my fury. For coming to my land and trying to steal it from me.

Hunger claws my gut.

But by the time I see the lights of the humans' ship and their strange robots guarding the once dusty ruins, my frustration wanes. All I want is to be back in my den with Daisy and coiled around her body. I worked the enormous knot out of my shaft during the journey, and my seed hasn't fully refilled it. The pressure, the tension in my groin has eased and with it some of my anger.

Except each time I glimpse my shaft, I snarl viciously, hating it. I am the biggest naga in all the land and for once, I hate it. Not even my father was as large as me. I used to revel in this knowledge, but I'm beginning to think I am cursed. *If I were a smaller male...*

Daisy is a small, human female. I don't want to bring her pain. If I bring her pain, she may not submit to me. She may refuse to let me touch her again.

She will see me as she saw the Python. I spit venom.

And I gave her freedom... I had done so as I left, unsure if I would ever come back, if it would even be possible with the tension wrecking my thoughts. At least behind the barrier of my home she would be safe, especially if I were to guard it and her from afar.

She could be the home's new master, keeping me and all else who might hurt her away from her. That way, I could ensure she is mine without fully giving her up.

I was an idiot.

If she locks me out, I will break the glass like Vagan had.

Until him, no other has ever been able to. But if Vagan can, so can I. Looking around at the shadowy forest on all sides, I clench my fists.

What if another male comes while I've been away? Or animals? Or creatures of the forest? What if she accidentally lets one in and I'm here at the facility where I know she is not? What if she leaves and gets attacked?

What if she comes looking for me?

I turn for home, leaving the humans and their creations alive, cursing my recent choices. Cursing many of the choices I have made.

It was idiotic of me to leave Daisy and my den. My body is weak and strained beyond its limit, from my mating heat and my wound. My head is a torrent of riotous thoughts. I dig my claws into my palms, seeking the blood under my skin. *I had her on my stem. I had her spread open upon my tail.*

And I left.

It's only proven to me that I am nothing more than a lowly, despicable reptile.

I wish I had never found that book.

She's the only thing that can cure me of these horrible thoughts and feelings. If I can't be a king for her, then how can I ever be a king again among my kind?

Slicing through the forest, across the gorge, I don't stop, needing to be back home, needing to see Daisy. I need to know that she is safe. The sun sets too soon, and it's dark before I reach the base of my mountain. Exhausted, I'm forced to stop. I can't risk ascending the cliff pass in the dark.

I can guard the path, though. Ensure no naga finds it, and protect Daisy from here. Pressing my hand to my chest, I lower to the ground, hiding within a pile of dead leaves. I've reopened my wound and fresh blood leaks through my fingers. Sleep finds me swiftly, despite not wanting it to.

I wake once, hearing movement but when the noises fade soon after, indicating it is not a large creature passing by, I fall back asleep.

The sun is high above me when I wake once more. I release a frustrated hiss. My knot is full to bursting again, but I find the pain in my chest gone. The wound has reclosed. I take to the mountain with renewed strength. What feels like an eternity passes before I see the glint of my den's windows.

I enter my home and dart my eyes around the space, finding everything the way it has always been, quiet and perfect, and...empty. Usually, I can feel Daisy's presence all around me. She's brought life into my world and into my home. Right now, my den feels lifeless.

A low hiss climbs my throat as my nostrils flare to take in the scent of the place.

There's no scent at all. I make my way to the lower rooms.

She is waiting for me there. She is always waiting for me.

I smile.

The door to my nest is open and I head straight for it, eagerness vibrating my nerves.

It's empty and perfectly made. The pillows, the bedding I once detested, all crisp and organized as it had been every day since the first day I'd come to this place. Slipping to the bathroom, it's also empty. I go to the closet next, and halt, seeing the collar I gave her, the diamond strings reattached to it lying where the sapphire necklace usually is.

Blood rushes through my veins.

It's the only thing in this wretched place that has changed—has ever changed. Floored, I stare at the diamond chains. Only noticing afterward that the picture of human males is also gone.

"Daisy!" I roar, leaving the closet. My gaze falls upon the cage.

I should have never let her out. I should have kept her locked in it forever, even if she hated me for it, even if she denied me, even if I never saw her smile again. I'd rather have my queen in a cage, where she's mine, where I can protect her and gaze upon her beauty, rather than free. Where she can be hurt, or worse. She isn't safe without me. She'll never be safe without me. I hiss deeply, reverberating my cowl.

Overcome with foreboding, I move to the playroom, hoping there's a slim chance she is within. But the mirrored wall is still in place... There's nothing but cold silence and my reptilian reflection glaring back at me. My hands shake.

She's gone.

She left.

The noise I heard last night...

A growl bursts from my throat as I pivot and tear out of my house.

TWENTY-FIVE

THE PIT

Daisy

"DAISY!"

I startle, turning around as my name echoes through the gorge.

Zaku?

Goosebumps rise as I hear my name again. I can't tell which direction it's coming from...whether it's ahead of me or behind.

I can't let him catch me.

Even if he's not with Vagan, Zaku will never let me near the facility, he'll never let me warn Shelby.

I catch my body against a tree and clutch it, holding myself upright. Pushing off the tree, I aim for the river in the distance. It's attached to the lake. Keeping high on the mountain ledges, I've kept it to my left, knowing I'll need to cross it to get to the facility.

But not yet...

It's the only river, and I remember seeing it below the

plateau the first day. I need to cross there to keep my positioning. If I cross too early, I could miss the facility entirely while in the forest. But if I can spy the plateau, keep it at my back, I can make it to the facility. I can.

"*DAISY!*"

I flinch.

But it's been hours and I still haven't located the plateau. I've circled boulders, ledges, even climbed one of the trees to get a view of where I am and where I'm positioned, but no plateau. The sheer edge and the steep climb to the plateau's bluff are unmistakable. There are no trees, no foliage after the dropoff.

Huffing out a ragged breath, I round another set of boulders, swiping the sweat off my brow.

And then I see it.

I nearly drop to my knees when I do. The plateau's sharp ledge.

I want to sob, half-terrified I was never going to find it, that I was lost, that I miscalculated.

I'm a pilot, not a ranger. I've been on and to many alien worlds, but rarely do I set foot on them.

It's time to cross the river and go straight north. Wiping my cheeks, I descend.

From one boulder to the next, from one rocky landing to a dead tree stump, I head for the river below. This side of the mountain has grown increasingly jagged with dirt and stone. There's barely any shade. Losing my footing on a shifting stone, I slip and land on my butt. Wiping the dirt off my palms, I try not to touch my face. My cheeks are burned from the Earth's sun. Sweat drips into my eyes, and I blink it out, wincing again.

When I hear the river, I sprint, wading into the reeds, and sinking into the water and mud. I push through the reeds until the water is up to my waist and the river opens up. Dipping under and cooling off, I wash the sweat off my face and drink all I can. I haven't encountered an apple tree or a berry bush in hours, and I need to keep my energy up for as long as possible. Hydration is key.

"*DAISY!*"

I lower into the water as my name echoes and then fades.

When Zaku's voice is gone, I glance at the barren slopes of the mountain behind me, expecting to see him charging down and toward me. When I don't, I say a silent prayer.

It's quiet as I dive into the water. It's a short distance to the other side. On the far shore, I position my back to the plateau. Taking a deep breath, I close my eyes and visualize the land, hoping to the stars that I'm right and the facility is in the spot I remember it to be.

I'm in the forest, on flat land. I have to be in the right area. I'll know for sure in a couple of miles.

I wring out my clothes and walk into the trees. Soon, the silence gives way to sounds.

Hissing fills my ears. First, it's on my right, and I drop and quiet my steps, and then it's on my left. My adrenaline surges and my stomach drops. *It's a good sign if I'm hearing other nagas*, I tell myself. I lick my lips and try to remain calm.

I should've considered there would still be nagas scouting the facility. If it's not Vagan who goes after Shelby, eventually one of the others might.

If they haven't already.

My fury at Peter—at this whole operation—slams through me. I grit my teeth and try not to scream.

I'll sneak in, find Shelby, and contact *The Dreadnaut*. *That's all you have to do.* Once Central Command knows what's going on, none of the rest matters. They'll save Gemma, they'll fire Peter, and they'll make a better deal with the nagas for their precious Lurker tech. A deal that doesn't include bartering flesh. This time tomorrow, the nightmare will be over.

I see the wall through the overgrowth and quietly move toward it. There's hissing behind me, though it's far off. But as I near, a low buzzing takes its place.

A scout. I crouch. Searching for it in the air, I spy the flying metal turret and let it see me. It stops, turns its guns on me, and flies in my direction.

I go still as it scans my face.

After a moment, it lowers its guns and I sag. The security systems still have me in their database. I move to the turret's side and open its panel, wiping the data off its system and powering the turret off, hiding it in the bushes. I turn to the wall afterward, heading for one of the entrances.

Something touches my leg.

Twisting around, I come face to face with a large, darkly-colored male coiled around a branch. Our eyes meet, and we stare at each other.

"Please let me go," I beg.

His expression doesn't change.

"My friend is in danger and so is her child. Please, if you have any mercy, you'll let me go."

"What is your name?" he rumbles.

"Daisy," I say, trembling.

"There's another calling that name." He tilts his head, glancing at the canopy. "It's on the wind."

"I know."

The male's eyes come back to me, darkening. "Are you in trouble as well?"

His question gives me pause. It's not something I'd

thought one of these aliens would ever ask. *Am I? I am.* I am in trouble, though it's not the type of trouble a stranger could ever help me with.

Right now, all I want is to make sure Shelby and her baby are safe. And if possible, to reach Central Command and help Gemma. After that? Thoughts of Zaku flick through my mind.

"I...I'm okay," I say.

The male regards me for a time. Waiting for him to snatch me or let me walk away, my heart pounds wildly. I brace for the former, for a fight. Slowly, I slip my hand into my pocket and grasp the nail file.

It's always the former.

He draws his tail away from me and vanishes into the trees.

I sag. *Thank you.*

I turn and run through the entrance before he changes his mind, pivoting behind a barricade. I take a look around. There's only me, the robots, and the ships on the newly-cleared field. None of the team is outside. Seeing everything the same way it was a couple of weeks ago saddens me. It also brings me some relief.

I'm not too late.

Glimpsing the sky, the sun is heading for the horizon.

It'll be dark in a couple of hours.

The day shift is ending soon, if it hasn't already. Everyone will retire to their quarters soon. Shelby will be working within the old facility or on the transport ship categorizing recent data—she's obsessed with Earth and the Lurkawathians—a little too obsessed. We haven't had many conversations in our short time together though each time we have had one, she brings up her work. She lives for it.

She loves it.

Something I have never really felt about my work...

Sneaking onto the transport ship will be risky, and riskier still is heading to the ship's bridge to contact Central Command. It would be better to wait for the night shift for that, I decide.

I dash to the ruins before I can change my mind. I've never been inside them, but others have mentioned that the old building is big. If it's big, there'll be lots of places to hide and to wait.

Coming to a stop at one of the partially fallen walls, I duck inside. The inside is a mess of rubble, but it's been cleaned out of all organic matter by the robots upon our arrival here. Hallways and rooms of dirt, mottled items, and old rusty metal greet me on every side. There are also lamps and beeping machines throughout, attached to computers under tarps. They hum softly in my ears.

I climb through another broken wall, deeper into the space where there are more shadows, rather than take the cleared hallways, and search for one of the team members, or for a place to hide.

Hearing footsteps, I duck behind a tarp and press my hands to my mouth.

The footsteps move past me and I peer over the tarp to see who it is. Squinting, I make out Collins' uniform. He turns left, down a different hallway, and toward the outside. I decide to go in the opposite direction. I don't want to encounter Collins any more than I want to run into Peter. I might just kill him and rid the universe of his presence if I do.

Seeing lights ahead of me and an open space, I slow and slip to the wall to look inside. I find what may have been a large atrium at one point, maybe a gym. The ceiling is caved in, and there's digging equipment. In the center is a giant pit with rusted pipes and old infrastructure bent up and out of the ground. More tarps and spotlights are blazing down into it.

There's also a lot of sentinel robots protecting the pit.

They're guarding it.

My curiosity piques. I can't see into the hole from my angle. Glancing around the room, it's empty but for the robots. I check behind me and there's no one coming.

Having only two ways to go, I enter the space, dodging to the right. The sentinels don't acknowledge me, staying angled to the pit. My brow furrows, and I move a little closer to see what it is they're focused on.

Could it be?

Is it?

What we came here to find?

I don't see anything at first, just dirt, cement blocks, and more pipes and wires than I can count. A flicker of blue light emerges, casting upon rocks from under the biggest tarp in the middle, and I suck in.

"Shelby?" I whisper.

TWENTY-SIX

LIES

Daisy

"COLLINS, if you're trying to scare me, fuck off," she says from somewhere below and out of my sight. "I am not in the mood."

My heart goes wild, and I scramble down into the pit before I can think otherwise. "It's not Collins, Shelby." Heading toward the deepest part of the pit, where tarps are covering it from my view, the blue light of Shelby's eyes brightens. It shifts in my direction. Shelby ducks her head under the tarp and blinks, turning off the light of her mechanical eyes.

"Daisy?" she says, her lips parting when she sees me. She stares as I rush over to her, taking her into my arms and hugging her to me, hard.

She's tense in my arms at first but then throws her arms around me with a cry. We hold onto each other tightly. I don't want to let her go. I thought I'd never see another human ever again. If I hold her hard enough, long enough, maybe I'll never be torn away again. She's warm. She's alive. The journey was worth it just for this hug.

But she pulls back and I let her go.

Her face is dirty, smudged with dirt and dust, and she's shaking.

"Daisy? How—how are you here? What happened? We need to get you to medical! Do the others know your back?" Shelby's questions fill my ears.

I grab her wrist. "I'm fine. I don't need medical attention. Though we need to go, and we need guns if they're around. I'll explain later, but we need to get you out of here. Now!"

The sentinels fly toward us from every side.

Shelby jerks her arm out of my grasp, stopping me. Fear lights her eyes as she looks at the sentinel drones. "I can't. Why do we need guns?"

The sentinels aim their lasers at me. "For protection. I'll explain later but right now we need to go," I tell her.

She shakes her head. It's then I notice the exhaustion on her face, the amount of dirt covering her. There are sweat stains on her clothes and her face looks long and winded. Her long hair is in a messy bun on the top of her head and some of her braids are slipping from it.

She's thinner than she was when I last saw her.

"What has happened to you?" I whisper. The last time I saw her, she was healthy, clean, and full of energy. Though angry too and filled with desperation for the situation we were in.

"I'm being watched," she whispers. "I can't go anywhere without guards, without Collins. Daisy, I'm so sorry—"

"I don't understand—"

"—I tried to contact Central Command, but Peter

stopped me. I can't go anywhere without them." She points behind me. "They'll shoot me if I try."

I look back at the sentinels now hovering around us.

Shelby continues, "You need to get out of here. It's not safe. Peter is not..."

"Not what?" I ask.

She shakes her head. "If we don't deliver..." she whispers. "If *I* don't deliver... Peter's head is on the block. All of our heads are. The Ketts took out *The Mercy*."

I still. *The Mercy* was the ship my father once commanded before he retired on *The Prime*. It was where I was born. It's also one of the biggest colony battleships in the entire fleet. A whole army of battleships was docked there.

Nearly a hundred thousand people lived and worked on *The Mercy*.

Dead. My heart stops. *They're dead now.*

"If Peter doesn't give Central Command what they want..."

I scrunch my face. "Stop. Just stop," I beg, reeling from the news. Losing *The Mercy* is a huge defeat, but there's nothing we can do about it here. "You're in trouble. There's a naga, a rabid one, coming for you. We have to get you out of here." I grab her hand. "I tried to kill him but these aliens don't die easily. They regenerate. We have to tell Central Command what's happening down here. Your baby is at risk."

Shelby tugs her hand from mine. "What are you talking about?"

"Vagan. I'm talking about Vagan. An alien who's after you, who's willing to kill me and—never mind. That's not all, the facility is surrounded by aliens. You're the only woman here. You're not safe and neither is your baby." I take her hand again and tug her after me.

"Daisy..." Shelby pulls from my grip. "I'm not pregnant."

I face her, not sure if I heard her correctly. "What?"

"I'm not pregnant," she repeats.

"Y-You miscarried?" I stutter.

Her face falls. "No."

It takes me a moment to realize what she's telling me. "You lied?"

"I was scared. Collins convinced me it was for the best. I've been doing everything I can to get you and Gemma help—"

"Wait. You were never pregnant?" I'm still not believing what she's saying.

"Daisy..."

I drop my hand. She's not pregnant. She never was?

"Are you okay?" Shelby reaches for me. Reeling, I turn from her.

She was never pregnant. My heart sinks further, and tears well. Shelby grabs my arm, I tug it out of her grasp.

She lied to save herself. She abandoned Gemma and me when our worlds fell apart. The fear I felt, the disbelief when Peter gathered Gemma, Shelby, and I to tell us what he plans on doing to us comes back to me. I had no lover, no friend, no one to turn to for help. Only two women, two strangers who served on the same ship.

"Daisy?" Shelby whispers my name. "I'm really sorry. I tried to buy an opportunity to help. I should've told you and Gemma. Collins said it was too risky."

I wipe my eyes with the back of my hands, hating the betrayal I'm feeling. I push through it. I try to, at least.

I never should have left Zaku. I should've waited for his

return, should've looked for *him*. I should've searched for Gemma.

I clench my hands. What am I going to do now? Can I even leave the facility without getting caught, or find my way to Zaku's mountain? Will I ever see him again?

"Please forgive me," Shelby begs. "I tried to use it to help us." She waves at the sentinels with defeat. "I tried."

I finally look at her, exhaling the betrayal. It doesn't change anything. "I forgive you," I choke. My voice is numb after I clear my throat. "Vagan is after you. We need to get you out of the facility before he or another, or several band together and come for you."

"What do they want?" she asks, her voice lowering.

"Nestmates? I was almost raped," I wheeze as flashes of the Python return. I push him out and think of Zaku instead and even the male I met outside. "Some are not bad... I have no idea what Gemma is going through. You're not safe. You need to get onto the transport ship—to *The Dreadnaut* if possible. That, or join me. There's a place you can hide. A place you'll be safe. Zaku has a den..." I trail off. "It doesn't matter, as long as you're not *here*. I need to get to the ship and send a message to Central Command." I turn to leave.

"Wait! The sentinels."

I pause. "They're watching you, not me. They still recognize me as part of the team."

"They'll shoot me if I follow you."

"Okay. I can turn them off manually." I glance at the turrets poised on us, shuddering some more. "Give me a minute."

"Shelby, who are you talking to?" Collins says from somewhere above us.

Going rigid, my toes curl and I reach for my nail file again. Shelby's eyes widen, and she tugs me toward the tarps she crawled out from under. "Hide," she whispers furiously.

I duck with her under the tarps. I thought I could trust Shelby—I know I still can. The knife she gave me saved me. I owe her, but my debt is cleared. There's nothing left for me here. I rub my chest, feeling heaviness there. She can come with me, or find her own way. She's more capable than I.

But there's still Gemma, and Peter to contend with. There are naga males still lurking outside the facility.

I wish they would attack, tear the facility down, and humanity can prevail and defeat the Ketts—that they'd start evacuating the planets in the Ketts' path instead and fleeing into a different part of the universe to rebuild.

The government will never give up its resources and lands. The upper castes can't fathom losing their wealth.

I wish I had made a case for those babies.

I wish for a lot of things. They're all just wishes. Wishes never come true. Gripping my nail file tight, I ready to stab Collins in the throat.

Why did I come here at all?

"I'm just cataloging my finds," Shelby calls out. "Have Nick and his team made any headway on the data?"

Collins grunts. Rocks shift as he nears and his footsteps get closer. "They're still deciphering the text, so no. Captain says we're all working through the night again. He wants an update. We're having the night meal with him tonight. He wants another test."

"Another one?" Shelby's face falls as we hold each other's gaze. "I don't want to eat with that fucker," she snarls. She lowers her voice to me. "I'll distract him. Go," she says, pointing to an opening through more pipes behind me.

"What about you?" I whisper. "The sentinels?"

"I'll be fine."

Collins sighs deeply and it's right outside the tarp. "I prepared a test already, so don't worry. I have it covered. Eating with him on the other hand, I can't change. If he's willing to share extra rations with us, we need to take advantage of that. You need to keep your strength up."

"Tests?" I ask.

"Pregnancy tests," Shelby says, shooing me to the other side of her tarp tent.

"They'll find out you lied, Shelby," I tell her, ducking under the other side. I crouch. "You can't fake a pregnancy forever."

She scrubs her face with her hands, and I almost feel bad. Almost.

"I'll be fine. Go, Daisy, please. I can take care of myself. I have Collins. Get to the ship. Tell them what's happening. Save us."

I see Collins' hand as he lifts the tarp. There's no way she'll be able to follow me now, and waiting is too risky. My heart falls further.

"I stole some water from John for you," Collins says, lifting the flap.

"Go," Shelby begs. With one last look, we turn from each other.

Hearing the tarp drop, I crawl away, finding another way out of the hole. I check to make sure he's within the tent before I move to the outer walls of the atrium and head back the way I came. The shadows have lengthened and I hurry my steps, dashing down the hallway, deciding I don't want to be here when night falls.

"Hold," someone says behind me.

I stop. My hands shake.

"What are you doing in here, and without your uniform... Wait... Officer Daisy? Is... No..."

I turn and face Captain Peter, and our eyes meet in the gloom. There's a light behind his back that casts his face in shadows.

Hatred bursts through me, hard and fast. "Peter," I breathe his name through gritted teeth, taking a step toward him. Fury is giving me courage I wouldn't usually have.

Seeing his shocked face, all I want suddenly is for him to feel what I've felt, what Gemma's felt, what Shelby feels. I want him to know the terror, the hopelessness, and the helplessness he's made us experience.

"How are you here?" He's as still as stone, and I hope it's because he's afraid. I take another step toward him. I am done being a victim. "Where did you..." He reaches for his gun.

"I wouldn't do that if I were you," I warn.

His hand pauses. "Daisy, let's talk—"

"Talk? You want to fucking talk? Now?"

He shakes his head.

I continue, "We are way beyond talking, you piece of shit." I rush forward and tackle him. He falls back into the wall. I hit him over and over with my fists, and he tries to push me away, tries to defend himself. "You son of a bitch!" I scream, aiming for his face, drilling him in the nose. I grab my nail file and slam the tip into his hand, puncturing it. "I will kill you!"

"Stop!" he yells, pushing at me, jerking his hand away, taking my nail file with it. I hit him some more. Enraged, all I want is to hurt him as much as I can for as long as I can. Blood surges through my veins.

"I said stop, damn it!" he roars as I curl my fingers and try clawing his face.

"Stop?" I shout. "You want me to stop? You should've thought of that before you left me on a plateau at the mercy of aliens! You should have thought about that when I was nearly killed!"

He struggles to get his gun free from his hip, and I throw my weight over him, grabbing his hand. I don't see his leg before it's too late. He kicks me hard in the gut, and I tumble backward with a gasp.

"Stupid bitch," he growls, yanking his gun from his waistband.

I turn and run as gunfire rings. I hear shouting from Collins and Shelby, and the buzz of the sentinels and drones floods my ears. Peter fires a shot as I duck through a crack in the outer wall. A blast goes off next to my head, sending rubble flying. I stumble. Catching my footing, I sprint across the open field.

Seeing the facility barrier all around me, I'll never make it to the forest alive.

"Stop her!" Peter shouts.

He gives chase. Shots ring out, and the dirt around my feet explodes.

"Daisy!" Shelby screams. "Run!"

Ducking my head, I pivot for the skiff to my left. Throwing my body against it, I slap my hand on the security panel and pray that it still registers me. When the door slides open, I scramble inside, slamming the door closed behind me. A bullet hits the glass by my head, pinging the inside of the vessel. Peter aims his gun at me as the rest of the team runs out of the transport ship. Several sprint for the skiff.

Turning to the controls, I power them on.

"Come on, come on, come on. Faster," I beg. The controls light up. Something zips by the window, forcing my eyes up. Several drones are right outside with their turret guns. They shoot at the windows. I swallow back my vomit.

The thrusters come to life and I crank the switches. I push my palm to the central orb. "Take me to *The Dreadnaut*," I order, checking that the coordinates to the warship hadn't changed, waiting anxiously for the skiff to connect to the main vessel. Whether it takes me there or not, connecting to it is all I need.

Something hits me to my right, rocking the skiff. The ship falters for a moment, losing its momentum. "Come on!"

"This is *The Dreadnaut*," a woman's voice says through the controls. "You do realize you're asking for clearance for a planetary transport skiff, right?"

"It's an emergency," I snap, pressing my palm hard to the central orb, forcing the vessel up. Gunfire rings in my ears, but the ship hoists into the air. Seeing the forest and the mountains over the barrier, I push my palm forward.

"You do not have clearance, Officer Daisy. I recommend you land," the woman says. "The skiff will not be able to make such a journey."

"Do you know what's happening down here?" I shout. "Captain Peter is trading lives for tech!"

The ship jerks, the sentinels fly out of my path, and I push the thrusters to the max, yanking the controls back. I see the barrier loom before me.

I'm not going to make it. "Please," I whisper. "Please."

At the last moment, the vessel clears the barrier, though a wrenching, screeching noise bursts my ears as the bottom of it scrapes it. I hit the trees, slicing through branches, barely evading the thick trunks.

"Turn back, Officer Daisy. You do not have clearance to use this skiff anymore, nor do you have access to *The Dreadnaut*. You are being insubordinate."

Hitting tree after tree, I make it above them, and I sag a little, angling the skiff higher, toward the mountains to the left of the plateau. I see it and the lake for a split second before I turn.

"You don't understand," I say, stumbling over my words, sweat pouring down my face. "Captain Peter is bartering the women on his team, even Officer Gemma—"

"I know—"

"—we're in trouble, we need backup..." I trail off. "You know?"

"I recommend you turn around and land," the woman says.

I start to shake. "You know?"

"If you do not turn back now, I will take away your access to fly and the skiff will no longer respond to you. It will fall."

"You know!?" I scream.

I focus on the mountains ahead of me, the sprawling forest.

"Turn back, Officer Daisy. Do not make me take away your access. The skiff is expensive."

The skiff is expensive. I want to laugh and sob.

Tears brim my eyes. I think of Peter and Gemma, and Zaku. The last couple of weeks flit through my mind. Zaku. I'd been happy. *With him.* Despite everything.

He cared for me. Me, *of all people.*

"Officer Daisy, I won't ask again. This is my final warning."

"I'm sorry," I whisper. "I'm so sorry." Sorry about Zaku, sorry that I couldn't save Shelby, sorry that I didn't get a chance to end Peter.

I hear a sigh and then everything goes silent. A thunderous noise builds from there, hollowing out my ears. I close my eyes and take a ragged breath.

She did it. She really fucking did it, taking away my access.

Something hits the skiff, knocking the vessel sideways. Pushing my hand to the orb, the ship doesn't right itself. I wipe them off with the back of my hands, nose-diving for the mountain.

I'm sorry.

TWENTY-SEVEN
A NEW PAIN

Zaku

I HOLD DAISY CLOSE, as close as I can without hurting her any more than she is. Days, I searched for her. Days, I thought I lost her, terrified I would never see her again. Now I have her in my arms, and I've never been in more pain.

She screams.

And screams and screams. Her body is burned—black and red—her clothes are charred, and her hair is nothing more than singed, smoking wisps around a swollen and mottled face.

I want to hold her close and take away her pain, except each time I move, she whimpers. Her screams fill my ears, and I beg for her to lose consciousness again. It's only when she's unconscious that I can breathe, that I can think straight. She's not cognizant of the pain when her mind is blank.

I barely acknowledge the others traveling with me. I do

not want them near her, I do not want to share her, but the other female, Gemma, insists on staying by Daisy's side. She is with Vruksha, as I suspected she would be—even I noticed how he fixated on her coloring. He has pined for his lost family for many years, and the other female's coloring is similar to that of the Pit Viper. He can be near Daisy, as he only has eyes for his claimed one.

But Azsote, the blasted Boomslang, is with us as well. He's the one who found Daisy, pulling her burning body from the wreckage of the ship she was in, and for that, he can live. For now.

He did not steal her while he had the chance. Instead, he sought me and brought me to Daisy's side. He told me Daisy said my name as he carried her out of the flames. Azsote wanted to honor her dying wish.

Her dying wish...
She will not die!

I will not let my queen leave me, not again! I will atone. I have to atone. I have made so many mistakes that I don't know where to begin. Making sure she lives and is comfortable is a start. Because if she dies... A shudder goes through me. If Daisy dies, there is nothing left for me to live for. I've been alone for so long before her, and I can't go back to that.

Azsote and the others are not the only ones who saw Daisy's ship fall from the sky. There are nagas in the shadows of the forest, lurking about. I need to keep her from them as much as I need to keep her alive.

Azsote and Vruksha bare their fangs at the others, saving me from the task of handling her broken form and guarding her as well. I am indebted to them.

Daisy shakes and screams, and I grit my teeth.

The trek back to my den is grueling, and it's not until

Daisy goes unconscious and stays that way—when I fear she will give in and let go—that we finally reach my home.

Only the medical pod can save her. Gemma, the other female, insists it's our only option. It's either try the pod, or make Daisy as comfortable as possible until she succumbs to her wounds, or until infection takes hold and kills her.

Still, I can't let her go, and it takes the others forcing Daisy out of my arms and holding me down on the floor before Daisy is placed in the machine. With Vruksha gripping my arms and Azsote on top of me, Gemma—with Vruksha's tail for help—settles Daisy in the machine. Gemma scrambles around it, figuring it out.

I roar.

Watching the glass of the pod shield Daisy's body from me and fill with smoke, nearly destroys me. But then the smoke clears and I see her again. The arms within the pod go to work and I'm released. Moving to her side, I beg to the skies for her to live. The house robots have maintained this machine as they have everything else in this wretched place. It should work. I will bring this place to the ground if it doesn't.

You are strong. Stronger than me.

The tension in Daisy's body goes away after the machine pokes her with needles. I fist my hands, waiting for her to wake up and see me. Instead, she doesn't wake at all.

What if she never wakes?

"Zaku?" the other female says my name. I snarl in response. I do not want to be bothered. After a few minutes, she says it again.

"What?" I snap.

"She's going to be asleep for a while. You should get some rest."

I hiss, low and annoyed.

"Leave him," Vruksha says. "He will do as he pleases."

Hours go by. Time stands still. I don't move, gazing at Daisy, unable to look away. I'm afraid if I do, she'll vanish. The day comes and goes, and so does the night. The house robots try to feed me and I ignore them, unable to stomach food, unable to do anything except wait. It's not until much later that I catch Azsote enter my home without being stopped, that it occurs to me others are here with me.

Seeing him through the open door of the room I'm in, he drags in a deer carcass, hauling it to the kitchen. Once there, he and Vruksha strip its hide off.

Confused, I study them for a while.

I don't like that they're here. I like it less that Daisy hasn't woken up. I turn to the female sleeping in a chair across from me. She hasn't moved from Daisy's side either.

Daisy is alive because of her.

I recall her taking charge by the crash site when I couldn't. I owe the other female for forcing me to face what I did not want to.

My eyes fall upon her bandaged feet, her shoddy clothes, and I leave quietly so I do not wake her, coming back with an armful of garments and some footwear from the closet below. I place the offering by the female's side. A gift for her help.

I eat the meat the robots bring me in silence, studying my guests, lulled by the constant beeping of the machine. It has been many years since I tolerated a guest. Clenching my hands, I keep my body still so I do not strike out.

There have been many changes in my life this season.

"You should get some rest." The female across from me sits up from her chair and rubs her eyes.

I hiss in warning. No one tells me what to do.

She is unbothered by it, standing to check Daisy's vitals.

"I'll be with her. I'll make sure nothing happens," she says. "I need her to live."

I slide my tail over the pod's glass. "Why?"

"Because this should have never happened. I should have been able to stop it, and Peter can't win." The female looks at me. "I care about her. If she dies, then I've failed."

The female's eyes hood, and she licks her lips. She curls her fingers on the glass beside my tail, keeping my gaze. "We both have failed if she diesss," I say. "Do you understand?"

"I do."

I nod. "If she dies, you will have failed me as well, Gemma."

Her brow furrows briefly, then smooths out. "I understand."

"Do not let the others near her," I add, tilting my head at Vruksha and Azsote. "I do not trust them."

"I won't."

With that, I settle down beside Daisy, pushing the rest of my tail over the pod. I close my eyes.

I wake to hushed voices sometime later. Female voices. I pull my addled mind out of the slumber it desperately needs when Daisy cries out.

The next second, I'm up and over her, gazing into her eyes. Or eye. The other is swollen shut. We stare at each other. There's so much I want to say, except my mouth doesn't open. Nothing comes out. She is not the Daisy I knew. She is different. There's pain in her that wasn't there before, and it's not physical pain. It's more than that, and I fear it's because of me.

"My queen," I say. "Forgive me."

TWENTY-EIGHT
A FRIGHTENING FACE

Daisy

THE DAYS BLUR. The pain ebbs and flows.

It's because of the pain that I know I'm alive. I wait for death to take me. I pray it does, I hurt so much.

Most of the time I feel nothing, stuck up with needles and tubes. I never thought I'd live, and each time I wake, the pain reminds me that I'm still alive. That I'm *going* to survive. It hurts, knowing I won't have an easy out. That whatever the medical pod is doing to me is working. When I woke the first time, it was to glass covering me, and Gemma's face. I finger the thin sheet draped over me, glad I can't see underneath it.

I've glimpsed my reflection in the pod's glass. It scares me.

I don't know who it is looking back at me anymore.

I manage to tell Gemma that *The Dreadnaut* knows what's happened to us and that they're in on it. At least someone in command is in on it. It means there will be no help coming, and I fear what it means in the future if they don't get the tech they're so desperately searching for. It's not like the war is over.

Earth is clear for travel. At least if sanctioned by Central Command. Others will come. It might take some time for them to get here, but they will come. The government is tyrannical, though they live by laws and codes. Others? Not so much.

But they won't be coming for Gemma or me. Or Shelby, or Peter, or anyone else.

Gemma says we have to help ourselves now. She's a flitting voice in my head. I think she's right. It's the last thing she tells me before she says she'll be returning soon, that she'll find a way for us to communicate.

I think I mentioned seeing Shelby to her as well, but I can't remember. I don't tell her about the lie. I tell her about *the Mercy*.

I beg her to stay. I fear for her safety. She says she is safe and not to worry about her. That I shouldn't focus on anything except getting better. She's a leader and I've always tested as a follower growing up. A sheep.

Gemma's been claimed by Vruksha, a red naga I sometimes see in a blur behind her. She has claimed him back. I see her leading him outside.

My head spins. The pod pumps me full of more drugs.

Zaku's claimed me... Have I claimed him too?

Should I claim him? He's sitting beside me, staring at me. I try to look at him but my eyes hurt. It makes me sad.

I wish... I stayed.

He's quiet, letting me rest, forcing me to rest. I don't want to rest anymore. I want to get out of the pod and get dressed. I want to bathe. I want to curl up in the coil of his tail. I want to pound my fists against his chest for leaving me when he did, of not telling me where he was going, of abandoning me after I spent days thinking he might be dead!

He won't let me do anything of the sort.

"Zaku," I rasp, trying to sit up. The glass shield of the pod moves back.

He shifts and gently puts his hand on my shoulder, keeping me down. "Do not move. You are not well yet."

I sigh. "I've been here forever." The fact that it's only been days should be astonishing to me. It should take me weeks to heal the way I am, months, years even. Then I remember it's advanced technology being used on me. This pod, while similar to those I've used before, is clearly superior. It's technology that humans like Peter are willing to sell their souls for.

Technology that can restore a human from critical condition to stable in no time at all, would be worth millions of credits. Zaku's home has more wealth than I can wrap my head around. I'd been flummoxed by the jewels, the warm water, the pleasure, when I should've been in awe of this pod.

I haven't been paying enough attention...

"Not forever, little human."

He settles back when I don't fight him. Managing to face him, fighting the taut wounds on my neck, I take him in.

He hasn't left my side, not once since I woke up. He gives me no privacy, hovering over me every second of every day. I don't think he's sleeping now that Gemma's left, and I worry for him. He's been wounded, and his chest is still healing. He needs sleep as well as food and rest.

"I wish I could regenerate too," I say.

"So do I."

Arguing with him to go take care of himself is futile. He

won't do it, not while I'm awake at least. I've tried and failed. But I feel better today, stronger. Perhaps it's the recent flood of meds. The pod is helping me heal rapidly, repairing my skin, numbing my nerves. "At least let me sit in a chair. If I can just take a dose of painkiller with me, I'll be fine," I beg. "I'd like to sit upright. I'd like to look at the trees and the gorge below."

"No."

"Please? Just to the window?"

His tail winds over the top of the pod, giving me his answer. "Daisy, not only have you been burned—"

I close my eye. The other one doesn't open any longer. "I don't want to know."

"—you've lost sight in one eye. Your arm is broken. You've also lost a significant amount of blood and you have third-degree burns down your body from your face to your hip. You are not going anywhere."

"I didn't want to know," I whisper. I'm damaged. I know this. I don't think I have hair anymore either. I don't... feel it. I didn't see it in the glass. There's a wounded person in it, not me.

"You must rest," he says.

"What about you?" I ask.

"Rest."

Heartbroken, I let sleep take me away.

When I wake next, the pod is changing my IVs, and it's dark. A single candle is lit, flickering shadows across the space. Zaku's beside me, reading. I've never seen him read before.

When he notices me, he puts the book down.

"What is it?" I ask, though it comes out as a croak.

He lifts the book. "An encyclopedia."

"What's that?"

His cowl flutters. "I think... It's a book of many subjects. There is a lot in it about the old world."

"Is it interesting?"

"I have read it before, so no. But it has subjects on human health, and I have no other books on the matter."

He goes silent, studying me, and the longer he does, the more nervous I get. I can't read his expression; shadows cling to his features. My eye is out of focus. I can't even sit up. My heart quickens uncomfortably the longer he studies me.

"Please stop looking at me," I whisper when it becomes too much, facing away.

He shifts, and I try curling into a ball to make my body small. "Why?" he rumbles.

"My face—"

"Is the same as it has always been."

Tears spring. "No, it's not. I've seen it. I'm not *me* anymore. I'll never be beautiful again for you. I'm—"

"Look."

I open my eye to find a mirror posed over me. "I don't want to see," I cry, turning away.

"*Look*, Daisy."

"Please don't make me."

He hisses. "You have nothing to fear, little mate."

Mate. He still claims me. My heart cracks and swells and I shudder.

Slowly I look into the mirror. Tears escape when I do, slipping down my cheek. Bleary, I blink them back until I face my reflection. It hurts. It hurts more than what's happened to my body.

I've always been Daisy, the daughter of a great commander. I've always looked like my father. I've always been that, and nothing more, until I was an orphan, a disappointment, and then a pilot, and then nothing at all. But it was *my* identity and no one else's. Now, like everything, it's gone. I don't know who I am anymore.

I don't know what I am anymore.

Why does everything have to come to an end?

The face staring back isn't me. It's also not the fearful thing I'd seen in the glass. It's my face, only different.

My hair is gone on the left side of my head, and shorn short on the right. My left eye is scarred, swollen, and closed. There are blotchy red burns all along the left side as well that goes down to my neck, shoulders, and lower still under the sheet, but the char of my skin is gone. And the right side of my face is almost entirely untouched. I have no eyebrows, and the one eye I can open is still bloodshot and red, still... I see me—*me*—behind the burns.

"Every day, you are healing. Every day, the pod grafts your skin. You're mending, Daisy, and you will live. Tomorrow you will be stronger, and you will be better. You will be closer to sitting up and looking out the window. You won't be alone."

I fall asleep staring at my reflection.

When I wake next, it's bright, and the pod is vibrating beneath me. My gaze goes to the ceiling—which is moving— and then to the view of the mountains next. Trying to sit upright, the pod stops as the glass above me shifts, and Zaku's hand is back on my shoulder, stopping me.

I glimpse him behind me, seeing he's rolling the pod across the main room. "I can sit up," I say softly.

"Not yet."

Sighing, I slump, and Zaku removes his hand from me, rolling me to the window. Once there, the glass screen of the pod lowers once more, and Zaku moves to my side with pillows under his arm. Carefully, he helps me rise and places them behind me.

I'm not sitting, but I'm a little more upright. Looking out the window I'm reminded there's a world beyond this glass. When he tries to move away, I reach for his hand.

"Stay with me."

He coils his tail under him, and we stare at the landscape together.

"Thank you," I whisper, just to fill the silence. He doesn't respond, and I get twitchy. "Can you tell me about your home?"

"What do you want to know?"

"Everything. Anything? I know so little about this planet. I want to know more. I've got nothing else to do."

Zaku's eyes twinkle in the glass. His tongue swipes his lower lip.

He tells me about the animals that scurry past the window first. Squirrels, rabbits, birds, and once he's done with the animals we see outside, he tells me about the animals we don't see. The pigs, the bears, and the monsters.

"Fearsome beasts once wandered this land, but they have been gone for many years now. They attacked indiscriminately, viciously, and so I and the other nagas who were strong of body and mind hunted them down."

"But monsters? Not just other animals?"

"The orbs did not know what they were. They are not of this land."

"Do the orbs know about you?" I ask.

His eyes pierce me and he doesn't answer. I let it be, already knowing his species is not from Earth. They can't be. Fifteen hundred years is a long time for a planet like Earth to be uninhabited, something would've returned in that time. The plants had, even animals. Why not other aliens, aliens that also worked with the Ketts? Every couple of hundred years or so, humans encounter a new alien species.

Shivering, I ask him what these monsters looked like, and where they came from, trying to glean more from Zaku's origins, only he shakes his head. "I have never seen them in my books. I do not know."

He shows me his encyclopedia, flipping to different points of interest he finds fascinating. One is a map of Earth and the old oceans. He can't fathom an ocean but thinks they must be several times larger than the lake.

I smile. "Much, much larger."

He tells me about his favorite battles. The nagas he's killed, and the skulls on his lawn that he enjoys the most, one being the head of a Death Adder—a notorious rapist and killer—that he and several other nagas took down many years prior.

As the sun sets, Zaku feeds me berries from his hand and tells me about his father.

"I was searching for him. I had not seen him for some time, and we often kept in communication. One day, I scented his body in the wind. I followed the scent and came upon his corpse. It... was mangled and broken, but not torn and bitten. I could not figure out how he died. He did not have the wounds that would indicate another naga had killed him, or a beast from the forest. For days, I stayed by his side, trying to figure out how a king, a male that even I feared could be dead. I needed to know. I had to know. And until then, I remained and kept the scavengers away from his corpse. On the third day, I realized a truth I didn't want to accept. There were steep cliffs nearby."

Zaku goes silent.

"Why?" I ask quietly. "Why would he do that?"

"I have never known, until recently... He was not the king he thought he was." Zaku's cowl falls. "Our females were dying. They were beginning to band together and leave us, to travel west. Rogue males were appearing and much more was lost in the shift. My father chased after things that I did not care about nor understand. It was wet that summer. Water fell from the sky for the first time. The skiesss opened up and water poured for weeks on end." Zaku shudders.

"Rain?" I say.

"Yes. Water that comes from the sky."

"I know what rain is, but here? That's not possible. The oceans are gone. The water has to come from somewhere to rain." My brow furrows.

I never paid attention to my history lessons and had very few on the ancient home planet, though it occurs to me that there's a lake here, and that shouldn't be. I saw no other bodies of water from the sky. Maybe the water is coming from under the ground?

Is the lake big enough to make rain? It can't be. Glancing at the trees in the gorge, I wonder how they're alive at all.

Perhaps that's why Central Command wants the technology here so much. My stomach drops and I try to push the feeling of unease away. It's not my problem. Still, I look at my hands and the scarring on them, tracing them with my fingertip.

"I do not know. Are there not oceans and lakes in space?"

"Not... quite. On other planets, yes, but not in space. It's not in one of your books?"

"Not that I have found. I have never thought much about it."

I turn back to the landscape, recalling what I've been told about the Lurkers and their precious tech. Even so, no tech could control the weather.

"I'm sorry about your father," I say.

"I am sorry about yours too."

I go still, my gaze finding him. He's looking at me and not out the window. He reaches over and cups my cheek where I'm not burned.

"I would have chosen to save the young as well. In that, you and I are alike," he rasps.

"Zaku..."

He drops his hand when I nuzzle it.

"Rest now. It's getting late." He rises and moves away.

"Zaku, wait," I say. He stops and comes back to my side. I grab his wrist and curl my fingers around it. "Why did you leave me?"

He tilts his head.

"In the shower," I clarify. "Why did you leave? Where did you go?"

"You were right," he says.

"Right about what?"

Instead of answering me, he leans down, putting his face before mine. I fall back upon the pillows. I lick my chapped lips when his mouth moves close.

But it doesn't fall upon mine. It doesn't kiss mine. He presses his lips to my forehead and slides his wrist out of my fingers. "You will always be my queen. Regardless of what I am, you will always be that."

And with the silence clouding in around me, he rolls me back to the room, breaking my heart.

TWENTY-NINE

THE HARD TRUTH

Daisy

ZAKU MAKES me stay in the pod until it stops grafting my skin and administering painkillers. And even then, he keeps his tail over the glass until my vitals are normal and stable. We don't talk again. Not after that last time. I try to start a conversation, but he dodges. I have never been stationary for so long before. It's worse because Zaku's pulling away. He's different around me. The days come and go and with each new sunrise, I'm stronger, healthier, better. The pod's AI verifies it.

It begins administering steroids, boosters, and stimulants to help return my strength.

When it starts to return, it returns fast.

Afterward, the pod began signaling low on stores, making Zaku erupt at the house. Like it's the house's fault. Seeing emotion from him brings me hope. Managing to calm him, I tell him I'm going to be fine, that we'll replace what is lost, that unless every hospital on Earth has miraculously vanished, there will be ruins for us to scavenge through. Later.

And then it occurred to me...

I'm making plans. Plans *here*, with Zaku. I didn't have a choice when I was stuck, though now that I'm not, now that I'm free, I can't help but think about my future.

I'm not going back to *The Dreadnaut*. I want nothing to do with them and the people who are in command. I can't help but think of them all as child killers. Dream destroyers. Though it's not true. There are good people. It's just... you have to break down too many walls to find them. And I'm tired, so very tired of doing that. I see those babies on the rooftop often in my head. Hearing Zaku's response—that he even heard my story at all—healed me more than the pod ever could.

He'd save them too.

I don't have to wonder if I made the right choice any longer.

We should have evacuated Colony 4. Not try to keep it. So many lives would have been saved if we had. *So many children...*

I want to be with him. We're more alike than I ever imagined. Sucking in a breath, it's deep and satisfying...and scentless.

He's sweet, kind, and patient, and not at all the Zaku who pulled me from the lake weeks ago—who chased me down and caught me up in his arms. And it scares me. It scares me as much as my choice to stay has.

Staring at my reflection in the window, I gently trace the wrinkles on my skin. I'll never look the way I did before the crash. I'll never be what I once was. I stretch out my fingers, loosening the scar tissue that's stiff between them, peering between them. The pod has been unable to return my sight, and I'm slowly getting used to my altered vision.

Facing the room, it's empty. There are no robots, no visitors, and no Zaku. He's around. I think...I hope he's just giving me some space.

Now that I can move freely, he's gone distant. He stiffens when I touch him, only giving me his tail to use as a crutch. Besides that, he's avoiding touching me at all.

Is it because of the way I look? Is he afraid he'll hurt me?

Hugging my body, I walk to the kitchen.

He says it's because I'm weak. I don't believe him. I need him. I need him so badly it hurts.

I miss him.

I can *feel* around him and not have to be ashamed of it.

I want my Zaku back.

Does he still want me?

I rub my face, wanting to rub it all away. Stinging my skin, I drop my hands. I hear the scuff of his scales sliding across the floor, and when I look up, I see Zaku entering the room. He catches my gaze as he closes the red door behind him but looks away.

He approaches me with something in his hand. Reaching out, he offers it to me. "Fresh clothes," he says, his voice a rumble.

I take them and hold them to my chest. "Thank you."

He makes his way over to the door. "I am going to harvest berries."

"Why won't you look at me?"

He stops. I step away from the counter, and toward him.

"Why won't you touch me?" I try to keep my voice from cracking. "It's been nearly two weeks," my voice cracks anyway. "Why?"

He tilts his head in my direction. "I don't want to hurt you."

I take another step. "You've never hurt me before. Why would you now? Tell me the truth." My voice gains steam. "Is it because of the way I look? Is it because I... I look this way?"

He pivots in my direction and hisses furiously, forcing me to lean back. His cowl expands, shuttering my view of everything else. The gold flecks in his dark eyes spark with anger. "Never say such a thing! You are the most beautiful creature in the world."

"But I'm not. I never was," I whisper, unable to hold his eyes. "I'm this," I run my hand down my chest and clutch the loose shirt I'm wearing. "I'm scarred."

His tail coils around where I stand. Zaku's fingers clasp my chin, and I squeeze my eye shut. He lifts my face. "Look at me."

I crack my eye open unwillingly. "I hate when you say that."

"No one is more beautiful than you. No one can be."

"Your lies are pretty."

"They are not liesss. I do not lie."

I swat his hand off me and turn away. I never cared about the way I looked, but now, it's a ball of pain in my chest. It's building, and each day it gets worse. If he hadn't regaled my looks so much... "Why won't you touch me then? Do you not want me anymore? There's something wrong and it's been wrong since the shower.."

Zaku's hissing deepens. "Daisssy—"

"Go. Leave," I snap, suddenly needing space before I become the weak creature I'm feeling right now, the weak creature he says I am. I don't want Zaku to see me vulnerable anymore.

He grabs my hand and spins me back to face him. "You do not get to tell me what to do," he growls.

I growl back. "The same goes for you."

His brow cocks, and I try tugging my hand from his grasp. His hold on me tightens. "I will not have you think you are not beautiful. You are healing, little one, and I am..."

"You're what?" I ask when he trails off.

His eyes shift away, and he shakes his head.

"You're what, Zaku? What's wrong? What happened during the shower? Why did you really leave?"

He hisses, releases my hand. "Don't."

"Don't? After all you've done? After bartering for me? Stealing me? Keeping me trapped and then caging me? You ask me to... *don't*?" Anger fills me, replacing my doubt. "I will not '*don't*.'"

Zaku's lips twist.

"Tell me!" I shout. "You wanted a mate so bad—you should know that mates talk! Contracted couples communicate! How am I supposed to feel if I don't know what's going on with you?" I lower my voice. "How can I believe your words if I don't know if there's any truth behind them? Let me trust you again. I want to trust you!"

When he stares at me, saying nothing, the numbness I had thought long gone returns hard and fast. I refuse to be deluded any longer. I refuse to live in a world where I'm unwanted any longer. I might not be the prodigy my father hoped I would be, but I survived without him.

I can survive without Zaku too. My soul splinters. I can make it here on Earth. There are entire cities, towns, buildings scattered across the land, and technology that I'm growing more comfortable with every day. I'll scavenge, stay low, and make my own way.

Perhaps I'll head west and seek out the missing naga females.

Yes. That's what I'll do. I'll join them.

Sanctuary. The word fills my head.

"Fine," I say, heading for the door.

My throat closes as I approach it. I haven't tried to leave and I don't know if it'll open for me. A hand slams on the glass before I can try. Zaku's claws streak across the door before curling into a fist in front of my face.

I swallow thickly, and then I smell it.

It. His scent.

"You are going nowhere," he growls.

THIRTY
THE LAST KING COBRA

Zaku

How DARE she try to leave?

I push away from the door, seeking to calm my rage. *Calm!* It's not something I've felt since Daisy. There's no calm anymore, only her. Her and my failures and the hard truth of my existence.

"You want to know the truth? Is that it?" I snap.

She slowly turns to face me and I lower to face her.

"Yes," she says. "More than anything."

"I'm going to hurt you." I slip my tongue out to taste her cheek. I can't help it. Not with the emotion etched on her face. I've been needing to taste her, desperate for it. I was tormented before I ran, and before her pain. I am in anguish now. The need, the endless throbbing, it will not stop.

It was easy to ignore for a time. Not anymore, not with her mending.

"Hurt me?"

"I am trying not to." My words come out through a

tightened throat. "Because I will. I will hurt you, and you will hate me. You will leave me, and I will have no choice but to let you go. That's the truth. I want you so much that I don't trust my strength, or my mind anymore. I am not..." I trail off, staring at the streak of saliva on her cheek from my tongue, wanting to lick it again.

It glistens like a beacon.

She pulls her arms to her chest. It means she's nervous. She's done it often, shielding herself from me, and only recently have I begun to realize *why*. I hiss deeply and thrust away from her before I do more than lick her face.

Daisy jerks forward. "Wait—don't!" She throws her arms around me.

I go rigid. My soul stills. If I move... I will feel her and I will fall.

"Don't go. Don't stop talking. Please, Zaku, I want to know what's wrong. I do." She pushes her face to my chest.

Should I tell her that I know nothing about who I am? Shaking, I inhale and embrace her to me, risking everything. "I do not know how to live with another. I do not know how to take care of you. Since I've had you, I have only brought you further into danger."

She lifts her head and looks at me. Her hair is beginning to grow back, her scars are fading, her self-assurance return-ing, helped by the stimulants from the pod. I have read everything I have on the machine—everything. The meds it administers, the sprays it covers her body with. But I don't have all the information or the skill to help in her recovery. I am ill-equipped.

I always have been.

"You have. You've put me in danger. But you've also done more for me than you could know."

"Yet you said so yourself. I have done nothing but hurt you."

"The cage? Yeah, that wasn't good. Bartering for females against their will? That's even worse."

I close my eyes.

"You've also saved me," she continues.

"It wasn't me who pulled you from the wreckage. It was Azsote."

"That's not what I'm talking about, Zaku." She reaches up and cups my cheek, and I tremble from her touch. "You've helped me realize I can be strong too. That there's more to life than war and death and laws and codes. That... life is more important than all of that. You realize that, right?"

"You cannot have a life with me."

Her brow furrows, and I hate seeing the softness from her gaze diminish. The hurt that crosses her face. She snatches her hand back and brings it to her chest like she's been burned. "I don't understand," she says.

Groaning, I put distance between us, moving back into the room. "I will hurt you. There will come a time where I can't hold back, or I will make another mistake, and I will betray you. I have almost done it already. It... will happen again."

"I don't—"

"The shower!" I roar, spinning on her and baring my fangs.

She flinches but doesn't recoil.

She should be running!

"You told me we weren't compatible, and I refused to believe it. I tried to mate with you anyway, even after the deal we made. I used your wish for freedom against you. My mind is not what it once was. My body is not the same. It hasn't been, not since I saw you. Look," I growl, swiping my claws across my tail. "Look at me! I am an animal!"

My member bursts forth, barely contained by the scales that hide it. Red, thick, and swollen, my knot beyond recognition. I grab my shaft and squeeze, and even without touching my bulge, spill pours out of me. "Look at it, at us, and tell me I won't hurt you!" Tearing my eyes away from my misery, I force them to Daisy, needing to see the horror return to her. "I will destroy you," I say, my voice lowering as my torment builds.

Except it's not horror that crosses her features. It's not disgust, or fear, or even the sadness that has been plaguing her. It's... something else. Something unexpected. She's staring at my shaft, and her chest rises and falls. Her nose twitches. Her cheeks pinken and then redden, and when they do, her lips part.

She takes a step toward me.

My arm snaps out to stop her. "If you come any closer, I don't know what will happen," I warn.

"Zaku," she says my name absently and then her eye rips from me to look at the floor, her brow furrowing, and if I didn't think her skin could heat any further, it does. She shakes once all over and grasps her shirt with straining fingers.

Her reaction confuses me.

"This is why I avoid you," I rasp. "I have felt what it's like to have you, to have you kill for me! And I have been cursed ever since. It is the least I deserve." Sweat beads her brow, and I fist my hands to stop from diving forward and licking it off. "I am not a king. I am not anything. I am becoming something I never wanted to be, a primal, nasty naga, one who deserves to have his spine removed from his body and wrapped around a tree. That is why I left. We're not compatible, nor should we ever be. You are a rare crea-ture, a human female, and I am nothing but a beast living in someone else's home, pretending to be something I am not."

She licks her lips and I nearly throw her to the ground and mount her. Pivoting to the door, I need to get away and now, or my worst fear will come true.

I grab the handle. "The place is yours. You will be safe here—I will make certain of it. I will keep these lands clear of any who might harm you and provide for you, but to ask me to stay? I can't. I would like to keep you, and I have tried, but I can't at the expense of your life. Do not ask such a thing of me. I am losing my mind."

I push the door open, shaking all over.

Daisy throws her arms around me. I crush the handle.

"Stupid, stupid, thick-headed male," she says against my back, her breath teasing my scales. I don't move, I don't dare, wrenching the metal between my fingers and closing my eyes. "You are so stupid."

"Is that...what thick-headed means?" I grit, remem-bering her calling me this. She climbs over my tail and pushes her body flush to my back.

It's too much. It's torture.

"Yes. That's what thick-headed means. I am not the weak creature you want to so badly believe I am. You are not leaving me. I am not asking."

I growl.

She continues like she has no idea that I am about to tear her clothes off and rut her across the floor. That I am about to add her bones to the ones outside. Agony floods me at the thought.

"I want to mate. I want to."

My claws crack, pushing into the metal. "I... It will not... work..."

"Then let me prove it to you. After everything, can you give me that?"

"A gift?" I wheeze, slicing my tongue with my fangs, swallowing blood and venom.

"Yes. A gift. One more gift."

How can I refuse?

"I will hurt you."

She laughs—laughs!—while pressing her soft lips to my spine. "No, Zaku, you won't."

My mind scrambles. I drop the metal shards and clasp her hand on my chest, feeling hope niggle its way into me. Horrible, damnable hope. She pulls away but takes my hand, coming to my side. I peer down at her.

Daisy gifts *me* a smile, and I am undone.

THIRTY-ONE
TAMING THE KING

Daisy

I LEAD Zaku back into his home. He's nervous, perhaps afraid? It's flattering and is giving me confidence. Confidence I have been in sore need of. I thought he didn't want me anymore. I'd been wrong.

"Wait," he rumbles, pulling his hand from mine. Before I can ask him why, he's slipping into the kitchen. When he returns, it's with a kitchen knife. He hands it to me and I eye it curiously.

"There are knives in the kitchen?" I've gone through every drawer several times over. I never found a knife. I assumed the robots had utensils attached to them, and Zaku used his claws for cutting the meat.

"They are kept locked and hidden."

"Why are you giving me this?" I ask, turning it over.

"So you have protection."

"I'm not going—"

Zaku stops me, lifting my chin with his fingers. "I vowed

I would never give you a reason to stab me like you had Vagan and the Python, but..." His eyes glint dark and gold. "I need you to know you will use it."

"I can't possibly—"

"Daisssy," he says, hissing my name unusually long.

Stunned by the anguish in his voice, I can't help but nod. "Okay," I whisper.

He closes his eyes and when he opens them, there's only hunger. Feverish hunger. The anguish is gone. I curl my fingers around the knife's handle, anxiety swirling through me. *He really is afraid he's going to hurt me.* Glimpsing his cock, I know why.

It's gone from a smooth shaft with a knot in the middle to a swollen battering ram. Veins pulse up and down its length, pushed out by the seed flooding it. It leaks, milky and wet from his tip, blooming the air with its scent. I'm addicted to it. I don't know why I'm not flopping on the floor, but I'm glad I'm not.

I want to be. I feel my body changing because of his scent. The sensation is exciting and pleasant. Some alien species change during certain cycles... I should've gotten my period by now, but I haven't.

And ovulating? I take shots to stop that from happening. All women do unless they plan to get pregnant with a contracted partner.

I haven't had a shot in several months though... Shaking the thought from my mind, I've missed many monthlies due to stress in my old line of work, and the shots last a while.

Zaku shifts and I jerk, realizing I've been staring at his cock again. Forcing my gaze to his face, blood trickles from the corner of his mouth.

My palms dampen with sweat. I retake his hand with

my free one and finish the descent. I'm going to claim him as Gemma has with her male.

With my confidence building, I approach the Zaku's nest. I haven't been in the lower parts of the house since the crash. First, because the stairs were too much for me, and then it was because of Zaku's indifference. I was afraid to crawl into it, only to lie amongst the soft bedding without him.

I stop at the edge, suddenly nervous again. I turn to face him.

"Remember the knife," he growls.

I look down at it in my hand and place it by the pillows. "I will. Lie back."

"Lie... back?"

"Yes," I respond quickly before I lose my nerve.

His eyes hood and my chest tightens. His tail thumps, but he listens to me, running the length of it against my leg as he moves past me. When he's positioned, leaning on the pillows with his arms folded behind his head, I gaze at him, unable to do anything else. *He's certain he's going to hurt me.*

He could. He's huge. I hear the door to the bedroom click close behind me, and I know it's his tailtip that has shut it.

It wraps around my ankle a moment later.

I pull off my loose clothes, avoiding looking at his cock. If I do... I'll just stare at it, and nothing will happen. The tension between my legs *wants* something to happen. It wants it badly.

His eyes shift over my naked body, and my spine straightens. He's seen me naked many times as the pod worked its magic on me. I'm not what I once was and he knows that. This is different though...

His tail tightens around my ankle. "Come here," he growls. "Or I will force it."

Heat rises to my cheeks. Crawling over his tail, I straddle him. His scent floods me, and my eye waters. Wetness leaks from me, and feeling his scales all along my sex, I push down into him. Male musk, sweet starsugar, and every smell I have ever loved enters me. I stare at his bulge and saliva gushes.

"Daisss—"

I grasp his knot with both hands and moan. Spill shoots out.

Zaku thrashes, sending me bouncing, he hisses and grasps the bedding, shredding it. I hold onto his cock, my sex slipping over his scales. He roars.

My mouth falls open and I dive forward, so hungry it hurts.

Zaku grabs hold of me as I squeeze his cock, forcing his seed out. Pressing my lips to his tip, I drink it down. Starving, I wrap my mouth on him and suck, becoming an uncivilized creature like him. A primitive creature who needs to devour or die. His body shakes as I suck him hard, tensing my jaw, swaying my face side to side, lashing my tongue. Grasping his knot, I knead it, needing more. Cum flows into my mouth like a river, and I take it all greedily.

I jerk up with a gasp, flinging my head back, catching my breath. Diving back down, I go for more.

He bellows raw, animalistic noises, bowing his chest over me, clawing my back with his nails, and toward my butt, hoisting it up.

It's not enough.

His seed slides down my throat like oil and into my belly. Fire erupts there, and I grip his shaft, massaging it for more. His spurts have me swallowing constantly. Precious seed leaks from my mouth, and I roll my hips. Tickling sensations pet my nerves, knotting up my insides. He grabs my butt and digs his claws into my cheeks, pushing my brow to his abs.

Zaku spreads my cheeks wide, and I clench hard, emptier than ever.

Almost faint, I pop off his cock and rub it hard up and down. Like a fountain, his cum releases. It splashes my face. I lick my lips.

"You taste how you smell," I moan.

Zaku strains upward, slamming his shaft back into my open mouth. "Daisssy," he hisses between the rabid sounds he's making. I squeeze his knot as my eye waters.

His fingers paw my sex and thrust into me. I lift off him again and inhale, wiping the cum off around my eyes. "We need to empty you," I say.

He groans, thrusting his fingers in and out of me. "I have tried."

"I haven't." Locked between his tail and his torso, I swirl my tongue over his tip.

He trembles, and I smile. His fingers strain, scissor, and I lift my butt higher for more.

"You... are... killing me," he grates thickly. "I am dying."

I run my tongue over his knot. "Have you cummed, Zaku?" I ask between licks.

He doesn't answer at first, his tail going tense, then quivering. "C-Cummed?"

"Orgasmed."

"I am—" he rumbles "—always spilling, always since you. I am... tormented! Tortured!" He roars as I find the groove around his cock where it hides inside his tail. My fingers explore the warm skin inside, searching for where his spill is stored. All I feel is smooth, warm skin.

Zaku falls back, tearing his fingers out of me, and the bed bounces. He grabs my hand and rips it from his tail slit. "Don't," he grits, squeezing my fingers.

"Does it hurt?" I ask.

His eyes are crazed, diabolical. Blood is smeared across his lips. I lean up and press my sex to his tail excitedly, rubbing it over him.

"It's too much. Too muuuch. The knife. Use the knife."

I swipe the cum off my lips, taking my hand back. His body convulses when I do. "Trust me?"

His cowl extends out. He exhales slowly. "Yesss," he hisses. "No. I do not trust myself."

Keeping his eyes, I slip my fingers back to the groove around his cock. His pupils expand, and his chest swells. My poor king is lost.

Poor, poor king. I slowly lower my face, keeping his gaze trapped. I push my mouth to his root and slide my tongue to the groove. I lick him within. Zaku falls back, pushing his pelvis up. With my free hands, I wrap them around his cock and work his length.

I need to get his seed out of him before there can be more...

Beyond tense, he goes completely still as I lash my tongue, moving it around the base of his cock. The noises he made before are gone. He's silent, shaking, and I almost feel bad for putting him in this position. I'm sending him to the edge. I'm trying to at least.

Just in case, I slide my hand up to the pillows and grasp the knife, bringing it toward me. Déjà vu hits, and I lick him faster.

Slicing my hand over his length, his knot is growing, rather than getting smaller. His tremors are joined by a deep, vibrating hiss that thrums my nerves. Clenching and desperate, I lave him with everything I have. I need him inside me, I need this to work, taking so much more from him than I'm giving.

His hisses deepen.

My skin prickles, my spine arches, and I cry out. Grasping his base, I rise over him.

He doesn't stop me, watching me through slitted, serpentine eyes. Eyes I don't recognize.

"My gift," I gasp, reaching down and pushing my fingers to tickle his cock's base as I lower my body onto him. His tip sinks into me and I rub the sensitive flesh in his slit hard. He grabs my hips, shunting up.

And spills and spills and spills. It invades me deeply, overflowing, leaking out around his shaft despite how stretched I am. Zaku's eyes roll into the back of his head, and his tail slithers around my body, caging me in a trap of swarming limbs. I lose sight of him as it gently coils around my head. He holds me still, emptying inside me.

Tensing, I realize the knife is out of my reach. *Is he...* His muscled tail and velvety scales is all I see. A thick wall of scales and tendons. Pleasure blooms despite being caged in his limbs and I moan from the onslaught.

He won't hurt me.

When I can't take anymore, I cry out and shoot off him, letting it empty out of me as well. His tail shifts and allows just enough room for me to relax. He continues to come, and I palm his knot, helping him. The moment my hand cups it, he thrusts me back down and forces me to take it inside me instead.

I cry out.

Minutes go by, maybe hours, and slowly the tension leaves his hands. We work the seed out of him together. Twitching, he lets me rise so his spill can trickle out of me again. My sex constricts. I feel what he's been feeling. Except it's me who's full now.

Gasping, his hisses remain deep and soothing and he tugs me off of him to lie me on his chest. I snuggle in, tracing the scales on his chest. I'm needy and hot, and I moan weakly. So tired and yet nowhere near as sated as he is.

Seed dries on my skin as he caresses my back.

"My queen. What a gift you have given me."

We drift.

THIRTY-TWO

GLASS

Daisy

THE GROUND SHAKES, and I open my eye. Zaku's over me, licking my neck, rubbing his cock against my leg. He's hissing again. It's that deep hiss I can't handle and I reach for the knife. But my eyes slice to the window where the glass is vibrating.

"What's that?" I ask.

Zaku's forked tongue dives into my ear, and I squeak. "My desperation."

Shunting my hips up, I tell him with my body that I need more than ear licks. The reverberating of the glass worsens, and my eye cuts to the window again, but then Zaku moves, blocking the view. Can his hissing do that? The tremors stop, though the nerve endings sparking throughout my body continue.

Vaguely aware that a robot is lasering the bedding, I try not to giggle from the absurdity.

Zaku sees my smile and gives me one back. I cup his

face and drag it down to mine. Warm, thick lips cover mine
—even his mouth is big—and he pushes his tongue into me. I
moan, sucking on his tongue.

He's between my legs, held open wide by the girth of
his upper tail. Something pushes between us and tickles me.
Zaku rises slightly and that *something* flicks my nub. His
tailtip. He pushes it inside me and flicks some more.

I moan, having been waiting for this for too long.
Needing him to claim me. Even if it does hurt...

My mouth parts to tell him this, and Zaku slides his
tongue down my throat, stopping me. Sputtering, I thrash,
and he slips it out. I inhale quickly as my throat contracts.
Tight and quivering, the muscles in my throat riot. His eyes
glint wickedly. He knows what he's doing to me. My eyes
water.

"You have broken me with your mouth, little female."

I swallow and he dives forward, thrusting his tongue
back down my throat.

Gagging, I grip his cowl. Invaded from both ends and
swollen with his seed. He groans and I feel it through my
entire body as he pushes against me. I press up into him, lost
in sensation, not sure if I want to get away or stay. My throat
tightens around his tongue as I try swallowing my hitches,
trying not to gag. He pulls out of me all at once, from both
ends.

Bereft, I collapse into the bedding, coughing.

Zaku peers down at me, pleased with himself. "Beautiful," he says.

Because of him, I'm beginning to think I might be. I
wipe the wetness gathering on my lashes off from his attack.

Gently, he caresses where my brow used to be above my
blinded eye. "I will make sure you see again, so you can see
what you are with clarity."

I hitch again for a different reason.

He rears and grabs my hips, rolling me onto my front, pushing against the back of my thighs. His prick nudges my sex. Curling my hands under my face, I brace for it. His tailtip returns and pets me, wrapping around my front. Needing something to hold onto, I grab it and bring it to my face and nuzzle it. The end flicks my lips and I lick it.

Zaku pushes his girth into me.

My sheath opens slowly for him, stretched tight, still half-fighting his invasion. I clamp my hands around his tailtip when he stops, when his bulge hits my opening, where it can go no further. I whimper.

"Let me mount you," he groans. "Let me in." His hands caress my buttocks, my backside, coaxing me. "Relax."

I take a deep breath.

Slowly, so slowly it's almost unbearable, he works his knot into me. I fight it unwillingly, moaning from the stretch, even though it's not nearly as big as it has been, it still stings. Liquid heat hits me deep within. He's already seeding me.

It helps—oh, how it helps. His spill is hot when fresh, and it ignites my insides. I bite down on the bedding.

His hips move to either side, stretching me further, working me open. Clenching hard around his shaft, part of me wants to fight him out of me, fearing it'll be too much. But then his hissing fills my ears and I relax again. I am not of his species. I don't know why his hissing, his scent is affecting me so much, but I'm grateful. His claws rub my opening.

"Relax," he rasps.

I take another breath, and when I do, he grips my hips and slams into me.

Rising, I scream. His knot pushes me from every side,

his tip bottoms out, and I blanch. He stops once he's seated, petting me all over, whispering compliments all around me. Compliments and scales and heat and musk entrap me. A wall of masculine fervor and I'm nothing but a lost creature caged within, forced to worship it, having entered the trap of my own volition. It's too much. Panting, I hold my body prone, waiting for the pressure to end. It doesn't.

"Zaku," I cry.

He pushes me back down to the bed and lowers his body to mine. He nuzzles the back of my head. "We fit, my queen, we fit."

Tears brim my eyes again as time stands still.

Zaku doesn't rut. He doesn't do anything but lick my ear, my cheek, slipping his forked tongue all over my face and giving me the time I need to accept him. After a while, I can't take it anymore, shifting my hips to get him to release me, ready to give up. Then I feel it again...

Pleasure. Deep, strange pleasure.

My body eases.

He seems to sense it because he rises and takes me with him. Seated on his prick, he wraps his arms around me, pushes his tailtip between my lips, and moves me on him just a little. His bulge rubs my sensitive spot unlike anything ever has. It's not like his tongue, or his fingers, or his tip. It rubs it like a puzzle piece, one that's been missing my whole life.

Is this how Gemma is with Vruksha? Is this why she claimed him? Did she feel this too?

My thoughts swirl, and I constrict.

"Zaku," I whisper his name again, easier this time. "What's happening to me?" I'm not like him. This doesn't happen to human female bodies.

"You are ovulating. I am heated. I can scent it. I did not know it at first, though I am sure of it now."

Air *wooshes* out. He pushes his tail hard against me, undulating ever so slightly.

Ovulating...

Pleasure explodes through my body. Falling forward into his banded arms, my sex quakes as an orgasm rends me. Brutal and devastating, I scramble, squirming, so full I might burst. Before it ends, before there's an ease, another one hits. Screams tear out of me. Zaku lifts me off him and then seats me back on his length mid-quiver. His bulge expands and then loosens as my sheath milks it. He empties into me. He does it again, ripping me off him only to put my body back upon his length. It hurts. It stings. And then it's rapture.

I'm helpless as another orgasm pummels me each time he connects us. Hips dancing, sexes swollen and raw, I unravel.

"My little flower has finally found her stem," Zaku growls, his knot thickening again. "You have shown me how to water you, and water you, I will."

I trust him. The knife clatters to the floor.

He pushes me forward, wraps his tail under me, and mounts me. I grasp his wrists now on either side of my head and cry out for more. Lost in the shunts, the violent thrusts, I forget the war, my past, the dark things that haunt me.

We fit.

Please don't crush me.

THIRTY-THREE

THE PLAYROOM

Daisy

"What's the deal with the... playroom?" I ask, peering at the door between the cage and the window. "Why is it just a room of mirrors? Do you know?"

Zaku's fingers whisper across my back, his tail piled in around me from every side. He's leaned up against it like some cocky prince. The appendage slithers closer, indicating he doesn't want me to move away from him. I move to my knees anyway and rest my elbows on it, looking at the door across the way.

We've been in his nest for days, unbothered by the outside world, choosing each other instead. The frenzy of our first mating continued, only paused for nourishment and medical scans to make sure I am still on the mend and that Zaku's and my's eagerness isn't doing something it shouldn't. I'm getting better every day. I have strength. My mind is my own again. I can stop the stimulants and boosters today.

Though I ache unlike ever before. Zaku is merciless and needy. His body won't stop producing seed at an alarming rate, and mating regularly is the only thing keeping his knot from growing too big. It's easier to take him when he's purged.

We do fit... with work.

He's certain the heat will come to an end... if only he can rut me one more time...

Still waiting for Zaku to answer me, I face him and tilt my head.

He hisses, captures me in his arms, and dives his tail into my sheath. I gasp, jerking upward from the invasion.

"It'sss not just mirrors," he growls as he stretches me wide, stroking my inner spot, making me tremble. I plant my hands on his chest to hold my body upright from the attack. With focused hunger in his dark eyes, he pulls out his tail and guides me down on his girth.

I squeeze him, not wholly prepared. He pushes through my slit's weak refusal and forces my acceptance. "Zaku," I moan, annoyed and... pleased.

He rocks my body upon him, having more than enough strength to sate his need despite my laziness. I feel his knot expand, his tailtip teasing my behind, and with another annoyed groan, I rub my clit. I want my answers.

Zaku grabs my hand, taking over.

I don't know which one of us releases first, only that for the next hour I ride his undulating tail a lot more vigorously after the first release he gives me. We continue until we're depleted, until all I want to do is curl up against his side and go back to sleep. He leaves me on the bed—sprawled out, drenched, and thirsty—to get me water. I gulp down the pitcher he returns with and rush to the bathroom afterward to clean up.

He follows me, bathes me, dives his tongue between my legs, and soothes my aches away.

When we leave and I'm dressed, I head straight for the playroom and cross my arms, waiting for him to join me. My gaze goes to the nest, which is being cleaned by the house robots.

I've found Zaku is a reader when he relaxes. Books from the upper part of the house are stacked up around our nest, hoarded from the house robots who want to gather them and put them back in their place. I asked them to politely stop.

But all they say is that they have been given an order from the master—the original one—to keep the place perfect for when he returns.

The robots gather the books and carry them out. I sigh.

I had argued that the old master is *not* going to return because he's dead. Of course, they ignored me. Not all of the lost technology is perfect, I realized then, though the jury is still out on the Lurker tech. I haven't seen any of it.

I almost feel for Peter and the others. Hopefully, they'll decide it's a lost cause and leave.

A woman can wish.

Zaku scowls at the house robots as he comes my way.

I turn and open the door, walking into the mirrored room. He joins me, leaving the majority of his tail outside. The room is small.

"All I see are mirrors," I say, walking around the space. "How does someone play in a space like this? Were ancient humans narcissistic?"

"I do not know. What I know about your kind and Earth's history is all from books and the house robots. My father searched for information, which, I believe, led him here. We did not often see each other near the end of his life." He moves to the mirror directly across from the door.

I pause. "Your father died here?"

Zaku's cowl flares. "He jumped off the top of this mountain, and I found his body out on the lawn. That is how I discovered this place."

"Oh..." My brow wrinkles. "I'm sorry, Zaku," I say, joining him at his side in front of the mirror. "I did not know it was here your father died."

"It was long ago. Many seasons have passed since then, and I have lost count. I no longer think of him unless he's brought to my thoughts."

Still, I can't imagine living in a place where I'd be reminded of my father's body. *The lawn... with all of the bones...*

Is his father among them? I don't ask. I'm not sure I want to know. That will be a question for another day.

"You... don't know how long you've been here?" I say instead.

"It takes effort to count the seasons when there are so many of them." Zaku goes to the side of the mirror, where it ends in the corner, and hooks his fingers behind it. I hear a snap and the mirror opens inward. On the other side is an ascending staircase. It's not like the others in the house. It's a cement staircase more appropriate in a government building or... *Facility?*

I freeze.

A cold draft hits me as small lights upon the walls flicker on, brightening up the gloom. The air is fresher, like it's coming from a breeze off of the mountain.

"Has this always been unlocked?"

"It is hidden. It does not need a lock if it's hidden," Zaku says as he pushes the mirror against the wall within, opening the passage up for both of us.

"I suppose that's logical," I grumble. "So I was never trapped in your room to begin with?"

"As I said, it is hidden, and there's no escape this way, only old things, and a sharp descent and death."

"Is this...where the robots go?"

"Yesss."

I study the staircase curiously. "Where does it lead?"

"Come. Maybe you can answer questions I haven't been able to. I have not been up here since..." he trails off.

I look at him. "Since?"

"Your ship came out of the sky and your male leader demanded to know the secrets of this land." Zaku slides forward but stops before the stairs and turns to me. When I join him, he offers me his hand.

I stutter, "L-Lurker tech?" I recall the picture in the closet, the frightening alien in the shadows. A picture I wish I had never seen. A picture I destroyed. A ghost that isn't mine and I refuse to let haunt me.

"I don't know."

As if my curiosity couldn't get worse, it does. I don't care about alien technology. That's not why I'm here. I'm here because the good pilots—the obedient ones, the less emotional ones—are all on the front lines or in active duty.

But the Lurker tech brought Zaku and I together, and if he has it, knowing about it might save us in the future, when others arrive. I take Zaku's hand and we climb the stairs, and for a time there's nothing but our ascent to fill the silence. The stairs wrap around and continue. Zaku carries me when my legs shake. There are no doors, nothing to break the bleak passageway. I get lightheaded after a few minutes.

Eventually, we come to a room when the stairs end. Ahead of us are double doors, but one is cracked open, letting in wind. Sunlight streaks through the gloom, filling my vision with dust motes. There are two more doors, one on either side.

Zaku sets me down. Saving the open door for last, I go to the right one first. The handle is crushed, and I wonder why it hasn't been repaired. Peering inside, I find a cavernous room filled with dormant house robots. Several are milling about, repairing their broken comrades. There are crates upon crates stacked in rows at the back. *A warehouse.*

Well... Now I know where the house robots go. I hum. Except there are so many of them, it gives me pause. Hundreds, maybe thousands. Why are there so many of them?

I head for the left door where I find the handle also destroyed. Inside is machinery I have no idea what's for.

When I look for Zaku to ask what it is, he's at the open door waiting for me. I close the one behind me and go to him. He swings it the rest of the way open, and I step out.

The sky greets me. Wind whips my clothes, and I shiver from the cold. We've climbed above Zaku's house, and higher still. But my attention doesn't stay on the sky, it goes to the ground.

"It's flat," I say. It's also partially cracked. Taking a few steps away, it appears to me like a landing pad. Ahead of me and to the left is a circular railing in the center, covered in rust. There are strange grooves on the ground. "What's this?"

"The relay."

"Relay two," I mumble. "The house mentioned it. That you were its new master. What does it do?"

"It controls the power in this area. There are others, though I don't know where they are located. Vagan knows where one is."

At the mention of Vagan, my heart drops.

"The power?" I ask, moving the subject away from him. "What power?"

"Do not move," Zaku warns suddenly and moves back toward the doors. Beside it is another door, another space I completely missed. He goes in it and the ground trembles. I catch the railing.

"What's happening?" I shout.

Inside the railing the mountain opens up, dropping and shifting into the rocks. Buzzing floods my ears and a big machine rises from the ground, streaked in brilliant lights of red and blue. The air heats around me. And with the machine are turrets, dozens of turrets. They aim their guns at me.

Hitching, I stop breathing. I don't dare.

"Zaku?" I whisper for him.

The turrets turn away. My shoulders sag and I back up.

When the machine fully emerges, the buzzing stops and Zaku is back at my side. Still, it takes a moment for my muscles to ease.

"This keeps the tech running across the land," he says as if the active turrets aren't worrisome. "This machine feeds it information. It stores it, moves it, collects it, and keeps the power on—electricity, humans call it? I think it is magic."

My lips part. "Science, not magic. Perhaps a battery of some sort, a server?"

"I don't know," Zaku rasps, coiling his tail around my legs. "All the information I have on it is within the room I was just within."

"And the house robots?"

"Keep their secrets to themselves."

Stepping out of Zaku's tail, I walk around the railing, and as I do, something zips by my head. It comes to a stop beside the relay and hovers. An orb. Like the one Vagan had. More of them appear, flying from every direction to hover around the relay. And not just orbs, other things too. Other machines I don't recognize.

I continue walking around the railing, watching them gather.

One by one, they fly away.

When I approach Zaku, he pulls me against his side. "If I turn it off... the machines die. They fall from the sky, they halt in their tracks, they stop. Everything stops."

"What do you mean stops?"

"The power leaves them, and when that happens the Earth begins to die."

My spine straightens at his words. How simple they are. And yet... how many answers it gives. I think of Central Command and Shelby, Gemma, and the nagas. Peter and the others. "Let's make sure it stays on then," I whisper.

Zaku leads me back to the doors and enters the side area. The relay drops back into the ground, and any remaining machines floating around it zip away.

Zaku's home isn't a home after all. It's a front.

A military one.

Why...

Waiting for him to emerge, I look out over the landscape, saying another useless wish. *Leave us alone.* My stomach churns and vertigo hits. Walking to the edge, I peer down and see the entrance to Zaku's home below. Recoiling, I back away. Something strange catches my attention, and my brow furrows.

To my left, past the lake and beyond the smaller mountain next to us, in the same direction as the facility, there's smoke. Wispy and rising into the sky, it's undeniably smoke. My stomach sinks recalling the trembling glass the other day while in Zaku's nest.

"Zaku!" I shout, dread and nausea rushing through me. "Something's wrong!" I curl my arms over my stomach as it upends.

He's at my side the next second, trapping me in his limbs. "Daisy?"

Shaking, I lift my arm and point in the direction. "Look. The facility," I rasp, feeling another wave of nausea hit. "Something's... wrong. There's smoke."

The roiling in my belly gets worse. Swallowing thickly, I taste bile in my throat.

"Daisy?"

"The smoke, Zaku, something's happened," I burst out, ignoring the nausea. I glance at him but he's not looking at the smoke, he's looking at me.

"We have to do something," I say, my breath hitching, the pain in my belly worsening. I go to look back and he captures my chin, forcing my gaze to remain on him. I furrow my brow.

"You have gone white," he growls.

"I'm...fine. The...smoke—" I don't get a chance to finish. I drop to the ground and vomit.

Zaku catches me in his arms, hissing furiously. My world grows dizzy. I try to speak but cough and hack and cough some more instead, vomiting between breaths.

He roars my name, lifting me in his arms. My world spins.

I cry out in pain as he rushes me down below.

Zaku

I can't get to the pod fast enough. Barreling through my den, each door, each room is a barrier I crash through. Wood, stone, and other materials go flying as I curl around Daisy's shaking form as I make my way to the main floor.

"Zaku," she groans, straining in my arms. "There's—there's something wrong! My stomach!" She screams.

I curse the enormity of my den.

The red door flies off the wall as I plow through it, bouncing down the hallway. I crush it under my tail as I slide into the room with the pod. I lay Daisy within it and immediately the machine goes to work.

She rolls over onto her side and curls into a fetal position. Sweat beads her brow and I wipe it off with the back of my fingers as the pod's shield rises over her. Her watery eye finds mine as I draw my hand back and it finishes closing her in.

"Zaku," she moans, burying her face in her hands.

"I will fix this, little mate," I say.

Her whole body trembles.

My hands open and close, clenching and unfurling, uncertain what to do, what to say. The pod scans her and one of the arms comes out to grasp her arm, pinning it from her body so it can take a sample of her blood. She presses her knees into her chest harder.

The pod releases another arm to take another one of her limbs and she fights it.

"Let it help you," I say, keeping my voice as calm as possible. It's a feat. "Let it help."

Daisy cries out.

My tail coils tight under me. I lean atop the glass and cover her as best I can. "Let it help, Daisy," I plead. "Look at me."

She quivers and slowly lets the pod take her limbs. The pod straightens her out and shifts her clothes.

"Look at me."

Daisy squeezes her eye closed briefly but then opens it. She blinks rapidly, meeting my gaze. "God I hate when you say that," she moans

"Good," I encourage her.

"*Administering relaxant*," the pod says.

I keep Daisy trapped with my gaze. She winces when the pod sticks her with an IV. Tears bead her lashes and I can see the worry cross her features, deep, concerning worry. The scales along my spine rise.

She begins to relax as the drugs enter her system. My claws streak the glass on either side of my head, trying to reach her through it to comfort her. I do it to stop from lashing out and breaking something. I don't see a wound on her body. There's no blood, no smell of infection, nothing.

Which means she's sick on the inside...

Have I mated her too roughly? Did we not wait long enough after her recovery?

"I cannot lose you, I will not lose you." Not again. Not so soon.

The pain etched over her vanishes and she inhales deeply. My thundering heart doesn't join her as she relaxes. I'm not sure if it ever will.

"*Scanning for infections.*"

"I'm feeling better—" she gasps, jerking, pressing her hand to her stomach. I jerk with her.

"Don't move," I order. It's as much for me as it is for her.

"Zaku! Something is happening, what's happening!" She tries to peer down at her belly. The pod's arms grab her and pin her flat. "It hurts!"

"*Please remain still.*"

I hiss wildly, wanting to tear my heart out of my chest with my claws. "What's wrong with her!?" I bellow at the machine.

Daisy's body strains.

The pod's glass lights up with color. It beeps and sticks Daisy with another needle. She fights harder against her bonds.

"*Administering a higher dose of relaxants and calmers.*"

I tear away from the pod before I break it.

"Zaku!" she screams.

Grazing my claws down my face, I draw blood, trying to hold in the fear spreading through me. Venom leaks from my fangs and I swallow it, slicing them across my tongue. I have only had Daisy for a short time. Too short. I can't lose her.

I can't! I roar, striking my tail against the wall, unable to keep calm any longer.

When the pod beeps again, I turn to it, ready to destroy it.

"*Scanning done.*"

I rush to Daisy's side and she's no longer fighting her restraints. She's breathing rapidly but the furrows on her face are gone. She's slumped, staring at the scans on the glass shield within the pod. Her lips part and she inhales once very hard. She stops shuddering. Her whole demeanor changes and some of my fear lifts.

The pod's restraints release her and her hands go to her belly.

"Daisy?" I ask, leaning back over her. "What's happening?" I don't look at her scans, unable to take my eyes off of her.

Her gaze meets mine.

"I'm pregnant." She brings her hands to her face and beams. "I'm pregnant!"

Stilling, unsure if I heard her correctly. "What?"

"Zaku!" She leans up on her elbows and the glass pulls back. She winces once but her smile quickly returns. "I'm going to be a mother!"

EPILOGUE

Zaku

A PING SOUNDS, and my body goes stiff. Tilting my head, I look at the entryway door.

"What was that?" Daisy asks.

I turn to her as she lifts her head from the book about advanced robotics she's reading.

She's fretting. She'd told me about this ship called *Mercy*. A ship where many humans have recently died. That is was the ship her father once commanded, and that she once lived on.

She told me of these…Ketts and how they are killing her people in droves. Females and children included. I flick my tail and hiss. They are the reason she's even on Earth right now. Humans are searching for an answer to a grave problem. They think the answers are here.

I'm not sure how I feel about this information. More humans means more females for the other nagas in search of a nestmate, but it also breeds uncertainty. Who will rule?

Daisy fears they will come. I am not so sure. No one has come before her. We have jewels, power, and knowledge, she says. This is all stuff her humans want and want badly. This, I understand. They will trade precious females for it.

She's nervous about the smoke. She fears for the human female called Shelby and her safety.

Above all, she's worried and excited about gestating. My queen wants to do something, anything, but I am against it. Over the last day, Daisy's spent a great deal of time in the robot room up in the mountain. She's decided it's her job to learn how they work and to reconfigure them before our litter comes.

She wants to use them as guards. Our personal army. She also wants to add a room called a nursery. She'd determined to get the robots to use their stored materials to build one for us.

First, the book on robotics, then I'll decide if she's capable for more than that in her current state. The pod says she's in her second trimester. Daisy is gestating quickly for a female human. Worry and excitement battle inside me as well.

Her stress is becoming my own. And so is her happiness.

I puff out my chest. Whatever happens, whatever comes, they'll have to go through me to get to Daisy and our litter. She has nothing to fear.

I always win.

"It's a visitor," I growl, severely unhappy at the prospect. If a naga is here to steal my female, I will string them up by their spine.

My den is camouflaged in the mountain and the pathways to this ancient place have long been overgrown with trees and bushes. I reassure her that she does not have to worry. Only the winding walkways along the mountainside are ever used.

Still... We have a litter to worry about now.

"A visitor?" Her face lights up. "Maybe it's Gemma. Maybe..." The color drains from her face. Her hands go to her stomach.

The ping chimes again, several times in rapid succession. Daisy stands, and I slice forward to stop her. "We don't know that. I will go first."

She nods.

Since her time in the pod yesterday, I have been edgy. I refuse to leave her side even for a second, fearful she will fall again. There are two in her litter, and as far as we both know, a human-naga child has never been born. We have decided to nest upstairs so she may be near the machine at all times. They are growing rapidly.

Already, she is showing.

The ping goes off again and again, rapidly, frantically. Daisy is right up on my tail, and I can sense her nervous energy. Each day, I am getting better at reading her, caring for her, loving her—as she calls it. I like it. It's a human thing, and I like it even more because of that.

I never told Daisy about the book of reptiles I once found, about the king cobra snakes within it, and how I resemble them. I'm not sure I ever will. I do not want her to see me as an animal...not with the family we are about to create.

A family.

I don't think I will believe it's happening until our litter is birthed, despite the proof. How fast things change.

"Do you think it has something to do with the explosion? The facility?" she asks. "I'm worried."

"It is not your problem anymore."

"I can't help it. You know I can't."

I turn to face her, cupping her shoulders, stopping her in the hallway. "You have to for the litter."

"Babies. Call them babies, I don't like you using the term litter. It makes me squeamish."

"Babies," I correct, holding her gaze. "It doesn't change my answer."

"I know." She sighs. "I have more important things to worry about. Still—"

"You will do nothing, nothing, until they are out of you safely."

"The pod says I'm healthy and fine. The babies are healthy and fine. I am gestating normally..." Her brow wrinkles. "Which is strange for the pod to say considering the circumstances."

"But I'm not," I tell her. "I am *not* fine." The corner of her lip twitches and the concern in her eyes diminishes. Grabbing her to me, I hold her close, shielding her with my body. "I am not fine and I won't be until I have you and our young coiled within my limbs."

The pinging continues.

"Zaku, you're emotionally manipulating me. I had a terrible case of morning sickness yesterday, that's all."

"Morning sickness is still sssicknessss."

Any sickness is bad in my mind. All sickness. Nagas don't get sick. It's a human thing. I've known Daisy was delicate since the moment I laid eyes on her, but illnesses never occurred to me. They didn't even occur to me after her crash. My mate can be hurt by things unseen, things I can't stop. This bothers me.

When the pinging of the door abruptly halts, Daisy pulls out of my arms. "The door."

"Stay here," I warn, pulling back. "Do not let whoever, whatever is out there see you. Not until we know it's safe."

Facing the entryway, I leave her in the shadows of the hallway. Outside, on the lawn, I see a flash of red.

Vruksha. I'd know his coloring anywhere. There is no naga left in the land that has his coloring. Slipping closer, his female comes into view. She's got her eyes shielded as she tries to peer through the window and into my den. She pulls back and steps away from the outer door when she sees me.

Of all the beings to disturb Daisy and me, at least it is the other human female and a naga I almost...*trust.* He helped me bring Daisy safely home. Regardless, I do not want them here despite this. Daisy is stressed, she worries greatly, and though seeing Gemma will bring her joy, it will ultimately cause her pain when they inevitably leave.

Because no one is allowed to live in my den that is not part of my nest. Especially another male who is not of my blood.

"Zaku!" Daisy yells, "What's outside?"

"Your friend."

She dashes out of the hallway and towards me. I knew she would.

Gemma throws her hands up into the air, clearly upset I have not let them in yet. Cowl flaring, keeping Daisy behind me, I unlock the door.

"Finally," the other female exclaims, barging in. "We have a problem." Vruksha's tail wraps around her middle, keeping her from going too far into my space. He slips forward and presses to her back, wrapping an arm around her as he meets my gaze.

"King Cobra," he says.

"Pit Viper."

We glare at each other. Muscles straining, we size each other up.

"We don't have time for this! The facility has been destroyed," Gemma says, pushing out of Vruksha's arms and going straight to Daisy, cupping her face. "I'm glad you're safe... you're mending fast." She pauses. "Really fast," she says, checking Daisy over.

Drawing back, I let Vruksha through. Daisy shakes her head. "I am, thanks to Zaku," Daisy says. "Destroyed? We saw the smoke. What about Shelby? Where's Shelby? Have you been there?" Her voice quickens.

Gemma faces Vruksha. The look they share isn't good.

It's then I notice how disheveled the other female is. There's dirt over her cheeks and hands. Her clothes are dirty and sweat stains on the front of her shirt. She carries a wooden spear with jagged metal plates at the end. *A weapon to defend herself with,* I presume. I glance at Daisy, realizing I have not given her such a thing. It is something I must remedy, and soon.

I cannot keep her contained in my home forever. She is a creature from the skies. She will not be content to hide behind walls.

I decide right then and there that I will not only make her bigger, but stronger as well.

Vruksha looks just as bad.

They have been traveling. Hard.

"Tell me!" Daisy demands when Gemma and Vruksha continue looking at each other. Gemma turns and walks to the seating area, sitting down and rubbing her hands all over her face. She peers at me.

"Can I have water, Zaku?" she asks.

I nod and move toward the kitchen. Vruksha stops me

and pushes past me, retrieving the water for his mate instead.

Returning to Daisy, who's followed Gemma to the seats, I pull her into me, knowing what's to come isn't going to be good for my mate. Vruksha joins us after handing Gemma her water. She gulps it quickly and swipes the back of her hand over her mouth.

"The facility is gone. The transport ship is...gone."

"Gone?" Daisy asks, confused.

"Just...gone."

"There's no ship exhaust in the sky. We would've seen it."

Gemma shakes her head. "I don't think it went back to The Dreadnaut."

"What do you mean?"

"Whoever took it, if someone did, they're still here. That's my only guess. Ship's don't just vanish."

"And the facility? Shelby? The smoke?" Daisy asks quickly.

Gemma's eyes flick to Vruksha briefly. "We were wondering if you guys might have...if Zaku..."

I hiss. "We have been *here*. If you think I went back to destroy the humans who have caused my mate so much pain, I have not. Daisy is my priority." I don't say that I haven't thought about it, a lot. About slipping out one night and traveling to the facility and breaking all of the humans' robots and machines, burning their ship, and killing those who try to stop me. I have fantasized about it.

When I thought Daisy and I were not meant to be, it was all I wanted to do. I have not thought about it since my queen has proven me so very wrong...

Gemma nods.

"You're dodging the questions," Daisy snaps. "What did you see?"

Vruksha growls. "Ruins and dust. Smoke and fire. There was only blood by the time we got there—"

"But Shelby could still be alive? She could be in the ship, right?" Daisy looks between Vruksha and Gemma. "Right?" She asks again when neither answer her.

"There's a hole, a giant pit where the facility used to be," Gemma breathes.

"And?"

"We searched everywhere we could. We couldn't find her. I know she's alive, I'm certain of it."

I coil my limbs closer to my mate. "And what do you want us to do about it?"

The other female sighs. "I was hoping you could tell me."

Daisy steps forward. "We need to find the ship."

"I don't think Shelby's on the ship."

"Where else would she be?"

"We talked briefly, Shelby and I. That's how we knew something had happened. She somehow connected into one of the orbs." Gemma reaches into the bag on her shoulder and pulls an orb out.

"And?"

"She said she was trapped with someone. That she's under the facility. Except there's nothing there. We searched the pit. She sounded desperate, Daisy, scared. Shelby doesn't get *scared*."

My gaze cuts to my mate. She's gone stiff, her face white. I tug her back to me. "We can't help you," I fire to the other female.

"Vagan..." Daisy whispers. "I should've forced Shelby to come with me."

Gemma stands. "Vagan? Who's Vagan?"

"Another naga male. He was on the plateau with Zaku and I." Vruksha answers. Gemma nods in remembrance. "He took part in the hunt."

"He was here," Daisy whispers. "He was crazed. I thought I'd killed him. I had hoped..." She trembles. "We have to help her, Zaku," Daisy looks up at me, her eyes fearful and pleading. "It's my fault."

"No."

"But—"

"No." I lower and place my hand on her stomach. "Remember the risk."

I feel the others staring at us. Daisy clenches her hands, closes her eye and then stares deep into mine. "You're right." She faces Gemma. "We can't go with you. I'm sorry, but Zaku's right. We can give you supplies, though, and food, water, a place to rest before you head out. If Shelby sounded scared, I would start with this Vagan."

"I know where his den is," Vruksha says.

Gemma continues to stare at my hand on Daisy's stomach but rips her gaze away when her mate speaks. "We'll go?" she asks.

He hisses. "Yesss, because there will be no peace unless we do. Peace is what I want."

Peace? My brow furrows, bending my scales.

Peace. I like this word.

It is what I want too, I realize. Peace, with Daisy. Peace in my land. Just... *Peace.*

"Thank you," Gemma whispers to Vruksha, reaching out and placing her hand on his arm. She faces us. "Thank you. We'll take those supplies if you're offering." She glances at Daisy's belly again. Her fingers touch her own stomach before they fall to her side.

"Save her," Daisy says. "Please. Do what I couldn't."

Gemma straightens. "We will."

The next night, when I have my mate back in our new nest by the pod, after Vruksha and Gemma have left, and my den is our own once more, I pull Daisy to my side where she likes to burrow against me. Because it is her favorite place to be, it is my favorite place to put her.

"You are worried," I say. "Do not worry any longer."

She sighs. "I can't help it."

"Vagan will not hurt this Shelby."

Daisy tilts her head to look at me. I brush my fingers through her short hair when she does. "How do you know? He tried to kill you, tried to take me. How can you say that?"

"I just know." Speaking of other nagas, especially males, is not something I often do. "He is...not a bad male. He can be trusted. He was not himself when he came here." My fangs drip when I remember how he attacked Daisy and me. "Though I will kill him if he ever comes near you again. Do not think of it any longer." I do not want her thinking of other males. "I have a gift for you."

Her lips flick upward and some of the worry leaves her face. "Another?"

"Another."

She perches on her elbows as I reach under the blankets where I have hidden her stolen gift. A prize I came across during my hunt this evening when she demanded apples. A craving, she said. Perhaps the first of many.

A symptom of gestation she has told me...

"I hope it will ease your mind," I say, bringing my gift forward from its hiding place. Handing her the delicate trophy, I know I won't get the same reaction as the head, or the jewels, but I am looking forward to it, like I'm looking forward to what happens next.

Daisy gently cups the gift between her hands. "A flower?"

"A daisy."

Transfixed, enchanted, her face lightens. Her eye clears, the scars smooth out. Her luscious lips part slightly and a whispering breath slips through them. I don't move, terrified if I do, she'll remember I'm here. I have not always been my best with her, I have failed a lot, but I am evolving and will continue to do so. I may not be a king in this world, but I am a king to her, and that is enough.

"Peace," I form the word with my mouth, uttering it in the silence.

She gently touches the petals with one of her fingers, feeling them, then feeling the fuzzy center at the flower's middle.

"It's beautiful," she whispers, smiling.

I pull her close, because I can. Because she's mine and I am hers.

Beautiful. Like you.

AUTHOR'S NOTE

Thank you for reading *King Cobra, Naga Brides Book Two*. If you liked the story or have a comment, please leave a review! Continue onto *Blue Coral* if you want to learn more about the ferocious naga males who rule Earth and all its secrets, and the strong women who love and worship them.

If you adore cyborgs, aliens, anti-heroes, and adventure, follow me on Facebook or through my blog online for information on new releases and updates.

Join my newsletter for the same information.
Naomi Lucas

Turn the page for Blue Coral, Naga Brides Book Three!

BLUE CORAL BLURB

NAGA BRIDES BOOK 3

When I see her, I have to have her.

The one they call Shelby.

But the humans have not given her to us. She remains behind the walls of the facility they have reclaimed. She remains with a male that does not DESERVE her.

This beautiful, enchanting creature with long black braids and bright eyes needs a real male, a master, a true protector. She needs me.

I will do whatever it takes to claim her.

I'll kill.

I'll cheat.

I'll steal.

No human, naga, or otherwise will keep us apart. Tonight, Shelby will be in my arms whether she wants to be or not.

To hell with the rest.

Click here to view more, or turn the page for chapter one...

BLUE CORAL TEASER

Blue Coral, Chapter One:

Shelby

"Why aren't you showing?"

I purse my lips and switch off the feed from my eyes. Wiping away the sweat gathered on my brow, I turn to Peter. My captain. Except he's not my captain anymore. He's the prick who's working me to the bone.

"I'm still in my first trimester, *Captain*. Most women don't show until the second. Your question is inappropriate," I say, unable to keep the hatred dripping from my voice. Glancing at the sentinels behind him, on either side of him, and the ones now circling me, I try not to shake. Peter has them guarding me night and day. Ever since a deal was struck with the locals—locals who shouldn't be here—and gave Gemma, *The Dreadnaut's* Communications Director and team's liaison, and Petty Officer Daisy to them. Daisy, our transport ship's pilot. The only one we had. *Dead...*

He's a fucking psycho. How are we going to get back to the main ship now that she's gone?

He wanted to hand me over to the locals too—for his precious tech, so he can please his bosses—but Collins, his second in command, wasn't about to have that.

Peter eyes me up and down. "I want another test done."

"I've already done three. I'm not doing another."

"This evening, come back to the ship and get it done."

Fisting my hands, I stop from hitting him. "Is that all, *Captain*?"

Peter glowers. His face is blotchy with sunburn, his eyes are red, and there are dark smudges beneath them. He hasn't shaved in weeks, and a beard is forming upon his once smooth jaw. His usually short hair is tousled, sticking up from grease. He hasn't showered in days, weeks maybe, and it shows. Then again, neither have I. He's not wearing his captain's uniform correctly. His blazer is off, and the top of his shirt is open, revealing the hair on the top of his chest.

If Central Command saw him, they'd dock his pay for the crime, maybe even replace him. He looks tired and weak and not like a leader at all.

He's not, not anymore. At least not to me. He's a piece of shit criminal who has bad karma coming for him, and as far as I can tell, he knows it. I hope. Part of me wants to empathize, part of me wants to help, but then thoughts of Gemma and Daisy arise and all I want is to see Peter burn. I think of what I've done and what my lies are going to cost me, and I hate him even more.

Because I'm not pregnant. I can't even get pregnant. It was part of the procedure done to me, a sacrifice I made for my work. No one seems to know that, though, and I'm glad. It's saved my life. For now.

I think.

It hasn't done anything for the guilt that's plaguing me. Guilt that keeps me up at night. Guilt that whispers in my ear and hisses, telling me I should be out in the forest like the others. I should be suffering like they have, like Gemma still might be. Like Daisy did...

"What have you discovered?" Peter asks. "Any closer to the source of the electrical spikes?"

"Not yet. The diggers are excavating slower now, so I believe we're close to something. Besides that, I've discovered nothing new."

"You said we'd have something by now."

"I can't crack the data cube your friend gave us. Not without access to the ship's terminal. And you've taken away my access to the ship," I scowl back. "I can't ramp up the diggers without compromising what we might find beneath the ground. If it's what we're searching for, Central Command will kill us all if we deliver them broken tech." I turn on my eyes and the blue light they cast falls upon Peter's face. "Tell me to ramp up the diggers. Go ahead." My eyes aren't just implants; they're implants with a purpose.

He scowls. "Your insubordination is tiresome. You'll be doing double shifts until your baby pops if you keep this up."

"It doesn't change the facts."

Peter takes a step towards me. I brace. Is he going to hit me?

"I want an update this evening, and that test," he says, keeping his hands at his sides. "Central Command wants an update and they want it now. Keep the diggers level, I'll let them know I am trusting your expertise," he spits. "They put you on my team for a reason. But remember, Shelby, your circumstances will only get worse if you don't deliver.

If you think I'm bad, you have no idea what can be done to you. I'm trying to be nice here, supportive even."

Right. Like trading me to one of the locals so they can eat me, or worse? Being raped? hurt? I keep the thought to myself. Saying it aloud might send him over the edge. And a man as desperate as Peter is frightening in itself. "Is that all?" I ask. Talking to him makes me tired. I'm already exhausted enough as is.

"Tonight, Shelby," he warns, eyeing me once more. "I want something to give to Central Command *tonight*. You hear me? You better come up with something."

He turns and climbs out of the pit, taking some of the sentinel robots with him. He's begun having them guard him since Daisy's return and big escape. I'm proud of my girl for attacking him, for busting his nose. She did what I couldn't. What none of us could.

I just wish I could have stopped her before she stole the skiff. Seeing it crash into the mountain destroyed something in me. Guilt has haunted me since.

You didn't have to die. Not for him, not for me, not for any of this. I told her to save us, I shouldn't have.

Not at the cost of your life...

Hearing Peter's footsteps fade, I slump, shuddering. I close my eyes hard. I'm the one who's supposed to save *them*. I'm the one who lied to do so. And look where it's gotten me? Nowhere.

Now, Daisy's dead. Gemma might be too.

You just have to outlast him. Once Command knows what he's done, you'll be rid of him. You'll be rid of him and they'll find Gemma and return her before anyone else dies.

I keep thinking this but as the days come and go, it's getting harder to believe it. Peter has me guarded at all times so I don't rat out what's happening down here, and to keep me working. But someone has had to have said something by now, right? The rest of the team is made up of men— Gemma, Daisy, and I were the only women on this mission, thank the nebulas—and not all of them like what he's done. I frown.

Collins hates Peter.

He still won't rat him out on my behalf.

I've known Collins for years, having encountered him again and again during academy training. He's the real reason I'm here at all. And yet, he's loyal to the bone to his captain. He recommended me for Earth's first excursion. We had a short, contracted relationship before the mission, but we terminated the contract once it was certain we would both be going landside. Jobs come first, after all. More so for him. And this job was important, extremely important. A dream job for me. A clear path to becoming a captain for him. We ended on good terms, on laughs, and even flirty excitement, over a drink.

I wasn't about to let our contract ruin our life's work, and neither was he.

Spending hours listening to Collins talk about his work killed any potential romanticism we could've had anyway, especially since he never gave me an ear in return when I wanted to talk about mine.

I shake my head. Is everyone here a coward?

Looking at my flat stomach, my chest constricts. If they're cowards, so am I.

"Hey, what's going on? Are you okay? What did the captain want?"

Speaking of Collins...

I glance up as he climbs down into the pit. Rubbing my face, I stand as he nears.

"Peter. Call him Peter, or scumbag. He's not a captain.

He doesn't deserve the title. Do not call him a captain when it's just us."

"Scumbag then." His eyes soften on me. "You okay? I brought you food." He hands me a canister and I snatch it from him, twisting the top off. The smell of oatmeal hits my nose and I tip it back, letting the warm sludge slide down my throat. I swallow it all, feeling a little better after my stomach's full.

When I lower it, I find him studying me. "You look tired," I say, handing him the empty canister. "Thank you."

"I wish I could have brought more. I hate seeing you like this."

"Peter still being flakey on the food?" I ask.

He sighs. "Now that Central Command wants to keep the team here for an extra month, yeah. Food is being rationed."

My heart drops into my stomach. "Wait? Another month? You're not serious?"

"I am, unfortunately. I came to tell you. We can make it through. You can make it through." Collins reaches out and pushes one of my braids behind my ear. "You're strong, that's why I like you so much. What did Peter want?"

I push his hand away, uncomfortable with the affection he continues to show me. More so now that we're pretending we're having a child... A fake child that Collins seems almost giddy about.

But another month of this? I try not to wilt.

Turning, I duck under the tarp before I do. Showing any vulnerability is bad in our profession. Collins follows me like I knew he would. Inside are my excavation tools and gear, even a cot because I'm not allowed back on the ship unless requested. Radars and trackers, scanners and chemicals are organized neatly upon rocks with flat surfaces. I've set up a makeshift laboratory and workstation.

Everything I need to collect, examine, and study any Lurker technology I come across. Most are contraptions I created, or have had a hand in creating. Alien technology can be very volatile, and handling it takes someone with knowledge, care, and a deep respect for it.

Lurkers nearly wiped humanity from existence, who knows what the pieces they've left behind might do?

To my left, is the hole at the bottom of the pit. Around the deepest parts are the diggers. They're carefully excavating through pipes, dirt, and stone. There are also my laser scanners collecting data, examining the hole continuously, sending it to the diggers, and my tablet.

"Shelby?"

Checking over the current data, new readings are saying the ground is getting warmer, and the electrical spikes higher. I narrow my eyes. Moving to the hole, I peer down, seeing... I narrow my eyes further. *Cement? Steel?*

Why would there be a foundation thirty feet under the facility?

Is there really a sublevel like I thought? A niggle of excitement rushes through me.

"Shelby?" Collins cups my shoulder and turns me to face him. "Dreadnaut to Shelby, what did the scumbag want?"

I blink. "What?"

He sighs. "Peter, Shelby, pay attention."

"Sorry, got distracted—"

"I know."

My lips purse. "He wants me to take another pregnancy test—"

"Are you fucking serious?"

"Yes. He's suspicious."

Collins turns and runs his fingers through his hair, dropping his head back in exasperation. "Well fuck, glad I came to check up on you. Now I'm going to have to get into the damn lab without being noticed again, fuck. A fourth fucking test?" He begins to pace. "What is wrong with that guy? Doesn't he know trading you to some alien savages isn't going to get him any closer to what he wants? Your expertise is priceless."

Collins is handsome, even the mess he is right now, his sharp features are nice to look at. His light grey eyes, mesmerizing. He's always been nice to look at. Unlike Peter, he's put effort into his appearance today. Thick biceps strain his jacket, his dark brown hair remains close to his head in the standard military cut, and there's not a single wrinkle in his suit. I've seen him chased by multitudes of women, only to ignore them. Why he contracted with me? I shake my head.

"Yep," I agree. "You could tell Central Command this," I add with a mumble under my breath. I look back into the pit. I knew there'd be a sublevel. I knew it.

"At least that means you'll be back aboard for the evening." Collins stops pacing and faces me. "I'll let you have my weekly shower slot."

"Do I smell that bad?" I huff absently, glancing back at him.

He smiles. "Like dirt."

"Thanks."

His hand cups my cheek. I go rigid as he presses his brow to mine. "I like the smell of dirt," he says, his voice lowering. "We can try for real, you know."

I pull away. "You know it's not possible." I regret contracting with him. He wants to sign another when the job is done and I don't. "I don't want children, not unless we defeat the Ketts. If that miracle happens, I'll get my eyes removed and my uterus replaced." Maybe.

"I'll defeat the Ketts for yo—"

The ground trembles. Collins and I shift apart. "What's that?" he asks.

"I...don't know."

My machines shake, and rubble slips in the hole, shifting pebbles and debris. My brow furrows. Tightening my hold on my tablet, the trembling stops. A few seconds pass and the dust settles. I inhale.

"What the hell was that?" Collins growls, walking away and lifting the tarp to check outside.

Heart thundering, I switch my eyes back on and lift my tablet to scan the readings. "A seismic wave maybe..."

"A what?"

The ground suddenly rocks under my feet. I fall to my knees, dropping my tablet as the tarp drapes atop me. "Collins!" I shout, struggling to raise it, to rise. "We need to get out of the pit! Now!" Catching my body, I try to stand again, only to be forced back to my knees as the rumbling worsens. Flapping plastic fills my ears as the tarp flutters. In the distance, someone shouts. Someone screams.

"Shelby where the fuck are you?" he yells to my left. "Something's going on."

The ground gives way beneath my feet and I start sliding toward the hole. "Here," I cry. I shunt to my left, grasping at the ground, barely keeping my body from tumbling in.

"Shelby, there's gunfire!"

Clawing away from the hole, the tarp envelops me, blanketing my vision. Sparks go off. A vacuous, hollowing groaning hums through the air from every direction. Gasping, I scramble towards Collins's voice, seeing him on his knees a few yards away, trying to rise himself. Wide, fearful eyes meet mine at the last second as the ground gives way under him.

"Collins!" I scream as he plummets out of my sight. "Collins!"

The tarp slides off me. Staring where Collins had just been, the atrium walls of the facility crumble. I struggle to reach a boulder and shield my head as the remaining ground forms pits. "Help!" I scream. Seeing a sentinel above me, I reach for it, praying it'll hold my weight. "Help!" I scream louder. "Somebody help me!"

Then I hear it, through the crashing, cracking, and violent shaking. My name deep and hurried, hissed through rough vocal cords.

"My Sssssshelby."

A flash of brilliant blue streaks across my eyes, coming towards me through the dust. The ground gives way under my knees just as arms clamp around my body.

We fall.

Interested in reading more? Click here!

Star Navigator

Venys Needs Men

To Touch a Dragon

To Mate a Dragon

To Wake a Dragon

Naga (Haime and Iskursu)

Valos of Sonhadra

Radiant

Standalones

Six Months with Cerberus

Made in the USA
Columbia, SC
19 May 2024